Erica Yeoman was .... irted writing eight years ago. .... eye informs her rich sense ....mberland landscape to life. This n....... ....erged from a passion for historical geography - a passion shared with her twin sister - which she taught in Edinburgh before she came to live in Northumberland. She lives in the ancient town of Alnwick and her painting of the Tree House appears on souvenirs at the famous Alnwick Castle Garden.

For Linda
love
Erica

20·11·10

Devil's Drove

ERICA YEOMAN

*The mind is its own place, and in itself
can make a Heav'n of Hell, a Hell of Heaven.*

John Milton

Copyright © 2010 Erica Yeoman

The right of Erica Yeoman to be identified as the Author of the Work has been asserted by her in accordance with the Copyright, Designs and Patents Act 1988

Apart from any use permitted under UK copyright law, this publication may only be reproduced, stored, or transmitted, in any form, or by any means, with prior permission in writing of the publishers or, in the case of reprographic production, in accordance with the terms of licences issued by the Copyright Licensing Agency.

All characters in this publication are fictitious and any resemblance to real persons, living or dead, is purely coincidental.

Published by Room To Write

Room To Write

www.roomtowrite.co.uk

ISBN 978-0-9564823-2-7

Designed and produced by HPM Group. Tel 0191 3006941
www.hpm.uk.com

For my family, past and present

Acknowledgements

I am deeply indebted to the inspirational help of novelist Wendy Robertson and her co-founders of *RoomToWrite*, Gillian Wales and Avril Joy. Also to Anne Ousby for her early encouragement as co-participant in our private publishing venture. I'm grateful to Pippa Robin, also Dave and Helmar Hurrell who showed me the magic of the Cheviots; and the Alnwick Playhouse Writer's Group for their twice-monthly injections of enthusiasm.

My love and thanks to husband Mike, for living with the novel and all that has meant to me.

Prologue

PLYMOUTH 1806.
Excitement churns my belly, battling my dread. We await the oncoming boats. The first one hits the side of the ship as loud as cannon fire and the crew cheers. For them, after months at sea there can be no more welcome boarding- party.

I stare down into a sea of bare flesh and bright red lips. The bumboat is here and our ship, harbour-calm, is about to be storm-tossed by women. The noise is deafening. I put my hands over my ears in mock horror and smirk at Jock pressed to the rail beside me.

'They sound like hungry gulls.'

'Aye laddie, they're greedy, but it's not food they're after.'

Does he think I'm stupid?

'So, Rory.' Jock Macnab slaps me on the back, his shortening of my name showing his improving temper; we've been too long at sea. 'We canna go ashore so Plymouth has come to us.'

'Only the women!' I retort. I can hear their laughter; their giggles mixing with the shouts of the ship's crew. It jars. Aye we've been too long away.

The first woman is climbing aboard. She sways against the side; her head bobs this way and that; her dress lifts in the Channel breeze. A shriek of merriment, 'Time enough for that, Nell,' as the girl below her smothers the wayward skirt. A head appears above the ship's rail and Jock seizes the woman's waist and pulls her on to the deck. She kisses him full on the mouth.

'Woa, girl, what a greeting, anyone would think we're related.'

'So where's the family loyalty?' I grin as the doxy looks him up and down and then with a shrug of her shoulders turns to me. What does she see, an inexperienced boy with anxious face? I've a good head of hair made fair by the Mediterranean sun and I've stubble on my chin; already I stand six inches above Macnab. But I do not get a second glance.

'O well plenty more fish in the sea.' But Jock frowns as another woman's eyes are fixed beyond us. If they don't fancy him, what chance have I?

'They should have let us ashore. We risk life and limb and for what?' Jock scowls. 'They say Trafalgar was a great victory but where's our reward?'

I eye the land so near and yet so far. The captain of the Royal Sovereign has put it out of bounds.

'Still the man's got sense,' Jock admits grudgingly, 'you wouldn't have seen me for dust. Press-ganged means easy come, but easy go.'

I bite my lip. I've chosen this life.

Jock grumbles on. 'One day they'll see the colour of my soles and then I swear I'll never sleep in the same bed two nights running. It'll be a wife in every port. Why here's my Plymouth wife now.' A woman, hair speckled grey, skin pock-marked is at his arm. She looks old enough to be his mother, though he's small, Jock is fit and wiry. The woman is very different she must have had a hard life.

He'll take any skirt. I stare in disbelief at Jock's retreating figure. How could the Scot fancy her? And who's he kidding, wife indeed?

He treats me as a child. My scrawny body shows my youth but I've men's urges. I'd planned to take my first woman in the back streets of Plymouth not here, on board ship in full view of my fellow crew. I want no-one to see my first fumbling.

The women swarm about the deck. Where are the pretty girls of my imagination? These are pitiable. I've heard the bumboat brings only the best looking. God help those left behind. And, what about the men, will the women close their eyes and noses when an unwashed seaman starved for months of his pleasure lies atop?

A crimson face leers just two inches from mine. Her breath is harbour-scum, ugh it's foul.

'Well, here's a beauty. I fancy you, though in truth, baby, you're not much older than this.' She pulls back her cloak. She is big with child. I turn and run, stumbling and falling over jutting feet and writhing bodies. The smell is nauseating, cheap scent and body fluids. The sounds are animal. Here can be no desire, just contempt. I'll be celibate for the rest of my days if it depends on this day's entertainment.

Hells bells, that was close. Give me the Frenchies any day. I catch sight of Vincent Byres, an officer and therefore, on pain of court-martial, mere spectator. He's at the far end of the quarter deck, his blond hair making him ever obvious.

He loiters by the mizzen topsail. Is he disgusted at the antics of his ship mates? It's unlikely from my reading of the man. He's a snooper. Intrigued I move along the deck, my chance now to snoop on him.

Byres is hiding a girl and this one is pretty. Already he has her skirts lifted and pinned to the sail upright. Inviting eyes seek conquest. She's better! By, she's definitely better. The officer holds the prize. But he dare make no coupling. The girl stands untaken. She catches sight of me and a slow smile crosses her face.

'That lad looks as though he wants a lesson?' Her voice is coaxing.

'Aye, and you're the teacher he needs.' Petty Officer Byres raises his finger and beckons and as I hesitate he moves snake quick and grabs my arm.

'Master Felton thinks he's a cut above the rest.' He sneers. 'Come say "please miss," ever so nicely. And the kind lady will show you a thing or two.'

She laughs with him and I struggle to free myself from his grasp.

'Let go of me.'

His adult strength drags me helpless to the girl. I can smell her excitement, her skin, her sweat. I've never known a woman. No need to find the back streets, no need to hide behind my innocence another day, my response is instant. What matter there is an audience to watch my entry into the world of men? It's just me and the girl. All noise stops. Am I in shock? One minute cheers and jeers then suddenly nothing. The watchers melt away. A new sound, footsteps ominous as fate shatter the silence. The Admiral has come from his cabin and is climbing the few steps that separate upper gun from quarter deck. Byres and the girl are nowhere to be seen.

I stand before Admiral Collingwood struggling to right my garments. Butter-fingered panic, sweat pours from every pore. Trousers up, I turn and face the great man. Eyes straight ahead I salute my hero. Unlike Nelson, this Commander is an imposing figure; it's no secret at St Vincent Collingwood's gunnery skills proved crucial, and at Trafalgar...Nelson died early in the battle.

'So boy?'

'Sir, I-I—-.'

'What's your name lad?' His face is father stern.

'Gregory Felton. Please sir!' I look him in the eye I've ever taken my punishment. The others have scuttled, left me alone to take the flack whilst they still get their pleasure, judging from the muffled sounds from the other decks. Typical!

He frowns. 'S-so lad, you're north-country.'

'Why aye, sir, Newcastle.'

'Newcastle!' Collingwood's grim mouth relaxes. 'Man, we're almost neighbours you and I.' He's lapsed into the north brogue. 'You'll know the border country.'

'That's wild, sir. I've never dared go there.' Still I wait for the rollicking.

'Not so tis God's own countree.' His tone is soft and reveals his longing. 'So lad, you're far from a father's hand.'

'This ship's my home.'

'Ah,' he looks sad, 'then you should go visit your family.' The Admiral fingers his shoulder epaulettes and stares unseeing over my shoulder.

'As Fleet Commander it'll be four years and more before I can return to Northumberland.' He sighs. 'When you go, bonnie lad, take with you a handful of acorns. His Majesty's Navy will ever need great ships of oak together with promising young men. Of which you may perhaps be one, some day?' His hawk eyes bore into me. Might I?—I hope so!

Of course he and I couldn't predict that ships wouldn't always from great oaks grow. But that encounter changed my life, Admiral Collingwood planting seeds in my mind that years later would lead me back north, back to his and my God's own countree. The wild border land that lay twixt England and Scotland.

1

1820 NORTHUMBERLAND.

Shuttered. The outside world is obliterated by the simple act of drawing wood across glass. Gregory's world is at once restricted. The only movement the spurt of flame struggling to take hold before another swathe of moist smoke splutters from the chimney. He cursed. Ahead stretched the long night hours, yet in the cold light of day the drawn-back shutters would reveal only the unfettered landscape and in it his solitude.

A smell pervaded the room. It was honest sweat, born of hard work and distance from water that caked the breast and coated the crotch. Gregory Felton put his head in his hands and moaned aloud. In his loneliness he was imagining Macnab and his shipboard companions. Befuddled, he sank his nose to his armpit, but there was no trace of a day's toil, honest or otherwise. He had bathed long and leisurely for no good reason. No-one sat the other side of the fireside. It mattered little whether he stank as high as a pile of rotting fish.

He sniffed the air; there was the coal smoke but there was something else besides, was it sweat-soaked crewmen? Below deck Macnab's smell had become his own, their hammocks just the statutory four feet apart; Jock's snores the nightly lullaby that sent the boy into a deep sleep, the man's morning farts bringing him back into the reality of life aboard ship. How he missed the crowded fellowship of his life at sea.

But now there was an added odour, the smell of hillside heather? He laughed scornfully as the aroma filled his nostrils. Tap, tap, there was a knock on the door. Now he was imagining sounds as well. He swore aloud and it echoed the soft knocking on wood.

'Who's there?' Gregory's voice was the croak of an old man unused to conversation. 'What do you want?' He staggered to his feet. His brain was playing tricks. No-one came to his door.

He could do with another drink. Even a glass in his hand would be tangible companion. On board ship there would have been mates to join in the harmless pastime. He told himself not to think of his old life. Comparing that energy and companionship with this place was apocalyptic. He might as well have been cast adrift in the middle of an ocean as come to this God-forsaken hole.

How far had he sunk that his mind was peopling his home with his old companions and now a new unknown visitor, some-one to help him empty a flagon? It was too late he had managed that particular task on his own account. He had long since finished the Communion wine.

The noise was loud enough to reach his fuddled brain.

'Who's there?' His repeated question coincided with a final harsh knock.

Silence! There was no-one, nothing to make him leave the faltering fire. He stared at the solid door and slowly it opened. He rubbed his eyes and there she was. An apparition he'd dreamed up in his lonely desperation.

She was beautiful. Her cloak hood rested on long neck and sloping shoulders so that her face was uncluttered and there for him to admire. Peat-dark eyes smiled back at him so that he could see and smell the heather. Long eyelashes curved up to her pencil straight brows, and wisps of hair fell down to her forehead in a high bank of furze. Her teeth showed her to be a young animal, white and unbroken.

He gawped at her. 'My God, who are you? Where do you come from?' The Communion wine had worked a miracle.

She laughed and it was a mountain stream cascading over unyielding rocks. She was the burn that thundered in spate feet from his door.

'My name is Kitty.' Her voice danced.

'Then I shall call you Kitty Linn,' he said and smiled. 'You come from the hills,' he pointed to the shuttered window, 'a turbulent mountain stream.'

She frowned. 'It's not water you'll be wanting. I'd not waste my muscles carrying that.' Her retort showed she had little time for his poetic imaginings. As she spoke she opened her cloak and Gregory began to tremble. Had the devil sent him the prostitute, the temptress who had been his shame? That single demeaning encounter enforcing even now his celibacy.

His eyes were playing tricks. He watched as she placed two ewers onto his desk. The earthenware was homespun and coarse.

'Grey hens filled with *morning dew*. I will bring more.'

The smell of peat flavoured whisky pervaded the room.

2

His God was a kindly God. He gave succour in strange ways. Gregory opened his eyes and saw a bright light striving to gain admittance to the room through the closed shutters. Yesterday they had seemed impregnable, but now thin shafts penetrated the gloom. Gregory watched the bands as they shimmered across his body. He stretched painfully. He'd slept beside the dead embers in the hearth. The floor was hard under his shins. He struggled to his feet and groaned as head and body became upright. Then he remembered. He felt a surge of spirits. The warmth of his God-sent vision filled him with an excitement long absent in his present depressed state.

The girl had been more beautiful than anything he could have thought up. He saw again her proud stance, the lift of her head, the smoothness of her skin. He felt his stab of disappointment at her bulging shape and the thought that she was heavy with child. Then she had opened her skirts and there had been the slim body. He felt weak at the memory. What had he expected? He gasped as he relived the moment. Right now a plunge into a cold upland stream would allay his ardour, but the image brought only instant arousal. Kitty Linn he had christened her, a cascading wild free-running torrent.

The name recall brought a smile to his lips. She was no figment of the imagination. 'Kitty Linn.' He whispered the words with reverence.

Of course the girl was real. She had stood there in the room, frowning at his flight of fancy, smiling at his eagerness. And she had brought him a present from her moorland home in jugs that were purpose-made. What had she called them, '*grey hens*' a poetic vessel for the meadow dew that was poesy itself?

Books and papers sprawled across his desk in an untidy heap. She'd moved them to one end to make room for the cream ewers, one small, one large; like mother hen and chick. He'd seen every gesture, every movement as the outside fog threatening the rectory all day cleared and in its place was bright moonlight. The grey hens looked so at home on his desk, as though they had come home to roost.

Had he tasted the whisky? With a shock of surprise he realised he could not remember. His eyes and every sense had been on the girl, she had bewitched him. He frowned and felt a stab of unease. A minister of the church yet he had so easily responded. Had Satan sent her? A beautiful girl bringing the devil drink and he had welcomed them both.

Gregory looked to his desk. It was the workplace of a priest with books and papers spilt everywhere. He moved to the pile of tomes that hid the flagons. His next Sunday sermon lay where he had thought to see the jugs. His large hands, more fit for the work of a navvy than the writings of a priest, fumbled with the untidy sprawl.

No hens. They had gone. But these were hens that could not move. He'd seen her place them on the desk, noted her long thin tapering fingers that looked as though they should hold a pen, not fastening her cloak against the inhospitable night.

His desperate eyes searched the room as though his life depended on seeing an enemy-free horizon. Furniture was sparse and functional, desk, chair and high book shelves. The mantlepiece was bare except for the Plymouth Crucifix, a daily reminder. The two ewers should be clearly visible, but they were not. The room showed no evidence that Kitty had ever been.

He strode to the window and with fumbling hands banged the shutters back against the recess walls. Morning sunlight burst into the room. Where were the whisky jugs brought to him by his night visitor? They did not exist and if that were the case, then neither did the girl. He had thought her up in his depraved longings.

Gregory man-handled the shutters. The day held nothing. Daylight was cruel. Only for him was the dark abyss where God had seen fit to send him. He seized his penknife. His hand no longer trembled. Slowly and deliberately he sank the blade into the wooden slats. SOLUS— SOLUS. God had ordained he should be alone, shipwrecked in no-man's land, adrift from his fellow men. He carved the word a dozen times into the yielding wood. Every incised letter spelt out the truth. SOLUS- he was alone.

Gregory stood by the empty hearth, his head bowed before the small crucifix. Now he was trembling. His palms stuck to the clean, smooth ivory and he could feel the thin, spare figure of Christ hanging, humiliated and scourged. He sank to his knees. But he knew there was little chance of easy redemption in a place like Thorneyburn.

3

Mist always dulled sound, now cleared there was a cacophony of noise as chaffinch and robin vied with each other. The burn bubbled in a deafening thunder that would have drowned conversation with any companion. It leapt in swift, gurgling descent down the hillside, curving and winding between its steep-sided banks away to its goal, the wide valley floor of the North Tyne. River bluffs impeded the view, but Gregory knew that if he followed the water he'd find human activity and that was what he craved most.

His church and rectory stood alone. It was a whole month since he had first trod the lonely track to his new home. He'd seen immediately that there was no need to climb a crow's nest to see that in the full three hundred and sixty degree sweep there was not another building in sight. The square-towered church and large stone house sat incongruous in the vast empty landscape. He had opened the newly-fashioned gate that separated rectory from church-yard and vowed as he looked at the virgin sward that his bones would never lie there.

From the age of twelve he'd assumed he would be buried at sea and he'd liked the idea that at the end he would find out what lay below, though for all of his twenty-nine years, Gregory had grudgingly accepted what lay on the surface. All he needed was to feel the sea-worthiness of the boat under his feet. Yet his new home appeared to be a craft close to foundering.

He'd opened the front door of the rectory with sinking heart. His fingers seeking the smooth shapes in his cloak pocket. The acorns plump and round were instant assurance, like Catholic rosary beads. He smoothed them again and at once the Protestant in him felt a stab of guilt. Here to spread the Government word established by the Church of England there could be no false sense of comfort. He smiled, little chance in a place like Thorneyburn. Yet hadn't the Admiral told him to go and plant acorns? If they could grow here, they could grow anywhere.

He stood at the study window and stared up into the surrounding hills. He remembered the Admiral's map showing a vast space with just drove roads cutting across its emptiness. He glowered at the blank. It would take the devil himself to make him penetrate into that remote, hostile land. He shivered, no, he must believe it was God who had sent him into this heathen wilderness, colluding with nature in its unnatural challenge. Why here? Why him? But he knew the answer. This was his punishment for the sins of his youth. And last night had been the first test.

The crisp cool air cleared his head as though he had doused it under cold water. He had need of company and at Greystead he would find it. The beautiful imaginings were devil-sent; reality distorted by his isolation. What he needed were good Christian folk who would seat him in their parlour and offer ale from a jug, not whisky from grey hens. Yes, that was what she had called them, a name he could not have conjured in a thousand years.

Greystead Rectory, his destination, was a mirror image of Thorneyburn. The Commissioners had come north to Newcastle, hired a coach with two dickeys, driven out into the wilds and in a few days had divided up the land into new parishes. Replicated churches and rectories stood almost within spitting distance of one another. They'd returned to London, no doubt happy men. It was not their job to conjure up a congregation.

Gregory waded the stream, the water tugged playfully at his boots and his feet moved with the current. It was not an unpleasant sensation being carried along in the flow. But of course danger lurked behind that character weakness. It was too easy to follow meekly where life led. Large boulders crowded midstream. He wedged his left foot between two of the rocks then lifted his other one out on to the opposite bank. Briefly he slipped in the mud then with a spurt of effort reached the flat haugh that skirted the river. He'd been equal to the challenge. With a grin he jumped back over on to the far side. It was a good game. His feet had hardly touched the water.

His nearest neighbours were accessible for the moment. Winter spate would make things very different, the crossing well nigh impossible. Gregory anticipated the challenge. Nothing would maroon him at Thorneyburn.

She watched him ford the stream then hesitate. Indecisive, she thought, just right for his line of work. He would have to run with the hare and hunt with the hounds: that was what his job entailed. Cecilia Howick stood at her father's study window perplexed, she saw him turn back the way he had come and re-cross the water. She let out a sigh of disappointment. The sight of an approaching figure had brought a surge of pleasure. Visitors to their off-the-beaten track home were few. Her father, the Reverend Thomas Howick could take them or leave them. She was different. Yes, her father was content with his lot and it showed in his placid face. No such acceptance lingered on the face of Gregory Felton. She watched as he approached the house, relieved at his reappearance, surprised at his antics crossing and re-crossing the obstacle water. He must like making things difficult for himself.

His forehead was creased in an uncompromising frown as he approached their rectory. Cecilia thought he might be a handsome man in a naval uniform but in the garb of a country parson he hardly merits notice. He stood irresolute making his long tapering face look even longer, though it was shortened by the cleft in his chin. Large ears stuck out from under his wide-brimmed black hat, though they were almost camouflaged by sandy coloured sideboards that curved naturally away from his face. She surmised in summer his hair would bleach to fair if freed to the open air, his eyes were already light brown, warm and friendly.

The Reverend Felton raised his hand to the front door. Even after a number of visits he could not obey her order to come round to the back one that would more than likely be open. Cecilia smoothed her hair from her forehead and puckered the neck of her blouse so that it curved about her round face. But her wiry hair was unruly and bounced back out of place and her collar sagged. What did it matter? There was probably flour on her cheek, and hairpins escaping from her bun.

'Gregory!' Cecilia's smile was genuine. She was pleased to see him. 'You are welcome.' Her voice cracked and he smiled to himself, they both knew hers would be as little used as his, even though she did not live alone.

'Is your Father at home? I would speak with him.' His hazel eyes blinked at her.

'He's at his prayers. You'll have to make do with me. I'm in need of conversation. I saw you practicing the high jump over the water.'

He grinned like a child. 'I thought to master such a hindrance. No barrier now, but in winter it would keep me from Greystead. And I would not want that to happen.'

Cecilia looked gratified. 'You are always welcome.'

'I come here for diversion. Though Greystead is even more isolated than my h-home.'

She nodded. 'Yes, it's a quiet backwater all right. Father is very happy. And a happy man finds any place his idyll.'

'He's to be envied, or perhaps I should say emulated. I'm less easily pleased.'

Cecilia looked sympathetic, but made no comment.

'And what of you, do you not find it very dull?' It was Gregory's turn to feel sympathy for the girl cut off in this isolated spot. No, she was no longer a girl. She was a mature woman, about his age and without a meaningful life of her own.

'Do you not find life here…, it's just that…?'

She laughed, but it was mirthless. 'Any other place and we wouldn't lose our voices through lack of use.'

'But you have your father?' Gregory questioned though he knew that the Reverend Howick would be unlikely to offer easy companionship.

'Wisdom lies in the acquisition of knowledge, not idle chat. Dear Papa spends all day in his library. He hardly knows the day of the week, though I do try to remember to tell him.'

'Good thing then that I've come. At least I know it's either Wednesday or Thursday.' Gregory's mock serious expression lightened and his whole face was transformed.

This time Cecilia's laugh was spontaneous. 'Yes, we have to laugh, don't we? Though, I believe God stretched his sense of humour when he put us here.'

'Indeed. Why else would he send Church of England padres to Catholic lands sequestered by the Government? Not the most tactful thing to do. We are the proverbial fish out of water.'

The girl nodded. Here was someone who saw and understood her loneliness. 'Yes, I have gills instead of ears.' She pulled back her hair and revealed surprisingly shapely specimens. Cecilia had not been furnished with many refined features.

Gregory shuffled his feet. Why had he come? For reassurance that he was not falling back into his old dissolute yearnings? He would have no such thoughts in the presence of Cecilia Howick; large, capable Cecilia.

'So, Gregory, I don't have all day to waste in chatter. Come into the kitchen.' Her pleasure had been brief. Now she was once more matter of fact. Obediently he followed her along the passage identical to his own and into the scullery that copied the Thorneyburn house in shape, though that was where the similarity ended. This place had a woman's hand.

He could smell warm scones fresh from the griddle. The upended flat iron showed it had already been used. Vegetables dug from the garden were piled for the scraping. Muddied woman-sized boots at the door revealed that Cecilia had been out into the garden to harvest her crop.

'So,' he said to fill the silence, 'you actually have something to show for your labours here. I wish I could say the same about my efforts.'

She looked at him, frowning slightly. 'Great oaks from little acorns grow.' She'd had enough of his miserable face.

Gregory nodded. 'I brought some acorns when I came north and I've planted them by the churchyard. I hope they will grow.' Cecilia made no reply. 'But I guess it's a forlorn hope in a place like this.'

'Why is that?' Cecelia's tone was sharp.

'So you obviously share Admiral Collingwood's optimism.'

She looked puzzled.

'On a far off day in Plymouth he told me to bring acorns to plant when I returned to Northumberland.' Gregory laughed. 'I cannot imagine he thought I would really do what he said. But he's always been my hero so I scooped up some of the oak fruits from Greenwich Park in a surge of optimism.' He looked rueful, 'I really believed then that the roomful of beneficent old men had handed me a future. With Napoleon out of the way, and my intended frigate mothballed where was an out-of-work padre to go? Fate and the custodians of the Greenwich Hospital came along in the nick of time.'

Cecilia began to scrape the carrots. The downward sweep of her knife was vehement. He'd annoyed her. Did she really believe her words about great oaks? He watched her in silence. He thought of her in the vegetable patch, her skirts tucked in her boots, her back arched in absorbing labour, her light auburn hair stringing untidily about her face. He thought of raised skirts with dark curls above. His knees went weak. Why had he come to Greystead, purely for human contact? Or had he come to test his resolve? Plain, stolid Cecilia would surely never rouse his baser instincts.

He coughed. 'You take pleasure in your harvest, as does your father. Both of you make the most of your situation.'

'And you?' Cecilia raised her eyes from the vegetables and looked him full in the face. 'Father says you preach the wrath of God.'

'Why not, but then there is no-one to hear?' Exasperation clouded his face.

'What did you expect? What did the Commissioners really expect when they created churches in a hot-bed of Presbyterianism so close to the Scottish border? See it as it is, an uphill challenge!'

Gregory stared at her. He felt her contempt. She stood tall and erect; she'd enough resolution for the two of them.

He sighed. 'I know your father does not worry about empty pews. I'm afraid I do.'

'Yes, father is on a higher plane. Where two or three are gathered together... Ah, here is the third member of the congregation.' Pastor Howick shuffled into the room. How well he fitted his saintly role: dishevelled, ill-kempt, Gregory knew he kept order for his mind. He didn't suffer from disturbing thoughts.

'My boy it is good to see you!' His voice boomed as though to reach the very last pew. 'To what do we owe this pleasure? Could you smell the scones? Or perhaps you anticipate the rabbit stew? Cecilia, you must lay another place.'

'Father, Gregory does not have all day to waste.' His daughter frowned, 'and neither do I.' She walked into the pantry and reappeared with a rabbit. She plonked it on to the marble-topped table and began to dismember it with an expert hand. Her hair fell forward and Gregory could no longer see the concentration on her intelligent face. Cecilia would have made a good surgeon. She's as thwarted as I am, he thought with a renewed stab of recognition.

He tried to appease her. 'Don't tell me, Cecilia you've already been out and caught the rabbit for the pot.'

Cecilia shook her head, 'No.' Her fingers explored the carcase. 'You know on a frosty night rabbits are supposed to grow fat. So this is a good one.'

'That's a relief. I was beginning to think there isn't anything you cannot do. I would have retreated with an even bigger inferiority complex. Going back over the Tyne I'd have sunk.'

Cecilia scraped her hair from her face and grinned at him. She had recovered from her bad humour. 'Yes, the river is rising. Gregory, come as often as you like! Soon it will come between us. You must stay to dinner.'

He shook his head. 'I must go and not disturb you further.'

Thomas Howick showed his disappointment. 'A wasted opportunity for intelligent conversation I enjoy your sea stories! It's not every day I talk with history. You will be able to tell your grandchildren you were at Trafalgar. Already you have lived a full life.'

'And now I vegetate.' It was out before he could stop himself.

'I don't like that expression.' Cecilia fixed him with an angry glare. 'It's misplaced. Vegetation does not stand still. It struggles to grow in whatever the soil and weather. You give in too easily I think. You should be grateful for your opportunity.'

'Cecilia.' Thomas Howick gently rebuked.

'Yes, she's right. My father used to say I lacked backbone, too easily dreaming about something I couldn't have. I...'

There was a knock on the door, first soft, then impatient when there was no immediate response. Gregory stopped in mid sentence and looked from Cecilia to her father. He felt a tightening about his chest. He'd come to Greystead, one burning enquiry on his lips. Who could be his night visitor? Surely the Howicks would have heard of her. They could confirm her existence. His mouth had not spoken her name, now there was no need. In one moment she would step into the room and this time he would see her not through a drunken haze but through eyes that could record every detail.

'O that will be the girl come for payment for the rabbit,' said Cecilia.

So they too had had an early visitor. 'The girl?' Gregory strove to keep his voice steady.

'Yes, the eggler.'

'Eggler?' Gregory sounded bemused. But then he'd not really expected her to announce the delivery of illicit whisky, not here not in this place.

'Yes, we buy butter and eggs from the local farms. It's the least we can do to spend precious pennies with them. Times are difficult. I will fetch the girl in and you can place an order.'

Gregory's heart beat fast. There would be no grey hens placed on the Howick table. That was night-hours trade. Dairy goods belonged to morning. There were footsteps in the passage. Kitty Linn was about to prove her existence and he would find immediate relief. He needed to know above all else that she was not the imagining of a sick mind.

The girl who came through the door was very young, thin and scrawny, with a pinched face and bad teeth. Her clothes were patched and poor. He had imagined a very different sight.

Cecilia saw the disappointment on Gregory's face. It was childlike in its blatant reaction. He showed his feelings too clearly. Not good when he had to stand in his pulpit above searching eyes. He should hide what he felt. What had he expected? Who did he think her visitor would be? It was hard to imagine. If it had been King George who had entered the kitchen Cecilia would have shown no reaction. For her life held few surprises. She'd been taught to accept with equanimity whatever happened. The next week would be like the next month, like the next year.

She stood at the window and watched his retreating figure. He looked what he was, a young man going into middle age with a figure that showed he sat too long over his desk. A tall man, his gait was stooped; perhaps he had spent too long below deck in the early years? His stride was slow, deliberate, as though he expected the ground to be pitted with obstruction. In this open sweeping land he looked small. Perhaps, she thought, when he'd breathed its air he'd lose his premature stoop and walk tall. Then I shall look up to him.

As he dropped down into the valley in the direction of the ford Gregory was lost to view. Cecilia smiled at the empty landscape. It looked better for his going. He had looked out of place, an infringement. His demeanour was of a lonely man and she had no wish to be reminded of that.

She plumped the sofa cushion with a loud thump and began to sing,

'Come ye thankful people come, raise the song of harvest home; all is safely gathered in, ere the winter storms begin.' She trailed her fingers over the piano and the room was filled with the melody of the harvest hymn. 'Wheat and tares together sown....' Abruptly she stopped playing. Could Gregory sing or not? It was something to discover? His visit had brightened the morning. He had a dry humour about him. Yes, Felton promised to improve on acquaintance for all his self doubt.

Gregory retraced his steps to his empty house, his pace slowing as he approached the dark, unlit windows. It stood stark against the sky line. Around it, small stunted hawthorn hugged the ground in twisted, gnarled shapes. No oaks here stood tall and proud. Perhaps one day it would be different?

4

The church was empty; stark and bare. The chill morning was trapped within the high stone walls, Gregory shivered. There was no welcome here. He knelt before the altar and he felt the dismay he carried with him like an early mantle of snow. It blanketed optimism and the order of things. How could he expect a flock to follow him when he could not muster the innate sense of survival required in the leader of the pack? Cecilia had been right to chastise him. Gregory rose from his knees. His mind could furnish no comfort.

The building was plain and functional, the walls bare. In this new church no lifespan had earned a lasting memorial. The slate was clean, awaiting the first mark. He squinted at the fresh plaster. Who would be written up for posterity, their good works left for future generations to applaud? It awaited names. And there would be none to commemorate unless he, Gregory Felton, did something to bring in a congregation.

It was warmer outside. He closed the stout oak door behind him, the one small entrance to the church lying below the squat tower at the western end. Should he leave the door open? Let in the thin autumn sunshine and any passerby? He laughed out loud at this preposterous thought. No-one came to Thorneyburn. Why had the good Lord's representatives built his church and that of the Reverend Howick where they served no purpose? He felt a mounting anger at those people in the south. No-one was remotely interested in the far corners of Northumberland. He scowled and began to walk. He was at his most resolute when his bad temper smouldered.

Greystead lay in the other direction. He would stay away from there. It was easy to seek the obvious comfort it offered, a good, scholarly man with intelligent conversation and a woman blessed as a home maker. Gregory reflected on Cecilia. For the woman read him. She wore her frustration on her sleeve though she didn't know it and he could give her no remedy.

He took the track that he'd travelled the first day but in the opposite direction. He remembered his dismay when suddenly it had stopped in the middle of nowhere and he had reached his destination. Disbelief, amazement had numbed his tired body. Today his spirits rose with every step as he walked the other way, away from his irrelevance.

The North Tyne lay far below him, the valley narrow, then broad, as the river meandered this way and that, pushing its banks to their furthest limits. He stopped and looked down at the water that carved out its own course. There was a sermon subject there. All he needed were ears to hear his words.

Two miles away lay the village of Falstone, the hub of the area. He could see the Presbyterian Church spire ahead of him, a beacon for any traveller. Every Sunday, so he'd heard, feet swarmed to its door; tracks from every hillside ended there. Did the congregation wend their way like unquestioning sheep, or was he up against an inspiring holy man?

This was sheep country, the soil meagre. About him Gregory could hear the bleating animals. The noise was reassuring. He felt his approach was being heralded, passed from one animal to the other. Named as the hills, the Cheviots dotted the landscape that sank southward from the high Scottish Border Ridge a dozen miles away. The bleating was loud and insistent and it was the collie dog that Gregory saw first before the man. It ran to him tail wagging, pleased at the unexpected meeting.

'Jed.' The voice was loud and curt and the dog slunk to the ground, ears, tail, body on level plane. The farmer was standing by the gate blocking his way.

'Good morning.' No response. Gregory added, 'It's a fine day.'

'There'll be snow before the day is out.'

'Goodness.' Surprised Gregory looked skyward. 'That's early.' Then to cover his note of disbelief, 'It takes an expert to know such things.'

'Aye, it's all a question of belonging. You're a stranger in these parts.'

Gregory was riled. The man knew very well who he was. He was about his own age, but there the similarity ended. He was a giant of a man, with strong weather-beaten face and hands that looked as though they might have built every stone wall in the area. Gregory's slighter though artisan hands looked woman-like in comparison as he stroked the dog.

'Jed, here boy.' The dog did his master's bidding.

'He has a fine coat.'

'Aye.'

Gregory turned to walk on. It was like talking to a stone wall. 'Fine for living outside.'

The man laughed. 'You'll wish for such a coat in your church. It'll not be the warmest place.'

'Indeed I shall.' Gregory turned around and held out his hand. 'I'm Gregory Felton. In truth I'm used to facing the elements.' He drew himself up to his full height, eye level with the man. 'You don't get much stormier than the Cape of Good Hope when the Roaring Forties are at your face. It makes this hillside feel like a Sunday afternoon stroll. Shall I be seeing you at Thorneyburn, Mr...?'

'Caleb Hunter.' Hand shake and words were clipped and grudging. 'No. I belong the U R C. And so does he, so it's no use trying to influence him.' He pointed to the dog. Gregory continued to fondle the collie, and for the first time the man smiled, a gaping hole of a mouth showing ragged teeth. 'Jed looks forward to his Sunday morning. It's his chance to get in out of the cold. The church is warm to him.'

'So he goes to church with you?' Gregory showed his surprise.

Caleb Hunter looked as though reply was a waste of breath. 'Why not? All the shepherd dogs go.'

Gregory nodded. 'So, I need to install rings for their leashes.'

Hunter looked unimpressed. 'Not necessary I assure you. They all lie at their master's feet, as obedient and open to the scriptures as any man. Some would say more. They're naturally compliant, they do as they are told.'

A smug look crossed Caleb Hunter's face. 'Come to think of it we're not so different from our dogs. Around here we worship where our fathers worshipped. It'll be no matter how fiery your sermon is. That'll not get a congregation into your fine new church.'

Gregory felt his growing irritation. The man was pure

antagonism. Then Hunter laughed. 'You'll not have heard about the time in Falstone when the dogs caused a stampede?'

'No.'

'It was the first time the Reverend allowed the dogs in. They lay like saints like I said through the service. But when the congregation stood for the blessing they thought it a sign it was over. They all, without exception, darted round and round the church looking to find the way out. It was pandemonium. Not so different from us humans, are they, all desperate to get out after a long boring sermon?'

'Good at least to see some genuine fervour.' Gregory smiled, stiffly.

They stood head to head. Hunter looked him straight in the eye. 'As I've said, man, religion isn't about inspiration. It's what your father and his father believed, or your master, in Jed's case.'

The man was goading him again, trying to get him to lose his temper. He bit his lip; it was like being on board ship when rank had been pulled. How he'd longed to give Byres a bloody nose. Now he'd the same urge.

'I tell you, Reverend, you'll find it hard to equal Jed at his job. You can herd and point in the right direction as long as you like, but you'll manage only a few stray sheep for your flock. Sheep heft to their own side of the hill.'

So Hunter wanted open confrontation. He would not get it from him. He made no reply.

The man laughed. 'Sheep seldom stray. But you will get a congregation.' He was smirking now. 'When there is winter snow, Falstone is a step too far.'

Hunter turned on his heel and with a gesture to his dog took the track to the village. There was no invitation to join him. The man's back told Gregory that he was on an impossible mission.

He looked at the village below. Falstone nestled beside the River North Tyne. It looked self-contained and smug. Judging from Farmer Hunter it was not the neutral territory he needed. Smoke coiled from chimneys on the small houses around the village square. Beside them nestled the Black Cock. The local hostelry had no spire to act as guide but it was a natural village meeting place. He imagined the noise and laughter emanating from its open door and windows. He had worked up a thirst. From his vantage point he could smell the camaraderie. Jed and his master would be as at home there as in the U R C church. The only difference there would be no blessing at the end to send them on their way.

Hunter reached the inn door and looked up to where Gregory was still standing, before he disappeared from view. Gregory pursed his lips. He knew he did not like the man. He was too smug by half. He thought with a stab of jealousy, Hunter is the kind of man who would know Kitty Linn. He turned back the way he had come.

The rectory door was open. There was noise coming from the entrance hall. Loud brush strokes swept the flag stones and the dust filtered up into the air before subsiding. The woman ceased in mid flight.

'Mind sir, you don't get swept up with the rubbish.' Her good humoured eyes peered up into his. Gregory smiled back.

'Mrs Dodds! You look as though you mean business. I'd better get out of your way.' She was tiny, wren-like and her movements were busy, just like the bird. She came twice a week to do for him. Cecilia had found her and, though the woman kept out of his way, she had made her presence felt. Water and polish and good food were her offering. She looked wholesome, her dress freshly laundered, her hair neatly tied so that not a wisp escaped.

'My study, Mrs Dodds have...?'

'I've already done your study, sir, as I knew you would want to be in there.'

'My desk?'

'I took the liberty of tidying your desk. I hope that was right.'

'Did you find anything that shouldn't be there?' It was a foolish question and sounded so.

The woman frowned. 'What could you be meaning by that?'

'Well I...I,' The second time that day Gregory was floundering. 'It's hard to explain, I....'

'Well, yes, Reverend, I did.' She peered up into his face and there was a slight frown. Gregory looked at the woman. Surely he could not have overlooked the hens of whisky? He had searched as though his very life had depended on them. Had they been there all along?

No. Disappointed, he watched Mrs Dodds put her hand into her apron pocket; no room to hide anything of significance there. Gregory could only wonder at the trifle. With a tut of satisfaction she found what she sought.

'See, sir these long black hairs caught between your papers?'

Gregory eyed the delicate tress and his face flamed. The woman laughed.

'Mind you wrap them round your wrist tonight and you'll be sure to dream of your true love.'

5

The whore's eyes were accusing, her brows were the shape of the hills about the rectory, her breasts were ice-smoothed, gentle, rolling country that he longed to explore. It was his recurring dream. Up in the deepest cleugh he would find her. Gregory woke in a sweat, and he started from the bed. He was shaking. The room was ice cold. Panic was a coating of frost that covered his limbs and made his feet skid to the window. He drew back the shutters. A thick covering of snow hid the land and highlighted the church of St Aidan. It stood like a white ghost, tall and spectral in the moonlight. Accusing eyes followed him back to the cold bed, but they were no longer those of the whore. They were the intelligent eyes of the man who had altered his life. They said he'd saved the nation; he'd certainly saved the easily-led boy that day in Plymouth.

The ship was man quiet. There was not a cloud to be seen in the blue sky above the Admiral's head.

'So, lad does this not remind you of a northern summer day? Not too hot, like Portugal, not too cool like the South Atlantic. Does it not make you just a little homesick?' The man's small humorous mouth smiled at him, his eyes under arched dark eyebrows were friendly.

'Aye, sir.' he gave the Admiral the answer he expected. 'Though, sir I can hardly remember it.'

'That is to be regretted. On such a day we should be in the Cheviots striding over the land of far horizons, crossing hill streams, reaching the feral goats in their high country, crushing the Scotsmen's heids underfoot.'

'But, sir?'

The Admiral laughed as he saw Gregory's surprise. 'Scotsman's heids? Tis the local name for cotton grass. There's no finer sight than a carpet of white cowering on an English hill top. Would you not agree?'

'I've never been north of Newcastle, sir.'

Collingwood looked disappointed. 'Then you need to be educated, lad. Come let me show you the promised land.'

The Admiral flattened the map across his desk. Gregory, awed to be standing in Collingwood's cabin, looked at the parchment and saw that it was no treasure-island map.

'This is a road map of Northumberland, lad, dated 1770.' Collingwood fingered the spread sheet. 'But it's hardly changed. Only Otterburn has been linked by road to Carter Bar since then.' He leaned closer to the almost empty map. 'It's the drove roads cutting through the hills that link Scotland and England. Clennell Street, you know, is wider than the Tyne Bridge. It's all of twenty feet across yet just a green road flattened by the feet of cattle heading for the city, not to mention those of tinkers, tailors, and invading Scots. And they're still used by smugglers.'

'The sun was na up, but the moon was down

For succour ye'se get nane frae me

Gai seek yor succour where ye paid blackmail

For, man! Ye ne'er paid money to me.'

There was an astonished silence. Collingwood looked as though he'd been hit.

'How came you by that, lad? You said you had not been into the Border Country.'

'No, but one doesn't need to travel to a place to know it. I know of Venice through the Bard's play though I have not sailed its canals.'

The Admiral threw back his head and laughed. Gregory grinned. What had made him so brave?

'You know the Border Ballads do you?' The Admiral beamed, 'Some would say they match the Shakespeare sonnets.'

'They are poems, very much of their place of origin.' Gregory aired his knowledge.

'So they are, lad. That's why I love them.' The Admiral touched his blue and gold epaulettes. 'I'd exchange these for the simple smock and a walking stick any day to roam those hills and a return in the evening to my fireside and family.' He paused, 'My son will be your age.' He looked at Gregory. 'I would he turn out such a one as you.'

Gregory showed his surprise as he related the story to Macnab.

'You'll not believe this, but I stood in the Admiral's cabin and we discussed poetry! And what's more the Admiral laughed!' Gregory described the scene blow by blow.

Macnab, listening to his breathless account looked sceptical. 'Ye're pulling ma leg, laddie, Everyone kens the man is melancholic. It's only his wee dog, Bounce, who brings a smile to his face.'

Gregory nodded. Collingwood's devotion to the small mongrel was common knowledge. Withdrawn and isolated by his position, the Admiral had no soul mate since he'd lost his friend Captain

Grindall to the command of another ship. It was lonely at the top. His dog received confessions and secrets, kept his counsel and at the end wagged his tail.

From that day Gregory joined the Admiral and Bounce. They made a trio.

In his Northumberland rectory Gregory was at his desk as soon as the early winter light allowed his eyes to scour the written word. It had been many days since he'd put on his reading glasses, and, figuratively speaking, his thinking cap. The memory of his conversation with Collingwood brought the usual glow of pleasure that was undimmed, even after a dozen years. Even now he marvelled at his cheek and how it had transformed his life, his knowledge of the Border Ballads gaining him the interest and fatherly care of his famous fellow countryman. He would not be a clergyman today except for his timely recitation of that poem. That morning in the great man's cabin had changed his life. He shuddered to think of the path he might have followed if he had continued to take part in the shameful activities common on his Majesty's ships. He had clung to his God-sent rescue however often the flesh had tempted.

He kept his head down the whole morning. He'd not penned a sermon in weeks. There had been neither the inspiration nor the audience to merit any thought provoking homily. The previous Sunday he had recited the one written for the Sabbath before that. He need not have worried; there was no one to accuse him of repetition. His brain was as unproductive as the scene before his window. Winter, as Hunter had forecast, had come early. Gregory felt a childish annoyance that the man's confident prediction had proved right. The snow, unsullied by footprints, curled against the church door, nature's barricade against any intrusion. The silence was tangible.

Here was peace and a perfect setting for a scholar lost in his books. For that was what he had become. Why had he buried his head so effectively in the Admiral's books? To please himself or the Admiral? It had been an opportunity that Gregory had seized with both hands, the jealousy of his ship-mates a small inconvenience. Jock had remained loyal as he listened to the latest facts gleaned by Gregory from Collingwood's library. All Scots were scholars he said even if they never opened a book

'Did you know, Jock, that when Julius Caesar came to England he didn't bother to go as far as Scotland?' Gregory passed on the information gleefully.

The large tomes kept the boy enthralled in his mentor's quarters long after he should have been in his bunk. Candle shadows became long and the dog Bounce stretched and stirred. He did not like sharing his master and Collingwood reprimanded the dog. 'If you were at home in Morpeth you'd have two children to share my attention.'

'Suffer little children to....' Gregory pondered the text. Was it appropriate and did he have any hopeful words to relay? He thought of the thin undernourished girl who had visited the Howick's kitchen, the eggler on her round with butter and eggs. Here was stark reality from the beautiful girl of his dream who'd plied less wholesome fare. And he too was a misfit; Thorneyburn was a place for a scholar, and he had thought himself one, but it was not enough. He envied Thomas Howick in his cocoon of knowledge. He still had a lot to learn. 'Suffer little children to come unto me.' He was one of them.

Physical labour was what he needed. He put on his boots and went out into the snow. He found a plank of wood in an outhouse and with it he cleared a path. His back arched and bent as he tackled the drift at the church door. The plank scraped against the stone in a noise that was as satisfying as a mason's chisel. He stood and rested on his improvised implement and surveyed his handiwork. He felt the gain from the physical activity and he had created a path to the church 'Now then, Lord,' he said aloud. 'It's up to you to send me feet to climb these steps.' He smiled to himself. That would be as big a miracle as any recorded in the Bible.

Sunshine percolated the church. It made the honey stone warm and inviting. Today could see the start of the congregation of names that one day would appear on the wall memorials. He pondered them; Hunter? Dodds? And soon, as word spread there would be more from the farms and cottages that pock-marked the area. Today they would choose to attend the nearest church. His clearing of a path to the door would not be in vain. Sheep heft to their side of the hill in inclement weather, Caleb Hunter had admitted the fact.

Gregory's text would be just that…HEFT TO YOUR SIDE OF THE HILL. Here and now, in a brand new church of God, in a new beginning, life's miracles will happen. They should look no further than their own back yards for reward and satisfaction. And he should start by heeding his own words. He gazed down the nave to the door. No screen separated it from the chancel and his view was uninterrupted. He was ready to greet the first arrival.

He waited. There were no hurrying feet. He strode to the door and opened it, placing a jamb of wood to secure it back. A closed door was uninviting. It made no difference. Gregory waited until a slow and painful dawning of the truth told him that today would see no hoped-for miracle; his homily would have to be kept for yet another week.

He closed the door behind him.

Greenhaugh was a cluster of cottages he'd passed on the day he had first come to Thorneyburn. Gregory knew there he would find Mrs Dodds and her family. He struggled through the snow. The going was flat, a mile back along the track that he'd followed with a growing feeling of unease just a few months before. It was the same feeling now in the opposite direction.

A thin wisp of smoke rose from the squat building. A single door and window were tight closed, would he beg, would he cajole?

It was the eggler girl who answered, her face pinched blue, her nose and eyes running. She wiped them with her hand. Gregory took a step back in surprise then assumed his full height. 'Today is the Sabbath. The good Lord does not take snow as an excuse for non attendance at church.' The girl looked blank. 'Does your mother not keep the Sabbath? I....'

'Mam,' the eggler called over her shoulder and it was Mrs Dodds who came to the door, incomprehension written all over her face. She looked harassed. She wore no Sunday-best clothing on her back but was dressed in her rectory cleaning garments... long grey skirt and blouse covered by a voluminous apron. Gregory held out his hand.

'I had hoped to see you in Church this Sunday, Mrs Dodds.'

'And so you will, Reverend. We plan to come to your service tomorrow.' The woman frowned. 'It is Saturday today.'

6

Mrs Dodds was surrounded by a skirt of children, different ages making an erratic hem line. Faces from a foot high to three feet looked up at Gregory, eyes the same blue material. Their laughter echoed that of their mother, an easy garment that was loose and free flowing. Gregory stared at them and felt a surge of annoyance. He pulled his cloak about him. The Christian cloth deserved respect and these children were laughing at him. Where was the joke? It was a simple mistake. And so very foolish.

Gregory began to laugh. It sounded strange but as the noise harmonised with the children it became an unaccompanied hymn that would have raised the rafters if they had been in Church. Mrs Dodds wiped her eyes as the tears streamed down her face and she blew her nose loudly.

'What else can we make, sir, if we don't make mistakes?'

'Indeed, Mrs Dodds, I should take that as my text for tomorrow.' He nodded ruefully. 'I should go home and rewrite my sermon.' He made no effort to go. The children moved to the door.

'Come in, sir. Jessie,' she addressed the little eggler. 'Go fetch Reverend Gregory a couple of eggs.'

Gregory protested and Mrs Dodds shook her head. 'They're from our hens, and good they are too.' She led the way into the cottage. The eggs were warm. He should have something in exchange to hand round, but their eyes held no expectation. The hearth was empty, not even ashes showed previous function. What had he to offer them? His harvest of books?

'Do you go to school?' He did not know even that. He felt ashamed of his lack of knowledge. The room was dark. Reading would be tiresome in such conditions. 'Can you read?' He addressed the eggler.

'Our Jessie can read. Miss Howick is teaching her. But as you can see, our crowded room isn't the best place.'

'Does she have a bedroom?' Gregory looked to the ladder that led above their heads.'

Mrs Dodds laughed. 'It's as black as night up there. Why have windows in a room where one goes only to sleep?'

'Then she must make use of my study.' Gregory smiled and felt further the rising of his spirits that had improved ever since he'd knocked on the cottage door. With a stab of chagrin he thought, so it's the thin, under nourished little girl that God intends to sit at my desk, not the dark-eyed temptress of my dreams. He sighed and felt a surge of hope.

'We shall be in Church tomorrow.' said Mrs Dodds

Gregory smiled. 'That's good to hear.'

'It is nearer than Falstone. Jessie will be glad. It'll give her longer at her studies.'

Outside, Gregory stood in the snow and looked about him. It was the same silent, white world that had existed before he'd gone into the cottage, but now it looked different. In the distance he could hear sheep bleating. Hadn't he come out to find his flock and already he'd rounded up those near at hand? It had taken only a knock at the door to start the count. He looked to the horizon. It was white and unbroken. There would be cleughs and hollows where sheltering sheep waited.

He walked northward following the Tarset stream until another burn joined forces. He was surrounded by water. And across the barricade water was a building, a sign of habitation at last. Gregory eyed the unwelcome-looking house, he even hesitated to call it such. Was it for man or animal?

The Bastle glowered down on him. He'd heard of such dwellings that housed both man and beast. Solid, unadorned, it was functional and safe. As in the cottage, there were few windows or doors, built in the days when more than likely it would be one's enemies that sought entrance. Gregory forded the stream, ice cold water brimming his boot. 1602 was carved above the lintel of the house, built beside the tower once fear of the marauding Scots was no more. Today animals and people no longer lived together.

Gregory knocked on the solid oak door. It looked unused. He frowned. He'd come this far and would not accept defeat. He hammered again and this time there was response. The door squealed its protest as it opened and an enquiring eye appeared at its edge. Caleb Hunter was unsmiling, his large face reddened, gargoyle-carved. The dog Jed welcomed, dancing about Gregory's feet as though the visitor was the last sheep to be gathered.

'Steady, boy.' Gregory put out a restraining hand. ' It's I who am the shepherd today. I am come to herd my flock.'

Caleb Hunter laughed. 'Then you should be ashamed of yourself, Felton. You're after another man's animals. Mother! Here's a reiver wanting entrance.' His laughter was a different sound from that of the children; theirs held mirth. Still, he held the door open and Gregory followed him into a hall and on into a parlour.

Mrs Hunter was seated by a roaring fire. She had tapestry in her hand, the red wool threads reflecting her long auburn hair. In the shadowed room she looked youthful, too young to be called mother by Caleb. A fine brocade dress circled tiny feet and her long neck held a small delicate head. She inclined it to Gregory and held out her hand.

'Our lad told we aboot ye. We waited for ye to come by.' She looked a duchess, sounded a servant.

Gregory took her hand gratefully. Here was a welcome he accepted out of all proportion to the offering.

'Mrs Hunter, it is kind of you. I apologise for not coming to see you sooner.'

'What matter! Caleb got wrong when he told me he'd met you and hadn't asked you to come by. I look for visitors.' Her voice changed. 'What do you think of our home? Is it not stylish?' Gregory looked about him. 'The latest fashion at its best, would you not say? Or it will be, when I've done with it.' Mrs Hunter leant to her foot stool and picked up an open book that she'd been reading as they entered. 'See, I have Thomas Hope's Household Furniture and Interior Decoration. Ye ken he spent eight years studying ruins in Europe and Egypt?'

Her son snorted his mirth. 'So, mother, you think we live in a ruin?'

His mother showed her displeasure. 'You know fine what I mean. Everyone knows of Egyptian art. We have Mr Napoleon to thank for that. Have you been to Egypt, Mr Felton?'

Gregory shook his head.

'Byron has called him a mere house finisher, Mr Hope I mean, not Napoleon, but there I cannot agree. He's changing fashion. I would have thought at the very least you would have sailed down or is it up the Nile, Mr Felton?'

'Mr Napoleon, as you rightly say, did dominate a few good years of my life, but Egypt's not a place I got to. I feel it a loss.' Gregory looked about the room. 'Our adversary is no longer able to enjoy works of art, unlike you, madam. He has only four walls and I think they will be but plastered. There will not be the fine tapestries you have here. Are they all your own work?'

Mrs Hunter looked gratified. 'Indeed sir. I learnt myself to embroider.' She passed the Hobbs book to her visitor. 'See for yourself, the furniture with which I wish to surround myself.' Gregory surveyed the gilt couch that bedecked the page. His hostess watched gratified as he began to flick through the pages. He felt a tinge of admiration for the woman. She was trying to make a silk purse out of a sow's ear.

Gregory thought so why not he? He should find useful employment, produce something to show for his efforts; something tangible. After all, didn't the devil find work for idle hands? His tools were idling in the outhouse, he had not made a single model ship since coming to Thorneyburn.

At the back of the book, a child's nursery and its fittings filled a whole page. On a shelf sat an open doll's house furnished from top to bottom. Yes, there was a task within his skills and when it was finished he could give it to Jessie. His pleasure at the thought of making such a toy showed on his face. His hostess mistook his look.

'So already you see the couch in my room? You, sir, shall be the first to be seated upon it.'

'Madame? I look forward to that.'

Her son was dismissive. 'You'd need a few sheep skins to pay for that and then even the Reverend in his Sunday best wouldn't be good enough to sit on it. Mam, enough of your fussing.'

Mrs Hunter tossed her head, 'My taste is way ahead of any of our neighbours.' She smoothed the silk skirt of her dress and preened her long neck.

'Mam, I'm sure the Reverend hasn't noticed. Anyway, he hasn't got all day, nor me neither.' Caleb turned his back on his mother and furrowed his eyebrows at Gregory. 'So then, what can we do for you?'

'I hope to see you at Saint Aidan's tomorrow. It is but a short walk and in this weather more accessible.'

Caleb grinned. 'You've got a point there. I should be able to stagger that distance, though it'll not be the weather that incapacitates me. It's already past my first dram. Have a drink with me and we'll seal our bargain on the whisky! I'll not take no for an answer, man.' as Gregory hesitated. 'One for the road, I've never known a Reverend yet to refuse.'

Mrs Hunter rose to her feet to follow her son's bidding. 'Mind it's the best stuff, woman, only quality for the parson.'

His mother glided to the door, her head held high her back straight. Her friends would hear of Caleb's new drinking companion.

Gregory reluctantly seated himself. Just one small measure, the winter afternoon was closing in.

The jug was coarse. It looked out of place in the over-furnished room. Gregory recognised it at once. It was the replica of the grey hen that had stood on his study desk, placed there by Kitty Linn. He breathed deeply, he could smell the distant heather moor and with it the morning dew.

7

Gregory had optimism a-plenty on this Sabbath morning. Was it God or the Dodds family who had granted him a second chance? This was the day when he would begin his ministry. He felt a great surge of good will. His brain was clear and racing.

Only yesterday, Caleb Hunter and he had drunk the nectar from the grey hen, neither wanting to be the first to concede defeat. His new found friend had thrust the flagon under his arm as he rose to take his leave.

'There's one for the road, Reverend, quite literally.' And the farmer's words followed him down the track and back over the burn, the precious liquid spilling out onto the pristine snow. The stain was brief. Gregory felt the impulse to bend down and scoop the treasure up into his mouth. It was a waste. He stared down at the brown liquid as it seeped over the virgin white. It was a pointer; for whom? His befuddled brain saw the mark left by the Hunters' dog for a local bitch. He laughed aloud. She will come again. Until then he held her grey hen.

She was fact. The jug was heavy. He carried it hugged to him like a sleeping child. He'd congratulated the Hunters on their whisky and the lady of the house looking suitably gratified made no reply. Caleb had winked a deep meaningful gesture, also unaccompanied by any explanation. Gregory made no enquiry; he'd the sense not to probe. Questions brought reluctance, time would tell. Eventually Caleb would boast it was in the nature of the man. He'd become taciturn as he drank and, but for his parting witticism, monosyllabic. Gregory realised with smug satisfaction that he could hold his drink better than his new-made friend, or rather drinking companion. Another drinking session or two and Hunter would reveal the source of his morning dew.

There was no dew this Sabbath morning. The ground was covered in an unbroken carpet of white, fringed with a sky as blue and beautiful as a tranquil sea. The colour dazzled the eyes and lifted the spirits. He'd bemoaned the emptiness of the landscape, its vastness emphasising his insecurity, but masked with snow he saw in it a new beauty waiting to be revealed.

It had snowed all night. The church door was again blocked. He must open it up to those who would track their way to the church in a few short hours.

His old life had been run on muscle power but, however tired, he'd never fallen asleep over a book. How he had soaked up the new knowledge. Macnab had said he could see the boy's head visibly grow. He'd laughed when the lad, on achieving midshipman, needed the same size of hat as Collingwood, easily beating that of Lord Nelson. It will be Admiral next for you, he'd said.

His learning had gained him no kudos with the rest of the crew whilst his whore encounter brought a constant sniggering behind the hand. He'd seen the contempt in the eyes of the girl and Vincent Byers' open scorn. It was the Admiral who had given no rebuke but instead had provided something to fill his mind. The long boring blockade of the Mediterranean ports that followed Trafalgar gave him his schooling.

Gregory stood in the pulpit and looked down on a dozen expectant faces. All those hours of study had brought him here.

'Are ye the wheat or are ye the tares?' The rhetorical question got no reply. But there was a flicker of interest on the upturned faces as they sought the relevance of the question to themselves. The good or the bad? An old harvest sermon, was it apt for this late harvest in snow when his flock had at last sought his side of the hill? Or a foolish enquiry and meaningless in hill country where animals not crops were of concern to the likes of the Hunter family. His text should have been obvious; the straying and saving of one sheep. Would Caleb Hunter search the last cleugh for a solitary buried animal?

Gregory thought not. Yet a solitary lamb for him would be worth the shepherding. And he had not just one but the beginnings of a flock. He looked down at the bent heads. Half a dozen pews held his first congregation, local families with names as yet unknown. They had followed the Dodds family, cutting a narrow track through the snow, following one in front of the other like the sheep out on the hillside, but eventually they would chose to come because of what he had to offer.

The Dodds family in their entirety had braved the weather and they filled a pew to the back of the church. Mother sat at the aisle end and then there was a descending order of height as if they had been measured before they took their seats. Uniformity went hand in hand with the spotless appearance of her flock. That their clothing was less than adequate on such a day seemed to give them little cause for complaint. They snuggled together under the watchful eye of the mother. The father sailor was the other side of the world.

One lamb stood out from the rest: the eggler girl. She was all of twelve years, his age when he had gone off to fight the French. But she looked much older than the morose, shy boy that he had been. The girl was tall for her age and held her head proud as though already she knew her worth. Seated beside her mother they were shoulder to shoulder. She sat Sabbath-restrained ready to be unleashed with the final blessing. There were no sheep dogs here, but he could imagine the energy released with the opening of the church door. The girl walked the hills in all weathers. He stared down at her. She had no need to answer his question. Tares were not part of her make-up.

God had sent the whore again last night and this time Gregory had taken his pleasure. But when he'd dared to look her in the face he'd seen her disdain. She had struggled with her skirts, tried to push him away with two large whisky hens and with one final effort she had crashed them across his skull.

There was no mark to his head, no scar to feel. Gregory was on his knees before the altar. The children had gone laughing out and away into the white hills. Gregory clasped his hands together. God had sent him to Thorneyburn to test him and find his ultimate salvation. In the cold light of day no track led to his temptress. Had she taken the place of the ship's whore? He saw they were one and the same. They were the tares in his field. But the wheat grew strong and her name was Jessie.

8

They came now to his church, Sunday morning after Sunday morning, even after the snow had melted away into the land and the hard ice of winter made their path more treacherous. They came of their own choice, the cottage families filing in ones and twos, his white-faced, hornless cheviot sheep that soon had names, characters and individuality that he found absorbing.

Reticent and shy, prickly and suspicious, all sitting on the edge of their seats, his aim to make them feel the pew backs. A path was worn to the church door. Lowered heads were raised, eyes fixed on his and he could put names to faces. Gradually they moved up the church. The early reticence of where to sit had meant them herding to the back but as the newness of the church and its incumbent had worn off they moved nearer like inquisitive animals. Now he stared down at Martin Dodds, brother-in-law to Mrs Dodds, and his family. As head of the extended family they sat directly in the pew in front, so as Jessie and family moved up the nave so did their cousins, keeping one jump ahead. Finally they could go no further and were seated so that Gregory could watch the ice on the man's head thaw and become a thin trickle down a runnel of wrinkled skin and end up escaping into his collar. He sat unmoving, his hands clasped tightly in his lap. Not so his two sons who sat fidgeting and bored and Gregory could sense rather than see the catapults that made their fingers itch. He wondered if perhaps they would be the ones to make the first impression on the unmarked walls and he had to hide his smile. Anything was better than nothing. He too had been a rebel once.

Their cousin had a name. She was Jessie. And it suited her. Matter of fact and old beyond her years, her brown eyes watchful, attentive, showing neither happiness nor displeasure.

Gregory walked to Greystead the day after the advent of his new congregation. Ignoring the front door, he knocked on the kitchen door and it was the eggler who opened it, Cecilia only just behind. Cecilia looked surprised and pleased to see him.

'I've been hearing from Jessie you achieved Morning Prayer yesterday. Hence you're self-satisfied look?' She laughed as Gregory changed his expression. 'I'm glad. Don't mind us. Father is quite happy to read aloud to me. He is the original contented scholar. His mind is as large as any cathedral congregation. And God, I think, likes the sound of father's voice. What's wrong with a soliloquy? You should hear Thomas Howick read Shakespeare.'

'I like you reciting it, miss.' Jessie's voice was enthusiastic.

Gregory was surprised at the girl's bravado and glad of it. Luckily for him, he'd not been tongue-tied in front of Collingwood; reciting the border ballad had been the best few words he had ever spoken. The sudden pleasure on the Admiral's face had been his invitation to a new and absorbing world just as now Jessie's obvious intelligence cried out for nurture.

Cecilia looked pleased at the girl's comment. 'It will not be long before you are as good as any of us. But the proof of the pudding is in the eating. Come, Reverend Felton and listen to my star piano pupil.'

'I am the only pupil you have.'

'That is very true. So your audience will have no chance for a comparison.' Cecilia as pedantic as the girl led them into the front room of the rectory. Again it was the exact copy of the Thorneyburn parlour but there again the comparison ended. Gregory spent his time divided between kitchen and study. His sitting room remained unused.

The Greystead furniture did not ape the fashion of Mrs Hunter but it had all the homely attributes of everyday, loved pieces in an eclectic collection.

The small grand piano was clearly well-used. A worn stool, its pattern long since removed, fronted the instrument, its top already open. There was no hesitancy or fumbling as the girl began to play. Cecilia caught Gregory's eye behind her back and there was a smile of satisfaction. Cecilia did not smile unnecessarily.

'May I introduce you to your future organist.'

Gregory bowed as the girl looked at him. Her eyes did not flicker. Complete conviction was written all over her face. Gregory thought here is an acorn ready to sprout ...?

As if Cecilia could read his thoughts she said, 'You've told me of the Admiral's acorns, here's one of the great oaks.'

'Yes, however thin the soil, however fierce the wind.' There was utter belief in his voice. At that moment Gregory could see the mature tree.

'Well I haven't got all day to waste. Your mother will be seeking you, child, and a busy parson needs to tend the entire vineyard not just the most fertile part.'

'Indeed.' Gregory pursed his lips. The girl's eyes were fixed on him. 'But I would like to help, Jessie?' He stroked his chin. 'I can offer her language. She could learn Latin?' He spoke over the child's head to Cecilia, reluctant to voice his offer and see doubt in the girl's eyes. What need did a peasant girl have of such knowledge?

'Latin did you say?' Jessie's face was a study. 'Then I could speak with the Romans.'

Cecilia threw back her head in a stuttering laugh of pleasure and disbelief. He joined in. A petulant look crossed the girl's face. Cecilia gave her a quick hug as she lifted her from the stool, 'Why not? It's an excellent idea, Reverend Felton. But come, eggler girl, back down to reality and on with your round. There are people eager for provisions, not notes of music or foreign words.'

Gregory hummed as he strode home, his mind full of beaten eggs and soliloquies and Latin phrases. He'd intended to seek out Caleb Hunter on the return journey, an offer of refreshment and a companionable chat there for the taking. But he crossed the Tyne river and turned away from the Tarset burn. Many times it was the smaller obstacles that proved the bigger problem.

He thought of the Hunter family as he strode home. He'd been gratified they'd turned up to his service; had felt a spasm of triumph when they entered the church and walked to the front of the nave, taking their place prominently below the pulpit. Theirs was not the symmetry of the family of his house keeper but a jagged drop, from son to mother; Caleb's large head obscuring the eldest Dodds girl, forcing Gregory to move to the furthest extremity of his vantage point.

He'd avoided eye contact with his pushy visitors and he felt the same reluctance now. It would be some time before he returned to their bastle; it held no welcome. He knew now he would never ask the question that had burned his lips on his first visit to the farmer's fortified home. Then he'd hardly been able to drink the whisky poured from the grey hen, so keen was he to know its provenance.

The ominous house stood away on the skyline. The stone was dark pigmented and from another quarry than his freestone house and it revealed a very different face. The fortified house was meant to keep out intruders: rectories surely said welcome.

He thought of Greystead. That had a welcome sign even before one stepped over the threshold; Cecilia made sure of that. Why had he gone there this morning? Had he gone there to boast of his new congregation? He hoped not. No, he'd wanted Cecilia to share his pleasure and there was the draw of home fire and good home baking. Yes he felt at home there. She was a woman as strong minded as any man.

Was she happy with her lot? No. That she was not. How thwarted was she in her father's house and so well equipped for better things. He felt the usual stab of sympathy and fellow feeling. She, like him was a caged lion. He remembered her delighted laugh at the precocity of her pupil and then her sudden apparent annoyance with both the girl and him. He saw again the child seated on the piano stool between them. Both Cecilia and he needed the challenge.

The Admiral's Latin Grammar awaited the pupil. It was well thumbed. Gregory fancied he could still smell the Mediterranean as he took it from the shelf and placed it on his desk. Those long weeks at sea, when they had sought to harry the French, had been the happiest of his life. Head bent over book, as though his very life depended on it, ignorance far greater an enemy than any Gallic menace.

She came; the eggler at the end of her round. And Gregory's pleasure at sight of the small figure and the jug of milk that she carried brought a smile to his face. How his old friend Jock Macnab would have laughed at his preference for the frothing white innocence, rather than the whisky that had once been his succour.

'Puella is a beautiful word.' Her voice caressed the sound. 'Our Jimmy is only a puer. I shall tell him so. He will not like to be so short and uninteresting. 'Homo,' she looked at Gregory a shy smile on her face 'it sounds sensible and matter of fact. Does it suit you?' She pursed her lips and gave no answer. 'What of Miss Howick? Femina, or matrona? Neither word is right for her. I cannot imagine her as a married lady.'

'Quite the little Homo sapiens talking,' Gregory said, 'sapiens or prudens, either would suit you.'

Jessie looked pleased. 'They are words to describe my mother. She is Mrs Prudens. She will like her new name.'

As Gregory wrote down the list of vocabulary for the next lesson, Jessie chatted nineteen to the dozen, Latin words releasing English ones she hardly knew existed.

'When I walk the hills I shall shout out the new words. We shall have the best educated sheep in the land. What is the word for sheep, so that I can tell them?'

'Ovis.'

'That's short like puer and easy to learn.'

'I am the Pastor for my flock. What do you think that word means?'

Jessie looked at him thoughtfully. 'Shepherd!' She was the sponge he had been and his study had become the ship's cabin that had widened his world.

In the time when he knew his pupil would be otherwise employed and his next sermon had been written, he walked abroad looking for wood. The trees stood out lone and beacon-like on the skyline or clustered in sociable groups in sheltered cleughs; sometimes they straddled along the winding water courses that descended the hills in hidden clefts. Where there were trees there was wood.

His wood-working tools had lain idle in his travel chest, unused and unwanted. Now they had purpose. He came home from his forays, pulling, carrying, dragging any offering. And the feeling of satisfaction as he stored his gleanings brought a smile to his face. A few steps led down under the church into a space directly below the nave. The architect in his wisdom had provided an underground room just waiting to become his workshop. Sawing and hammering rose as hymns to the vaulted ceiling above, and his tenor voice descanted the refrain. Solus, alone had been a sad word that had entered his very soul. Now it was no longer part of his vocabulary.

The creation took shape; wood, nails, imagination where knowledge was lacking. The idea had come from Mrs Hunter's furnishing book. The doll's house had been in the imaginary child's nursery. It had instantly appealed to the child in him. How splendid to build your house of dreams. He would build no rectory too bleak; no cottage too humble; no bastle too repelling. He closed his eyes and recalled a house he had seen in the Balearic Islands with white wood that reflected the sun and windows that were large enough to let in the sun. How the Dodds children would love it.

9

The curlew heralded the spring, late returned to the hill country. It called invitingly over the moor. Lazy sun struggled back over the horizon. Peat-stained the Tarset burn bubbled from the winter hills. Long blocked by snow, valleys that dissected the Cheviots were now open passes. Gregory felt restless. It was not a day to descend into his carpenter's workshop or sit idle at his study desk.

A cool invigorating breeze lifted his spirits and his wide purposeful strides soon had his blood racing. It was a day when the mist hugged the valley bottom in a narrow confining line. He had soon risen above it.

'Are we going to talk to the Romans?' The voice, eager and breathless made him start. His thoughts had been miles away. 'I think my vocabulary is good enough now.' Jessie, her arms and legs bare and unfettered, looked the hill sprite.

'Why not, Jessie I am sure they would talk to you if they could?' Gregory smiled down at the girl but she was an unwelcome intrusion. For once he needed solitude.

'But they can.' Jessie's voice showed her pique. 'They had mouths and ears just like us.'

'Of course, so then, what do you think they would want to hear?' Gregory sought to indulge the girl. 'Would you talk to them about your farm round, your brothers and sisters?'

'O, no.' Her tone was dismissive. 'I shall tell them how much I admire their Julius Caesar.'

Gregory looked surprised. 'But he invaded our land. We would not have welcomed Napoleon Bonaparte. So why the Romans?'

'They brought fine buildings and roads and villas and....'

'Not here in Northumberland. The Great Wall south of us kept them from these parts. This is not villa country. The Romans liked their comfort you know.' He pulled a face, 'and I don't blame them.'

'They are here. I shall take you to them then you will believe me.' The child sounded her scorn.

Gregory was amused. 'So tell me where is the wide-ditched metalled road that we should be travelling on? I see only the pebbles that farmer Hunter has laid to aid access to the farm. And we shall soon have left them behind.'

Jessie didn't bother to answer but there was a stubborn tilt of her head and a look of total conviction as she turned north easterly to the wide expanse of hills that ran unbroken to the skyline. Gregory stifled a sigh. Their road was green and soft and was easy walking. Now in springtime it was not cluttered in waist high bracken, and indolent flies were only just appearing. The hills lay pale and serene and waiting.

Before, he'd walked them only in his imagination and from the memory of Admiral Collingwood: longing and separation from his home had nurtured the eminent sailor's knowledge and he'd painted a landscape that, city-born, Gregory could not visualise. Together they had climbed in their imagination from the craggy ridges of fell sandstone, resistant to erosion but worn into strange shapes by water and wind, to the granite core that lifted Cheviot summit in a boggy alliance with Hedgehope Hill. They had walked the white lands, grass covered, and the black lands that sprouted heather, all cut deep by impatient streams.

His new guide was equally passionate. 'Kielder means violent stream.' Jessie mouthed the fact above the noise of the water; she'd become teacher of a subject that both Admiral and peasant girl thought worth the learning. With a stab of guilt Gregory acknowledged his resistance up until now to be the pupil. He'd humoured the home-sick Collingwood in his imagined land sorties.

'You shall teach me about the hills, Jessie. I shall become your pupil.'

'Oh, no. They are not a subject like Latin. They are just there and always have been.' Jessie's rebuttal was loud and dismissive. Gregory smiled to himself. The role he'd suggested for the girl was alien and quite beyond her imagining, teacher and pupil reversed. They walked in silence; hills crested, valleys used to regain breath.

She was a collie dog. He walked obediently, leading the way though the girl was only inches behind his long strides, nudging him, shepherding him to he knew not where, but keeping him on the right track. He did know he couldn't stop for if he did, there would be the metaphorical snap at the heels just to show who was really in control.

The girl was agile, her feet instinctively sensing the way, her rope shoes and thick mother-knitted socks as confident as drover's boots.

'Never step on the bright green.' she instructed as she took a wide detour. 'It is sphagnum moss beautiful but unreliable and sometimes treacherous.'

Gregory muttered his thanks. 'You'll keep me on the straight and narrow.' He sounded impressed. 'So tell me where we are going.'

He looked up into the sky, it was high and blue and in the distance a great swirl of upward moving cloud mountained the horizon. He felt a corresponding uplift of his spirits. On such a day he was ready for the wider landscape.

'Go back, go back.' The warning rasped through the silence, a sudden note of alarm that stopped Gregory in his tracks. 'Go back.' The strident order came from the rock crag blocking their way. But there was no movement, no sign of life from the bare rock pedestal, even more isolated and remote than his church pulpit. The rock rent by dark cracks stood stark on the hillside. Someone could be hiding. Jessie just inches behind urged him forward. 'Go back.' The grouse, sandstone-coloured, menaced.

'You mind yourself, Mrs Grouse, or Mr Hunter will come to shoot you. And if not, the Romans will snare you for the pot.'

Gregory watched the bird hover above the rocks. It was agitated, warning them to go no further. 'Will the Romans be hostile? Or are they friendly?' He was impatient. He had humoured the girl long enough. Even the bird was telling them to stop. 'Admit to me, Jessie. You have brought me out here on a wild goose chase or is it a grouse hunt?' He smiled at the girl, not wanting to dampen her enthusiasm. 'It's a good joke but one I think that has gone on long enough.' He did not like to think of the miles they'd covered. 'Your Romans, you know, can no longer be here.'

'But they are,' Jessie hesitated, her face flushed, 'though I have not spoken to them. Not yet.'

'You foolish girl, why do I listen?' Gregory exploded in anger, 'No, it is I who am foolish heeding such fanciful tales.'

Only later when he described the scene to Cecilia did he have the grace to feel ashamed. And she of course had no sympathy for the situation in which he had found himself. He should never have believed the girl's story in the first place. Did he not know he was as gullible as the child?

'It is true I have not spoken to them. I thought they would not understand me.' Jessie raised her head and there was a look of haughty defiance in her logical explanation. 'But I have seen them, and now I have the right words.' Abruptly, she turned from him and, forsaking her sheep-dog role, spurted ahead. A surprised Gregory swore as he was forced to follow in pursuit.

As they rounded the rocks, all speech was drowned by a crescendo of noise from an almost vertical stream, angrily descending the slope. Jessie filled her lungs with a deep breath of hill air and shouted. 'This is the place of the Roaring Stream and the foreign invaders.'

The thawed winter snows echoed through the valley in a crescendo of noise and spray. The grouse screamed again its warning, 'Go back.' The hillside rose above them and for a bizarre moment Gregory thought to see sentries on the sudden wall of rock, so much it seemed the wild and inhospitable land of Roman cohort sorties. He admitted this further folly to Cecilia, but from then on his story was edited. How could he have admitted the rest to her?

Large, worked, stone blocks stopped their way. They piled one on top of another in a man-made wall, and between them a track led through what had obviously been a gateway. Gregory stopped in amazement.

'You're right, Jessie, the Romans were here.' His words were apologetic, 'How clever of you to find this fort.' He looked about him in undisguised excitement. 'This surely must have been on the very edge of the Roman Empire.' To the south Hadrian's Great Wall had kept back the barbarians, northward the border of Scotland rested in the encircling hills. 'Not a posting many would be happy with. There must have been at least five hundred men here; just imagine the place in the height of winter.'

Jessie beamed at Gregory's enthusiasm. 'I've seen people here when there was snow on the ground.' She looked up at him shyly. 'I was not close enough to see whether they were happy or not.'

Gregory shivered. 'I would presume not. Did they have cloaks over their togas?'

'The man I saw did not even have a uniform. It would be long since worn out.' She sounded impatient. 'The girl was covered in sheep skins.'

'Go back, go back.' The bird wheeled above their heads, its cry impatient and angry.

Jessie couldn't contain her excitement. 'Salute,' she called down into the empty fort and Gregory joined in the greeting, his laugh rolling over the deserted ground between the old walled ramparts. There was no answer. Jessie called again. 'Salute.'

Gregory addressed his young companion. 'I'm going to give you five out of ten, Jessie. The Romans were here, but now their stone has been used by someone else to build a house in the fort.' He pointed to the mean dwelling that hugged the far wall. Smoke was coiling from the central chimney. 'Someone has been expedient and made use of the old barracks.'

The girl took his hand and began to pull him towards the house.

'They are Romans'

'The ghosts here will be Roman.' He smiled at the girl as they stepped amongst the grassed ridges. 'Here would be the headquarters, here the bathhouse, here the granaries.' He followed the recognised-layout of all Roman forts, learned from the Admiral's books and now traced out there on the hillside. At that moment Collingwood's cabin seemed very close. They walked together towards the one standing building.

Sunlight streamed on to the bare flesh. The woman was bathing, crouched beside the stream, holding her long hair aside as the water from the jug cascaded between her breasts and down on to her naked thighs. Gregory and Jessie stared at the Roman carving that now graced the wall of the cottage.

'How do you like Venus and her attendant nymphs?' The voice startled, Gregory spun round.

'Perhaps it was warmer here then. Or was the scene just in the imagination of a homesick soldier?' We shall never know.' Sparkling eyes teased, as the newcomer pointed to the ancient stone frieze.

'Kitty Linn.' Gregory's voice was a whisper.

'Salute.' said Jessie in a rush of happiness.

10

'So she does exist.' Gregory's words were foolish. Did he say it for his sake or the child's?

'Are you Venus?' Jessie's voice was a whisper.

'I'm no Goddess, am I Rector?' She smiled at Gregory. 'He calls me Kitty Linn.'

Jessie could not contain her disappointment. 'So you know her. Why did you say you didn't?' The childs face was a picture.

Gregory did not like to think what his face must reveal. He fought to regain his composure. Kitty was openly amused.

'So, Rector, you are here. I wondered how long it would take.'

Gregory frowned. 'You knew I would come?' His words were lame, and his next ones were no better. 'I thought you were a figment of my imagination. Hardly something I would follow on a fool's chase.'

'Fool's chase?' She repeated his words with raised eyebrows. 'Do you take yourself for a fool? You saw me with your own two eyes and surely your calling would say you should have blind faith. But no matter, "Seek and ye shall find." ' Her smile was gentle.

'Hunt the Romans, hunt the Romans.' Jessie began to skip round the two adults, bored by their words, 'Hunt the Romans, and we've found one.' She was unable to contain her excitement.

'Romans? I'm not as old as that.' Kitty laughed, 'but we have made use of their old home.' She pointed at the tell-tale Roman stones built into the cottage walls. 'Welcome to Bremenium, though we have no sign on the door.'

'You took back the flagons.' Gregory had eyes only for the woman.

'Yes, how foolish to come to the rectory in the first place. The mist must have got into my brain. It was very thick. I thought I was at another's house. I came back later to retrieve them.' Her laugh filled the ancient fort. 'It would be wrong to put temptation in the way of a parson.'

'There was no fear of that.' Gregory was curt.

'No? You were laid out by the hearth, your breath....' She shrugged her shoulders and looked at the silent child. 'No matter, so then, lassie, what can I give you? We have fresh spring water? Come with me and we will fill the jug.' Was there a hint of disdain in her voice?

Gregory watched the two go happily, hand in hand, down to the stream. The coarse flagon held carelessly in the woman's other hand. She offered whisky or water, depending on the company. He still had the ewer, given to him by Caleb Hunter. Had it been the Hunter house that she had meant to visit? Yes, the bastle had been her destination. He felt a tinge of jealousy of the local farmer who belonged to this land, who enjoyed his drink and made no secret of it. She would not laugh at him. She had laughed at Gregory; a clergyman with thoughts other-worldly, yet weak enough to drink the communion wine.

Her face was dirty, her hem trailed. No, she was no Goddess. He watched them climb back up from the source of water. Good clean liquid cascaded down the side of the jug and it bubbled as she poured it into beakers and silently offered it to her uninvited guests.

She had washed her face in the stream. It shone fresh, red-cheeked, healthy, gone was the voluptuous mystery of her clandestine winter visit. She was homespun in her simple home, a very different girl. And this wild place suited her. Here she was no fish out of water, yet he floundered still in his allotted place.

Her dress was coarse woven cloth and it hugged her figure. He looked away. There was a vegetable patch behind the cottage and evidence of fresh digging. She was another Cecilia. But there were differences. The growing season would be shorter up here. And he could not bear to think of her bending over the garden patch.

He took the proffered water without a thank you. He could not trust his voice. Jessie was not so inhibited.

She looked at her hostess. 'So, you don't speak Latin after all.' Jessie sounded disappointed.

'Do you?'

'O, yes. Well, I'm learning.' She looked to Gregory and he nodded.

'I could teach you, lady.' Jessie flushed and Gregory nodded his assent.

'We could come together, Jessie.' He tried to keep his voice steady. What better way to fill his leisure time than walk the hills with the eggler girl, their destination Kitty, an unlikely parishioner who awaited his counsel?

'So then, Jessie that means you will come again if you can find the way. It is a wild place we do not have many callers.'

'I thought Thorneyburn was remote, but this....' Gregory looked about the spot forsaken by history.

'Were you about to say God-forsaken? That's how I like it.' Mischievous eyes laughed back at him.

'Indeed.'

'So is it to be your mission to alter that?'

'Perhaps, though of course my parishioners are my first priority.' Pomposity hid his growing excitement. Here was reality more intriguing than all his wild imaginings. Up in the border land with Scotland lived a girl who, on lonely hill paths, smuggled its fabled drink to the homes and farms in the patch of northern England that was his parish; and Kitty Linn whisky-runner had brought her trade uninvited to his study desk.

His thoughts made him a silent companion on the return trek, but Jessie chatted. She had shown her disbelieving teacher a genuine Roman fort and, what was more, one that was lived in. It no longer mattered to her that the inhabitants were not real Romans. 'Salute' would resound again.

11

Tearing leaves from home-grown lettuce plants, placed in the middle of the table for all to grab, was the highlight of the visit. It was a pastime more suited to hutched rabbits and Gregory could hardly hide his amazement. He avoided catching Cecilia's eye. He might very well disgrace himself.

It was an unlikely group assembled at the invitation of Mrs Hunter the following Sunday. Gregory, gratified that the woman and her son came occasionally to his church, accepted, with unusual lack of hesitation, to join them and some of their friends in an informal supper. Perhaps she has got her new couch and we are to admire it, he had said to Cecilia and she had answered with a scornful raise of her eyebrows. He was pleased that she and her father were to be there. Cecilia, in her no-nonsense attitude, would be equal to Mrs Hunter. And who else might have been invited? It promised to be a memorable evening.

The bastle house furnishings were the height of comfort and Mrs Hunter bedecked in a fine crimson gown, strove to be the perfect hostess. 'Help tha self. We dinna stand on ceremony here.'

Caleb Hunter, unheeding of their guests, seized some lettuce for himself and stuffed it into his mouth. The soil from the newly-pulled plant sprinkled on to the tablecloth, peppering the pristine white in a shower of dark peat. There was a shocked silence from the assembled visitors. Cecilia's shoulders twitched. Gregory thought, now I have seen it all. This is a God-forsaken place. Jungle savages behaved thus. He had become a missionary in all but name.

What would his shipmates make of his new acquaintances? Effete Byres would have worn his supercilious smile the whole evening, Jock Macnab would have joined in with relish.

The serving girl brought in a large leg of lamb and he wondered if the protocol was to tear the flesh as they did the lettuce. He recoiled. But Caleb took up a large knife and expertly carved. The meat was the best Gregory had ever eaten.

'I suppose the ewe has only just stepped from moor to plate. It did not have far to go. That was excellent.' Gregory smiled his appreciation with words meant to appeal to Cecilia. It was cruel.

Mrs Hunter was gratified. 'There's nothing like home-grown animal on one's table.' Gregory had a vision of the beast astride the white cloth. He choked into his handkerchief.

'Tis simple food but the best, take more, Rector, you need feeding up. Though I'm glad to see you are not the pale thin parson you were a few weeks ago.' Mrs Hunter smiled benevolently.

'His colour is from the open moor.' Cecilia frowned across the table at him. 'Young Jessie led him quite a dance last week. She took him over into Redesdale.'

'That was way beyond your bounds. Seeking out the far heathen were you?' Hunter was amused. 'Are there not enough of us here?'

'Heathen?' Gregory sounded his surprise. 'I thought they were all God- fearing in those parts.'

'Don't you believe it. Border troubles may have belonged to another century. But they are still wild men up there. I tell yer, there's no better pastime than stepping on Scotsmen's heids and trampling them into the ground.'

Cecilia frowned at her host but Gregory laughed, 'Ah, you've not got the better of me there. I've seen the hillside covered with Scotsmen's heids, and it's a fine sight.' He turned to Cecilia, 'That's what they call cotton grass in these parts.'

Caleb looked impressed. 'You're learning Felton. Another twenty years and you might be one of us.'

'I've known that fact since I was a boy.' Gregory sounded defensive, then with a wicked smile, 'Admiral Collingwood told me.'

Mrs Hunter gasped with pleasure at the name of the famous man. 'Why, Mr Felton, if only the dear, good man were still alive, you might have brought him to our humble castle.' She had raised their status.

'So were you really out seeking congregation?' Cecilia interrupted, eying Gregory, a questioning irritation written all over her face. 'That would be more plausible than young Jessie's version.'

Gregory frowned. 'Do not accept all that she says. She has flights of fancy.'

'Well, it certainly sounded strange. You're right to look uncomfortable, Parson Felton.' Cecilia's laugh would have sounded in Redesdale. 'Chasing Roman goddesses figured in her version.'

'Why no?' Mrs Hunters eyes lit up and her fork clattered on to her plate. The new rector was more interesting than she had thought possible.

'Watch it, Felton.' Her son pursed his lips. 'Loneliness can breed madness.'

'So they say, Hunter. Is counting sheep the answer?' Gregory smiled at his host, but felt an irritation both with the man and with

Cecilia; even more so with his friend. She had sought to make him look ridiculous in the assembled company. She'd known the Hunter family would jump at the opportunity to laugh at him. So be it, they could all laugh at him. And he would play to their game.

'Yes, truth to say, I found a goddess.' He surveyed the table. Cecilia raised her eyebrows and their hostess gasped out loud. Suddenly Gregory was beginning to enjoy himself. He could act the simpleton when he wished. He remembered the bumboat at Plymouth and Macnab's amusement at the boy's reaction to the female invasion.

'Yes, I actually touched her.' He was more daring.

'She was real?' Mrs Hunter's voice was scarcely audible. Cecilia was no longer hiding her disbelief.

'A lovely smooth, rounded Venus.' The women mirrored their incredulity. Gregory burst out laughing. He'd gone too far for a gentleman of the cloth: his old wicked sense of humour had not surfaced before in this unfunny land. 'I jest of course, ladies.'

Mrs Hunter looked disappointed. 'Tut, tut, I believe every word from the mouth of a Reverend.'

'Not this one,' said Cecilia.

'The Goddess in question was a carving. It was on an old slab inserted into a cottage wall.' Disappointment and scorn were equal expressions on his listeners' faces. 'A relict of the past, Jessie was right. The Romans had been there, but not for a very long time.'

He looked round the table. He'd had the last laugh. He felt good; company, not of his choosing, had made him want to jest again. And yes, he would apologise later to Cecilia for his behaviour. Yet she had instigated the conversation, aware of what she was doing.

The fact jarred. He would never admit to her the existence of Kitty Lynn. He took a gasp of air. Yes the beautiful girl was flesh and blood.

'I do not like waste.' Thomas Howick filled the silence. 'It's good that the stone has been re-used. It has happened through the decades, the re-use of material for new buildings. Roman Temple sites became Christian churches, Spanish Cathedrals changed into Muslim Mosques, and sometimes back again, depending on who held power.'

'Yes,' Gregory was quick to agree. 'A holy site is a holy site.'

'So, it is strange, gentlemen that your new churches, Thorneyburn and Greystead, are both built on unholy sites?' Caleb Hunter eyed the two incumbents. 'Neither of you have history to back up your presence.' There was silence and he continued. 'No precedent, I'm afraid, however many old books you consult. Why were they built? We all know they are not needed.'

Gregory speechless was unable to think of a compelling reason to convince his host or indeed himself.

'Now then, our Caleb, you are being rude to your guests. Cecilia, perhaps we should now withdraw.' Mrs Hunter half rose but when her guest made no attempt to follow her, she subsided back on to her chair.

Gregory got to his feet. He stammered...'I hope, Mrs Hunter, that in a short time our ministry will answer your son's question. It is a challenge I face.'

Caleb smirked. 'What I've said is a fact, Mother, whether you like it or not; redundant padres in redundant livings.' Her son was openly enjoying himself. 'In fact we have two white elephants, so then, gentlemen, here is a question for you. When your churches are torn down through lack of use, what do you think they will build in their place?'

There was an awkward silence. Gregory thought he should have a clever answer, but his new-found pleasure had already gone. A sheep farmer should not be allowed to get the better of him. And yet he had.

Cecilia looked hopefully from him to her father and back again for a retort that would put their host in his place. When there was none forthcoming, she said,

'One day, folk will flock here.'

The three men looked at her. 'I see perhaps a dual use.' Cecilia, determined to be one up on her host, extemporised. 'The church walls are empty now, waiting to be filled. We could cover them with works of art.'

'That's a good idea, Cecilia' Gregory was eager to agree.

'Yes, figures on the wall, just like the fourteenth-century painting in Hexham Abbey.' She warmed to her subject. 'They look like Northumbrians.'

'Local saints and sinners,' Caleb guffawed 'one wall would be rather empty. I leave you to guess which one.' There was a murmur of amusement. 'I shall sit where I can see both groups. Let us take the ladies first. You, Miss Howick, will certainly be on the good wall. And on the other...?' Caleb paused melodramatically. 'Who would you suggest, Felton?' There was mischief on his face.

'Who do you think, Mother, is destined to stand opposite our worthy guest here, some voluptuous sinner perhaps who would be good to look at?'

Mrs Hunter did not pause for an answer. 'Why, Kitty without a doubt.'

Her son laughed. 'Of course, Mother, there was only one answer. You will agree with us, Rector?' Gregory felt his face flame.

Cecilia raised her eyebrows in surprise, incomprehension written all over her face.

Hunter's fist hit the table. 'No, we can do without the portrait gallery. Let's return to my premise, that our new church has no place in the landscape.' It was his turn to sound petulant; he had already drunk too much.

He said, 'An alehouse would be my choice to occupy the site. Then we would not have to make do with a painted image on a wall. The barmaid would be real flesh and blood. Again, wouldn't you agree, Felton, there is only one candidate?'

'It could only be Kitty,' chorused Mrs Hunter.

Cecilia looked from Hunter to Gregory, her annoyance obvious; liking to be part of the main thrust in any discussion, not the tongue-tied girl she now appeared. That she was not and never would be.

'Gentlemen, you would appear to be more favoured than I. Unfortunately, I am unacquainted with your friend, Kitty. Perhaps you would be so kind as to explain the lady.'

'Lady!' Hunter's laugh was a snort. 'She is not for the likes of you, Miss Howick. She does not mix in your circles.'

'Oh?' Cecilia raised her eyebrows. 'I do not have a circle but a straight path leading to friends.' She looked toward Gregory, trying to re-establish their former rapport. She'd enjoyed their shared amusement, and then somewhere she had lost him. It had been when someone called Kitty had been mentioned. This Kitty had invaded the room as surely as if she had walked in through the door.

12

The sun streamed through the window, casting mosaic squares of light behind the pulpit, making it the obvious candidate for Cecilia's wall of saints. And in most people's eyes she would take pride of place there. She would gaze down at all future congregations from her lofty position and they would see her worth; reassuring and incorruptible.

Opposite, the side stood in deep shadow; that was Hunter's sinner's wall. One did not need to have too fertile an imagination to see the local farmer in his muddy boots and his equally muddy character destined to join the damned. Gregory laughed out loud; he had no compulsion to save the man from his fate. How childish. He sobered. On which wall did he belong? There was no straight answer. He was in limbo, neither place as yet ordained for him.

'Not all that far off thirty and still it's not obvious on which wall I will stand.' It was a sobering thought. 'So here and now my life is at a crossroads. It will be my time at Thorneyburn that will decide where my figure will finally rest.'

He spoke into the empty church, and the words rebounded. He had no desire to spend eternity beside Hunter, but then neither did the thought of standing beside Cecilia for evermore hold any great excitement. Was he good or bad?

He believed in both God and the devil, and with that indecision he belonged in neither camp. He thought if I had paints I would draw Hunter's outline right now in the allotted place. Then his resolve would be simple; to make sure he did not stand next to the farmer in the Great Judgement Gallery.

Caleb Hunter was not likely to enter the church door again, at least not until it had become his local alehouse. Hunter had thrown down the challenge and Gregory welcomed it. The man was right, the church looked ill at ease, hardly established. It was up to him to anchor the new vessel. God in his wisdom had brought Gregory to this inauspicious spot and with his help he would turn it into a holy site that would last a thousand years. It was not his Garden of Eden awaiting the temptations of the Serpent but it was the next best thing. He fell to his knees in front of the altar and the Admiral's voice echoed in his ears.

'Just as I have planted oaks in my lands deep in the Cheviot Hills so, lad, you will plant hope in the souls of men.'

How strange that his Christian mission to Northumberland had sent him to a church that was as alien on its site as Collingwood's oak trees were in theirs.

Gregory's knees had gone dead: he'd been lost in thought. Collingwood had started him on this journey. He, a man who would go down in history, had heeded and rescued a lad destined for the lower deck and all its profanity. He looked up again at the sun-dappled wall and thought, there my place must be.

But standing beside Cecilia? Average height, unremarkable features, hair neither dark nor fair, a kindness mixed with a sharp tongue. He could stand by a worse companion in life and then finally in death. He squinted at the wall. He could almost see the drab colours of her cloak standing beside his clergy black, their hands held lightly in a show of affection and respect.

There was a burst of sunlight on to the wall. Gregory rubbed his eyes Cecilia was in shadow and another girl filled the space.

Her hair was black, polished in the warm light; her figure, clothed in a simple cloak from head to foot, looked innocent and matronly. She held no whisky keg but a simple cross, and she smiled serenely. Gregory groaned aloud. He knew now this girl lived and breathed an uninvited intrusion into his planned and ordered life. She was no imaginary drawing on a plastered wall.

Angrily, he turned his back on the empty space. His wild imaginings would lead him to perdition. He strode down the nave. No images conflicted except that of Kitty. How could she have earned her place on the sunny side? Was he being shown the way for his own salvation? Just as he had been saved so would he save the whisky runner. Was she the reason he had come to Thorneyburn?

There was no grouse to call her warning, "go back, go back"; no small girl to show him the way. It was all so easy his feet sped across the bracken and heather, avoiding the moss bogs and the rocky outcrops. The goddess Venus pointed the way to his Christian mission. The door of the cottage was open. God was a good God.

Voices, Gregory hesitated, she had someone there. He'd come a long way for nothing. He banged on the door and it was loud enough to cause the conversation to cease. Silence, then shuffling noises and hasty feet before a figure emerged into the passage. Gregory thought, what is my excuse? I no longer have the Roman reason. He stuttered, 'Good morning, I was passing your door.'

Dishevelled, she stood in the doorway and stared at him, and there was no answering smile at his foolish words. A man's voice had murmured with her. So there was a man in her life. Of course, how could he have thought otherwise? She had a husband to keep her beyond his thoughts and desires. The feeling of disappointment was a body blow. How could he have imagined that a girl like that would not have a companion? They married young in such places. His thoughts raced. He stood foolishly spinning his pastor's hat in his trembling hand. What possible reason could he have to be there? How ridiculous his 'just passing' had sounded.

'So the Romans have brought you back.' There was a guffaw of laughter as another figure emerged from the cottage. 'You haven't changed much from when you were a boy devouring the Admiral's history books.'

Gregory almost choked in his surprise. There was a face he knew, older, more lined, but the twinkling eyes of Jock Macnab grinned back at him. He stood now beside Kitty his arm about the girl's waist. Gregory stared in disbelief. It could not be his old shipmate with this wild young girl. Yet he remembered the bumboat.

'Jock!' The two men fell on each other in an embrace that dissolved the years.

At last Gregory held his old shipmate at arm's length and surveyed him as though he would never take his eyes from him again. How he had loved the man, fretted at their parting, and now he was just inches away.

'It's a miracle, a miracle.' Tears welled in his eyes and hastily he brushed them aside. 'Why here? What brings you to this place?' He surveyed the man who had kept him sane in the below-deck life on board ship. 'It's so good to see you. Let me look at you.'

In the intervening years Jock's dark hair had thinned though, either side of his crown were dark wavy tufts; a few more lines creased his forehead but there were still the wide-set eyes and generous mouth that gave him a permanently pleased expression.

'My daughter told me...'

'Daughter!' Gregory's loud exclamation made a bird rise into the sky, it's twittering, strident and alarmed. Gregory looked from the girl to the man. ' Kitty is your daughter?'

Macnab was delighted. 'Did you not think I could sire such a beautiful creature?'

'Of course, I...it was not that, I just...'

Macnab eyed his confusion. 'It's quite a surprise, Rory, lad.' He slipped easily into using the old nickname. 'I'll warrant you that.'

'Man, you throw not just one surprise at me but two.' He looked from the girl to his friend in utter disbelief, his moistened eyes filled with incredulity.

'When Kitty told me of her visitors who hunted Romans I did wonder who on earth they could be. I need not have wasted my thoughts. Still the same old Rory lost somewhere up in the clouds. And frae your garb, somewhere nearer heaven than when I spied ye last.'

'So its Rory is it?' The girl spoke for the first time. She had been unusually quiet. 'You never left your visiting card when you came before. Were you really looking for m-my father?' There was a note of suspicion in her voice and a cagey look crossed her face.

Gregory shook his head he could not trust his voice. His emotion at seeing his old friend and the use of his youthful name threatened to engulf him. At last he stuttered, 'How could I possibly know Jock was your father and he'd be here?'

'Well, it's to be hoped you didn't know my whereabouts.' Jock slapped him on the back. 'Do you remember I swore once I got away from the navy's clutches I would not sleep in the same bed two nights running? I always keep a promise.'

Gregory frowned. He remembered well the wily Scot had threatened to be ever on the run. Surely that necessity had long ceased to be? 'But, Jock, can you not rest your head in the same bed? There can be no reason now to keep you on the move.'

Jock shrugged his shoulders and grinned at him, 'Old habits die hard, laddie. But it's good to have you here. Come, no need to keep you standing.' He seized Gregory's hand indicating that he should follow him inside. He laughed. 'Do you remember I always said we were natural enemies, coming from the borderlands of Scotland and England and you would be as well never to turn your back on me. You took it so seriously, you were always so impressionable. Come!'

He led him into the dark interior of the cottage. 'I passed last night under my daughter's roof, today I shall seek another place to rest my head. How lucky indeed that I was here at the moment you were passing by.' His deep laugh was still too big for his body.

'Lucky indeed or just God's will.' Gregory sounded his belief. He still couldn't believe it. His early morning trek had brought both father and daughter into his life. They stood now side by side. He visualised the church wall. Would their pose one day be replicated there? Kitty smiling serenely, her long dress, high collared, a cross in her hand. Equally improbable was Jock. He grinned to himself. It would take a great leap of imagination to place him amongst the saints.

'So, daughter, what refreshment do you have to offer our friend?' Jock turned to his daughter.

'Of course, what am I doing just standing here? The excitement makes me forget my manners.'

As she spoke she turned to the small table that clung to the far wall and gathered up the glasses already there. A dark substance stained the base, and a whiff of whisky filled the air. Gregory eyed the vessels in her hand. He thought of Caleb's naming her barmaid at his alehouse. Yes, she'd fit well into the job; she could handle three glasses as easily as two. There were three glasses. It meant three people seated at the table: one woman's voice and two men's. One man had taken the back door.

13

A man stood out on the skyline in the late afternoon. His step was hurried, though his gait showed the pack on his back to be heavy. A stranger yet he would seem to know his destination. An unknown man, Gregory thought of Kitty's other visitor, but knew it was not he. This man came from the opposite direction.

Gregory watched the lolloping walk, and guessed he was a sailor and with that he was hit by a wave of nostalgia. He had found his old sea friend, Jock Macnab, he could hardly believe his luck.

Kitty Linn had become Kitty Macnab. He turned in the direction of the rectory. How strange, mystery and distance and exotic name had made the girl appealing. Now the acquisition of a father and down-to-earth name had made her a mortal just like anyone else. Her simple dress had been drab, her dishevelled hair had failed to hide tired eyes. That they were the same twinkling brown of Jock lent her a familiarity that held no allure. Her hands, he had noticed, were work-worn with jagged broken nails. She was half-way to redemption.

There must be other trades for a girl of her age and connections, than the spreading abroad of illicit whisky. And what of Jock? He was no settled town-dweller even now his early experience had made him wary, spending no two nights in the same place? Yet the War was over, the press-gangs no longer brought the dreaded knock at the door and still his behaviour revealed him to be an un-quiet man. Did Kitty Linn sleep easily in her bed? He would pray she did. God grant her an untroubled conscience, whatever her name.

But the doubt lingered. Were father and daughter hand in glove in the illicit trade?

He dragged into his workshop the large branch of beech that he'd gathered as he dropped down into the valley. What could he fashion from it? Already the doll's house had shape and soon it would require furniture. The plaything filled his days, the planning, the building, the working of the wood. He could hardly wait to see the pleasure of the Dodds family, not only children but mother also. He must go over to Greystead and ask Cecilia if she had any material she no longer needed. He had needle skill from his shipboard days enough to make not only bedding but clothes for the figures he intended to fashion.

The house required mother, father and children. Then it would be a happy one.

The thunderstorm came in the night. Lightening flared the dark and thunder drummed around the valley so that Gregory dreamed he was in the midst of an almighty battle. It was a surprise attack and he was not ready. Macnab's face leered over him. But he is not my enemy. Gregory struggled out of bed, and splashed his face with water from the jug, pouring it thinly into the ewer. Mrs Dodds did not come on Sunday to housekeep.

Water rushed off the hills, even though the rain had stopped. He stared resentfully at the burn. It was all of three feet higher and the youthful stream had become an angry, adult white with fury. Gregory was unable to contain his frustration. There was no firm ground on which he could land; no leap would be high enough to take him safely across and find his footing. The rectory of Greystead, the other white elephant in the landscape, stood beyond his reach.

No feet struggled through the deluge to the church door. He stood and waited in vain. He'd accepted the Hunters would drift back to Falstone, but on such a day? And where indeed were the Dodds family? He could not see them as fair- weather Christians. Jessie, the eggler, was abroad in all weathers. Only the Sabbath day did she cease her labour and then eagerly she sought the morning service. She absorbed facts as avidly as peat took in water. One day there would be an outpouring of knowledge that would become a flood.

He went down the six steps into his workroom. Here he could usefully employ his time. He unlocked the door and the doll's house met his gaze. It gleamed white and dazzling, alien in the over-cast gloom of Thorneyburn. But then, he had no desire to replicate the mundane. Here was a dream house for the child with imagination, a Mediterranean house suited to the shores of Spain.

Gregory took up a piece of wood and began to fashion a figure. He would work off his headache; frustration at the morning emptiness of the church had been almost tangible. Then he had thought to go to Greystead and its comforts even though it was the Sabbath, and he had been equally frustrated. He cut deep into the wood. It was becoming natural to turn to Cecilia when he was out of sorts. He needed the common sense calming effect she had on him.

He looked at the wood and frowned. Which member of the family to start? The mother figure was all important in the Dodd's family but the real one was no plaything, too cast down by the constant battle for survival. Cecilia was too predictable, just not toy material. Kitty would offer long hours of fun, an exotic dark-haired figure that would sit well in the white house.

Black wool from a misfit in one of Hunter's flock of Cheviots was already in his collection; it was more than enough to make her lustrous hair. But would Cecilia have cloth to match the character?

And the father? A sailor would be at home on the shores of the Mediterranean, and everyday handling would bring him closer to his children. He'd seen the returned traveller, stark on the skyline, a man with the ocean in his step. His advent was reason enough for the family's absence from church. He put down wood and tool. The seaman father could wait another day and then he could be fashioned from real life.

He closed his study door behind him and found the wine. It was going to be many hours before he would have human contact again. Not until Mrs Dodds appeared in the morning would he have need of his vocal chords.

Next day, midday, and there was still no sign of the woman. His irritation grew with each passing hour. The husband would be here for a few short days, her dependence on the rectory for the family sustenance, was on-going. She should remember that. He could not settle; his writing held no attraction. The sermon from yesterday had been undelivered. There was no reason to put pen to paper. And the doll's house held no pleasure. Why make a plaything for Jessie and her siblings when they had at hand what they wanted? It was surely he who needed such a distraction to fill his empty life. He took the few strides to the church and fell to his knees. "Please God, banish such foolishness. Preserve my sanity, Thy will, oh Lord."

The child was standing at the end of the nave watching him. She stood irresolute. 'Jessie.' She did not reply. 'Gracious, child, I expected you to be happy now your father is home.' Gregory smiled at the girl. 'You should be all smiles. Tell your mother it does not matter about the rectory. First things first.'

'She could not come. My father is sick. He lies in his bed. He has fever and this morning the rash appeared.' Her voice was scarcely a whisper. Gregory's heart sank.

'Oh, God.' He crossed himself.

'It appeared first of all on his forehead, but by bedtime, his whole face was covered. This morning mam says it has spread to his body. He has headache and aches all over. Just now he v…vomited.' The facts fell from her lips to mingle with the large tear on her cheek. 'It was as if all our hugs had been just too much for him. Please, pastor, do not let him die.'

14

'The rash will turn to blisters, and the lesions will become pustules that seep a foul fluid and then the scabs will appear.'

'Smallpox.' Cecilia's voice was scarcely a whisper. Gregory stood on her kitchen threshold.

'I best not enter your house.' He shifted his position from step back down to flagged yard. 'There can be no close contact. 'T'is best to breathe God's fresh air. Everyone should stay in their own home, I....'

'But, the family will need help. Poor Maria Dodds she must be at her wit's end,' she protested.

'But there should be no close contact. I have already closed the church,' He smiled ruefully, 'An unnecessary precaution I know in the circumstances. They are not exactly banging on the door.'

'They might very well be soon enough.'

Gregory frowned and fingered the large church key deposited in his deep inner pocket. He brought it out and gazed at it lying in his hand. It looked solid and dependable. He sighed.

'You are right. I must go back and open up the church.' But he stood where he was. 'I feel physically sickened by the intrusion of the dread disease into their—our lives. We will surely be affected. I pray not.' he held her look then dropped his gaze. 'How am I to explain God's purpose?' He sounded the child.

'Folk round here needed little excuse to turn their backs on my church. They are no God-fearing community but they don't deserve this pestilence.' There was silence.

He had come for Cecilia's reassurance, but her usually placid façade had gone. She looked flushed and unhappy and he peered fearfully at her. No-one was immune.

Gregory raised his hand and began to count. He got to ten and stopped.

'Death usually occurs between the tenth and sixteenth days of the illness.' He did not add that death is a mercy. He had seen the disease before. Gregory stared again at Cecilia's heightened colour, imagination led to fear. And there was one name that hung in the air between them.

'It is on the palms of the hands and the soles of the feet where the blisters merge and sheets of skin fall off exposing the underlying flesh.' He was crucifying himself. He needed to share his unhappy knowledge. Cecilia was strong and resourceful.

She made no response, but instinctively moved towards him, and then stopped.

'What we know fills us with uncertainty; what we do not know, fills us with hope.' She raised herself to her full height. 'We need your prayers, Gregory, not your unhappy experience.'

'Yes, I believe that God is a good God,' he nodded his head, 'whilst pestilence comes from the devil and it is he now who holds sway in the Dodds home.'

'No.' Cecilia raised her voice. 'The cottage is already cramped, there is no room for such a creature. We must not fear the worst. The children live their lives in the open. They are healthy, especially Jessie.'

Her name had been spoken, the intelligent, sensible child who had brought light into both their lives. 'Our little puella!' Gregory's voice broke and without another word he turned on his heel.

Cecelia breathed in deeply, once twice, three times. The cool upland air entered her lungs and she smiled, like the overcrowded cottage there would be no room for the deadly contagion within her. No room at the inn.

Her instinct was to go straight in, but she knocked on the stout door and when there was no answer she lifted the latch. The metal hinge protested loudly at the interruption and for a moment as she entered the room she thought it was empty. It was crowded with silence. The stench of illness and fear had usurped the space. Her basket slid on the polished surface of the table and the basin of broth clinked against the plate of shortbread; the huddled figures sat like statues, only young Jimmy Dodds looked up at the sound.

'I am become the eggler today. You must eat to keep up your strength.'

Jessic rose from the floor.

'You are very kind, miss. Here, children!' She handed round the goodies, but hesitated to take one for herself.

'Come now, Jessie. Your mother does not need to be nursing you as well.' She looked to the stair where muffled footsteps above showed Maria Dodds to be attending to her sick husband. 'Eat up, Jessie. We want no more patients.'

'Aye, to be sure.' The girl put the biscuit to her mouth and took a bite.

Cecelia clucked her approval and moved across the floor. She found the window but it was tightly sealed. Defeated she moved back to the door and opened it.

'You cannot sit around all day. Off you go outside and search the hedgerows, see if the borage is growing yet. Roots or leaves, both will do. Your father has fever, we must dispel it. The syrup we make will get rid of the heat and it will help the sores. Jessie you know where to find the plant.'

'Aye, miss.' The girl nodded with a half smile and took the hand of her young sister. Cecelia watched them disappear. The mission gave them purpose and it was out in the fresh air. When they returned their arms were laden. Jessie's face was flushed with success. 'This will make him better. You know everything miss. What is the Latin for healer?'

'Medicus I think.' She looked at the girl. She looked peaky. 'Jessie are you alright?'

'I'll take some of the borage medicine, miss. Then I will be.'

Cecilia collected the new Latin vocabulary words from Gregory before she visited the next day. Anything to take the child's attention—salubris, sanus, healthful, healthy; that's what she must stay.

The girl's hand was weak as she took the list. It was clammy and warm. Cecelia could feel the panic rising in her throat.

'See you learn the spellings before your next lesson.' Her voice was sharp.

The two mounds were not mole hills in the churchyard. One large, one small, the father and now the child. There had been ten days between the digging. With the second came the beginning of a line of exposed brown earth, scarring the spring green; two lesions that would scab then crust and peel and finally lie below the long grass;

a disfigurement that would, come time, look as though it had always been.

The rain fell on the huddled figures, natural tears in place of the dry eyes that could not comprehend their loss. It was too large and beyond their reasoning. Mrs Dodds stood with her children, but it was not the neat and ordered line of the church pew. There was a gap between the woman and her brood. Jessie had been near to her shoulder, now there was an unnatural space, a jagged drop to the one who had taken her place.

Gregory and Cecilia watched the depleted family walk back down the lane. They walked, weighed down by their grief, oblivious of the weather and their rain-soaked garments. When the group had finally disappeared round the bend in the track, Cecilia looked to her companion, but without a word he turned on his heel; he had no use for idle comfort. She saw him walk past the open Church door and make for the steps that led to the basement. The tall man whom she had glimpsed only last week had become shrunken and bowed.

The banging was strident. The axe cut deep into the flesh of the trunk splintering the wood, over and over again so that the sharp slivers caught her on the last step of the descent. The wooden spelk cut into her arm. Five minutes and his energy had gone. He stopped abruptly, then slowly he moved over to his work table and lifted the axe; the doll's house, white and gleaming would take one blow.

'Gregory no you must not do that.' She ran to him and her hand seized his. The weapon stood poised and then with a cry of anger he threw it across the floor. It skidded into the solid sandstone wall.

He turned his back on her and his shoulders crumpled. Cecilia stood silent. There was nothing to say.

She waited for his fury to subside. She looked about her, at the obvious industry of the place. Here Gregory spent his time. Their Greystead church crypt was unused. Here was Gregory's below decks. His tools hung in an ordered line, the wood in neat piles of size and origin; paints and brushes were materials ready to hand; she recognised her last summer muslin.

The doll's house was raised on a plinth. It was beautiful. She smiled her surprise and pleasure. The white-painted boards looked as though already they had felt the rays of the sun. At the wide windows her muslin, now curtains, waited to flutter in the imaginary breeze.

She saw the joy he had imagined. She felt his despair. Their eggler could never have dreamed up such a toy but Gregory, child-like, had done it for her.

Cecilia picked up two small figures discarded on the play kitchen floor, one completed in every minute detail, midshipman with immaculate uniform fashioned from one of her father's navy smocks. Its creator had laboured long and lovingly and factually on a sailor returned to a happy, comfortable home. Was it Gregory or Peter Dodds he had fashioned to be head of the house? The hair had been gorse dyed. Whoever it represented it no longer mattered; there was no little girl to enjoy her plaything.

The sailor had come home and when he left for his final journey he had taken Jessie with him. One day she would have walked away from the place and its servitude of her own accord. Cecilia shivered, despite her heavy black clothes. She was tied to this place. Jessie had been poised like a young bird ready to escape. It was not to be.

The low ceiling was just inches from their heads, the stone a substitute for the ship's below-deck timbers; it was little wonder that this was the one place where Gregory felt at home. Here in this confined place, his life had become focused on an imaginary wooden house filled with make-believe figures. She picked up the woman who was half complete; she had long black hair and a bright red skirt. It had taken much searching of her closet to come up with the scarlet gingham. She stood the figure beside the sailor and stared at the couple.

They no longer looked the harmless playthings meant for Jessie and her siblings. She caught sight of the axe that Gregory had thrown to the ground and she felt an impulse to shatter the manicured figures into unrecognisable shapes.

Why didn't Gregory live in the real world? Accept it for what it was instead of dreaming about things that could not be? Why fill his life with toys? And did he really imagine that the oak trees flourished where the Admiral had planted them more in hope than expectation all those years ago?

'Gregory, you have unlocked the Church door again.'

There was a snort of derision and the face he turned to her had an unpleasant smile. 'Yes, can't you see the crowds?'

'The church will be unused for many weeks. It is right to turn the key. Only isolation will stop the spread of the disease. It means you are free. You are no longer bound to Thorneyburn. You should go away from here.'

He stared back at her, his eyes were glazed. She repeated, 'You must go away.'

She forced out the words she knew she needed to say though it hurt. His visits to their home, once his need had become hers. They were birds of a feather, he and she both buried in a backwater that offered nothing but frustration. The difference was she knew there was little chance of anything better; he had not yet learned that lesson. She looked at the doll's house and sudden tears pricked her eyes. This white house had been his light at the end of the tunnel.

'I cannot go.' He sounded torn. 'What of the Dodds family? They'll need my pastoral care.'

'My father and I can comfort them. Mrs Dodds will need a woman's concern. And if you go, she'll not have to leave the family to come to the rectory. The other children need her with them even more so now.'

He turned to look at her and for the first time she saw some reaction.

His face was long and drawn. His hands smoothed his chin. 'Where would I go, to Newcastle to the bleak, cheerless house of my father, now retired and elderly? I was not welcome the last time I went. ' She put a hand on his arm. 'There would be no cheer. There never was.' He shook his head.

'Walk out to the far horizon, and then further still, Gregory. See that beyond our view there is another world.' She saw him shudder. 'Go on pilgrimage, and on the way find yourself. You do not know it now but one day you will want to come back. Here to us. We shall be waiting for you.' Her words showed her compassion, but also her hope.

He picked the axe from the ground, and methodically laid it beside the rest of his tools. Slowly he shook his head. 'I cannot go.

It would be like leaving the sinking ship. It's not the time. What sort of an example would I be? But thank you, Cecilia.

'Oh, Gregory, I feel you should go but I also feel you should stay.' Her sigh was heart-felt. 'How events can alter our natures. I don't often vacillate so.' She held out her hand to him. He drew away from her.

'I must go to the Dodds family, though I can take them little comfort.'

'Then show them your grief.'

'Will every seed planted here wither and die?' Gregory's voice broke.

'Plants that are tender do not flourish in poor soil. However much care they receive. It's a sad fact that any gardener will tell you.' Gregory caught hold of Cecilia's hand. She could feel his agitation.

'I know only too well the limitations of my Ministry.'

15

The moon was high. It shone as broad as day. He could not spend another night at Thorneyburn. He needed water: the sound, the smell, the feel. God was near when he was surrounded by water. And he needed Him now. He remembered the time when he found his faith.

The moon shimmered over the Mediterranean, a long path of silver that ended at his feet on the deck. It looked solid and, suddenly, he'd felt the urge to place his feet on the path that he knew led to his future. God was calling him. With that belief he could achieve anything. The Admiral standing beside him had placed a hand on his young companion's arm.

'Remember, Gregory,' he'd said, 'there are many drove roads, some dangerous, some easy. God shows you them all but it is your choice alone. I chose the Navy not to the benefit of my family, I might add.' Abruptly the Admiral turned on his heel. Were there regrets? No way was easy.

'My path is in the service of God.' Gregory whispered half to himself. 'Yes in the dark of the devil I have seen the light. He began to shake. He had seen a vision beautiful and beguiling. The moon had shone for him on the darkest night; his path had been ordained.

He watched the trim figure of Cecilia mount the steps from his basement refuge and close the door behind her. She'd witnessed his temptation, his show of uncontrolled anger and he felt ashamed.

She'd suggested escape but her concern had strengthened his resolve to stay. Someone cared what happened to him and it meant a lot. Cecilia was a good friend. She had a better understanding of people than he. She had told him to go comfort the Dodds family, He would go before night set in, it promised to be long and dark.

The simple cottage appeared empty. The door was firmly shut and there was no light emanating from the window that fronted the street. Nothing to show it still held life. But as he approached sound proved there was someone inside. An unearthly keening shook the wattle and burst into the night. It was an unholy noise, and it made him stop in his tracks. It was the sound he had been close to making ever since he had learned of Jessie's death. His fist sought the door. He prayed that he could find the right words; on his first visit he had not even known which day of the week it was. The moaning did not stop. He hesitated and then with a new sense of resolve he lifted the latch.

They turned in one movement and an engulfing wave hit his lonely figure. It was a mixture of despair, hate, contempt and he felt himself drowning in the tidal wave.

'Get ye gone, Reverend. You are no wanted here. You and your God could not save her.' Martin Dodds mouthed their rejection.

Gregory opened his mouth but no sound came.

The night was dark, Rectory and Church black shapes. But he needed no light to see the solid stone that was his home and his work. In the few months of his residence their shape had become familiar. He had walked the hills but the tracks had always led back.

Now in the blackness there was no ordained path. God had forsaken him, the devil beckoned, calling him away from the scene of his failure. The devil's drove road led away from there, away into the hills and into oblivion. Did the path lead back? He did not know. He heard again the noise of the sea and its mirage path. It had been the wrong path.

He walked the mile to where the Tarrat met the Tarset. At the confluence was a hidden cleft where rocks and boulders and bushes fought for foothold. He'd been there before. It had become his place of solace, a lonely hidden watery place that seeped into the soul. The water was loud, it roared its presence. He sat on a jutting boulder and cupped his hands in the stream. Its iciness made him gasp. It trickled into his mouth. Here he had felt close to God, but now there was no communion; his God was an unkind God. Thorneyburn was no place for him.

He thought of Jessie. Her future, her promise; the eggler girl purveying her healthy produce; eggs, milk, butter, cheese, the staff of life, only hers had been broken, caught suddenly in a hidden cleft. He felt his despair. His life was useless. The inky blankness showed his failure. With the return of the sailor, God's hand had removed Gregory's future. Ironic indeed that pestilence had come from the sea to this susceptible land.

He staggered to his feet. His old friend Macnab was within reach. Jock would help him get his feet back onto the ground. The Admiral had said there were many drove roads through the Cheviot Hills, he'd meant through life itself. He only had to find the right track.

16

He knew the sound even before he caught sight of her. The cart she pushed splashed over the stones in yet another stream that trickled south, seeking the mother river. It was loaded and she struggled. He saw the cloths that lay innocently on their moving counter; he guessed what lay beneath. On her cart lay temptation and he struggled with his anger, but Kitty Linn was moving in the opposite direction.

'Rory!' She used her father's nickname for him. 'You're an early bird. You must have been walking half the night.' The April morning was chill and the sun was only just rising above the Border Hills. He gave no response. He had walked since the first glimmer of light and he no longer noticed the temperature. His collar was open at the neck and the clothing, from his impecunious student days made him the itinerant. He carried nothing to show his calling. He had left it all far behind.

They stood indecisive in the shallow stream. The water trickled lazily about their feet and about the cart wheels. It would seem flesh and wood were going nowhere, anchored far down into the water by hidden chains. She could see his hesitancy and she frowned.

'Take a drink with me?' Her voice showed her uncertainty. Seizing a jug from the top of the cart, she bent down into the stream, her skirt hem soaking up the water as she scooped it into the ewer. Silently he watched her as she filled a cup and handed it to him. He drank greedily and handed it back and she repeated her movements, but taking long slow gulps of the cold drink as though she would lengthen their meeting.

'Will you breakfast?' Hesitantly she took a rough loaf and breaking a piece off she handed it to Gregory. It was solid and verging on stale but it was what he needed and he could feel his displeasure disappear with the food. Again she duplicated the action, though her portion was smaller. He hoped he had not deprived her of her food for the coming day.

'Where are you heading?' But already he knew the answer. She would be tracing his steps but they would lead not to Thorneyburn, that had been a mistake she had not repeated, but to the bastle door of Caleb Hunter. It would open readily and she would be welcomed gushingly by Mrs Hunter and by Caleb? Was it just the whisky that would make him open the door to her? Had Mrs Hunter got her gilt sofa yet? Would Kitty be the first to be seated on it, whisky smuggler and outlaw, except in name, seated beside the common woman dressed as a duchess? In this remote land anything was possible.

Kitty smiled at him. It was easy and unforced. Had he laughed aloud? The ready amusement in her eyes was an instant answer. They were the colour of a peat-stained burn and her skin was the cream of the matt grass that covered the land as far as the eye could see. The girl, out in all weathers and conditions, had skin that was as soft as dew. Morning dew, the name spoke of freshness and innocence. He looked at his companion as her hands delved into the inwards of the cart to rearrange its contents. Today, she was the quiet stream, no cataract upset the calm. Yet what did her hands disturb? What hidden goods lay below those on display? Hers was innocence that went just skin deep.

He peered into the cart and saw for the first time the trade she showed to the daylight world; milk in the coarse jugs, two bowls of eggs and rounds of cheese. These were natural products of the land and they belonged not here but in the cart trundled by a small girl with Latin words on her tongue. A lump came into his throat. Her goodness had counted for nothing; he had been unable to save her; he together with his God. He turned away from Kitty to look back the way he had come. He had failed. What use his platitudes, his words of hope? Martin Dodds had been right to spurn them.

'Hepzibah Hunter is where I'm headed.' The girl's voice brought him back with a start. 'You will have met her?' Kitty's voice was filled with amusement. 'Tell me you know her and I have not just dreamed her up.'

Gregory smiled at her words. 'That would be impossible. She is beyond belief. Is that her name? It suits her well.'

'All façade, our fine lady.' The girl pursed her lips, on her a pout equally childish and of the coquette.

'So, Reverend, is it important what we show to the world, appearances do they matter?' Her face was mock serious but her eyes still danced; he knew she was teasing him.

'Do we think any more of her for her fine dresses and her almost fashionable furniture?'

'I think not. But....' He hesitated, 'it gives her contentment. She is not torn by doubt.'

'You are right. You are a forgiving man. Hepzibah is a woman to be envied.'

'Oh, no certainly not by you.' He stopped, and then as she looked questioning. 'You seem to me to be content with your lot.'

She looked at him and her brow furrowed. She placed her hands on the cart as though she would move on but her feet remained firm. 'One day, Reverend, you will not condemn me as you do now.'

'That I do not.' His words rang false.

'Well then, I shall hope to stand at least equal in your eyes with Hepzibah. That is something to aim for.' She was now openly laughing at him. 'From my outward appearance I'm content, so that is enough?'

'You twist my words.' He felt a rising anger. 'Innocence both on the outside and inside is to be sought in all of God's creatures. It is what we should strive for, though few of us are lucky enough to achieve. Jessie had both in abundance.'

'Jessie?' Kitty smiled. 'Yes, a sweet, innocent child indeed.'

'So, it is hard to accept.'

'Accept what?'

'Our Lord in his wisdom has taken her to himself.'

'What do you mean?'

'Poor, Jessie.' He strove to speak the words. 'The child is dead.' His shaking voice was echoed by a gasp of horror from the girl. 'It was the smallpox.'

Kitty buried her face in her hands and her shoulders shook.

'Her sailor father brought with him the dread disease. My churchyard has the first graves.' He faltered and gently she put a hand on his arm.

'Now I see the reason for your sorrow.' Impulsively she seized his hands. 'It is sad the loss of one so young.' Kitty spoke almost in a whisper. 'So, Jessie is the load you carry. It's a weight that hinders your journey.'

'She is my journey.' Gregory stood with head bowed, their hands anchored now as their feet. He could feel the caress of her breath on his moistened cheek.

'My father said you carry the troubles of the world. It should not be. Your shoulders are broad but not that wide.' She removed her hand and turned to the cart as if to find profitable usage. 'Your load will lighten, though she will never be forgotten. Jessie was one to be remembered.' She paused and her tone lightened. 'My father has told me of you. Your melancholy is not an immoveable weight. You are one who could enjoy life. He told me that you had a sense of fun when you were a boy.'

Gregory's face relaxed. 'Did he say that? We had many jokes, he and I.'

'Do you seek him now?'

'I am headed for Hethpool where Admiral Collingwood owned land. He planted oak trees there. I go to check they flourish.'

She looked amused. 'Do you joke?' Gregory looked aggrieved. 'Well no matter, but you are somewhat off course. You should be headed east.'

They turned in the direction she pointed, and saw the horseman descending upon them. Kitty's hands went immediately to the cart and Gregory felt her stiffen.

The man looked official. Small, dapper, close shaven, his eyes ran ahead of his steed. He gathered pace at sight of the couple and both he and the horse exhaled steaming breath in the cool morning as they drew alongside.

Gregory raised his hand in greeting. 'It's a fine morning.'

'Aye.' The newcomer squinted down at them and then, as if he felt disadvantaged, dismounted. Gregory reckoned he had already had a long ride. 'Well met, I've not seen a solitary soul for miles. It's enough to make a man lose his vocal chords.'

'Aye it's remote.' Gregory nodded agreement.

'Though not as lonely as you might expect. You would be surprised at the people we do meet when we want to. His Majesty's Excise men can sniff out their prey.'

'Prey! That is an unhappy word to use on such a day. It speaks of the innocent animal going about its business, only to be trapped by a cruel hunter.' Gregory looked condemning.

The man scowled. 'Innocence, I assure you is only in the eye of the beholder. The Hawk will hover and swoop, he will take the mouse, but already the victim will have taken his own innocence in the form of a slug.'

Gregory laughed. 'That is very true. But I assure you we are the slugs.' The wave of his hand included Kitty, standing beside her cart, for once wordless.

The Excise man looked almost uncomfortable. 'I do not allot who is predator, who is the victim.' He paused, 'That is until I have proof.' He looked toward Kitty. Gregory stood motionless but alert; he was enjoying the encounter. The official was small in stature and he felt the superiority of pulpit to pew.

'Then sir! We must not delay you further. Besides, this lady has a way to go with her produce and already the milk could be on the turn. The coolness of the early hour has no hidden reason other than she would avoid the heat of the sun.'

'May I offer you a drink, Sir?' Kitty's voice had lost its normal lilt; it sounded flat and compliant. Gregory thought her voice for me had held another note.

'No-no thank, you.' The man sounded impatient. 'Milk is not my drink.' Gregory imagined the confiscated whisky, the hoard of illicit drink stacked in His Majesty's pound finding its way no further. The man's red face was not just from long rides in inclement weather. He had behind him a hard night of drinking. Slowly he remounted his patient horse.

'We'll keep our eyes open for suspicious persons.'

They laughed when the man was a spot on the skyline.

'Your offer of milk almost made the man throw up.'

'And you naming us as lowly slugs embarrassed him.' Kitty's voice was filled with laughter and Gregory felt her gratitude.

Why had he protected her? Why hadn't he lifted the cover on her wares? Illicit goods, the excise man was actively seeking. The man had stood inches from his prey. Gregory had known his duty yet his words had sought to fox the hunter. Why had he done it?

His complicity had saved her. He had been unable to protect Jessie the innocent, but he'd helped the sinner. Was that not his calling? And the wayward child of his friend, Macnab, was surely a fitting candidate.

17

He needed more than anything the companionship of below deck. Sooner or later he would find his old friend, somewhere out there hidden in a fold of hillside or cresting an open height. That was the nature of the man, a chameleon character, reticent or sociable depending on the place he frequented. He envied him his adaptability.

The girl had assumed that Gregory sought his old shipmate, and her words told him Macnab was not averse to his company, reminiscing about their shipboard life, he'd remembered Gregory's sense of fun.

How the years had changed him. Few had seen that side of his character. Was that why he'd teased one of his Majesty's excise men as he stood feet away from contraband goods, complicit throughout the encounter? How Jock would revel in Gregory and the girl, self-designated under-life, pitting their wits against a predator hovering to pounce.

Under-life was to be trodden underfoot. That was not the fate he wanted for Kitty. He felt a sense of unease. But the girl was a survivor; she courted adventure, inches away from danger, yet she'd remained icy calm.

Gregory relished the prospect of recounting the tale to Jock. But the man came and went, never more than one night in the same bed. Necessity or choice, the latter surely and his daughter was as restless. She would be unlikely to return to the fort before the next day at the earliest, given mission and distance. It meant Gregory that night could make the most of the cottage roof over his head. The man would appear sooner or later.

He felt a rising of spirits when the small squat building solitary within the Roman fort came into view. Gregory sank down on the turf beside the front door and rested his head on the carved stone, now part of the façade of Kitty's home. The curves of the goddess indented his scalp. Unsettled, he got to his feet and entered the dark interior.

There was little to show it was home; just four stone walls, turf roof, hearth, and beside it, a box bed with thin pallet. Winter chill still lingered; the summer heating of stone would come grudgingly. But inside the wind was banned. He could hear only a gentle murmur as it swirled about the chimney. Where would Kitty rest her head this night? Did Hepzibah Hunter have a gilt bed?

Night dark came early and the pallet felt as soft as hillside heather. He was very tired. The silence covered him in a deep, dreamless sleep yet at the first faint sound he was wide awake. He lay holding his breath. Footsteps crossed the stone flags and feet climbed the wooden surround of the bed. Gregory could hardly breathe. Should he speak, put out a hand to show there was already someone in the bed? The newcomer was asleep as soon as head touched the pallet. Familiar noises and smells soon told the sleepless man with whom he shared a bed.

Tears welled silently and fell onto the bed he shared with Jock. He cried for the years that had seemed to offer so much and yet were unfulfilled. And now in the dark and the silence he cried for Jessie. How could God let her ray of light be dimmed? His was a demanding God and for him there was no comfort. Finally he slept.

He did not feel the man's hands pull the cover about his shoulders in the early morning.

The smell pervaded the room and the sizzling fat was an alarm call that would have woken the dead. Gregory raised himself on one arm and smiled at the sight of his friend bent over the pan on the hearth. Rashers of bacon and two yellow eggs were lovingly slid on to two plates warming over the burning wood as he joined his companion beside the fire. They sat bestride the grate on two low stools and their feast was wordless. Two hunks of stale bread wiped the fat so that the plates looked as though they did not need to go near water.

'When was the last time I enjoyed a meal like that?' Gregory sighed as a mug of scalding tea was put into his hand. 'That was better than ship's biscuits and rancid water.' He grinned. 'Jock, you're a magician. You conjured that from nothing.'

His companion pointed to the furthest corner of the room. In the dark recess a cured ham hung from the rafters. It was much depleted, and told of a long winter. 'Kitty collects the eggs from the farms and takes them to the towns. It is a small trade but it does.'

Gregory made no reply. Did her father know of her accidental visit to his rectory with the morning dew? Perhaps not, but he knew, as well as his old shipmate, that it was whisky not dairy produce that bought the ham.

He drained the dregs of his drink. If he half closed his eyes he could be back on board, bemoaning with Jock the lack of an extra rum ration as reward for their victory at Trafalgar. The Scot had been furious, like a bear with a sore head. Now, the man had more than enough alcohol on tap.

As if Jock could read his thoughts he said.

'Do you remember, lad, our fighting over the tot of rum.' He laughed, 'It was harmless fun.'

'Between you and me perhaps but not Byres, how I hated him. Now it is hard to remember why.'

Jock laughed. 'You teased him mercilessly.'

'Did I?'

'Yes, you were always playing tricks on him. Like the time you carved a dog turd from a piece of wood and placed it in his bunk and said you'd seen the Admiral's little Bounce sniffing around.'

'He deserved all he got, the pompous ass.'

'You've changed Rory.' Jock studied his visitor's face. 'Your eyes are sad, and there's a puckered brow. Your laugh was infectious. Now, I'm in no danger from catching the disease.'

'Then you should have been there yesterday morning when I met your daughter. It was hard not to laugh.'

Jock looked quizzical. 'You met Kitty?'

'Yes, going south.'

'Ah, as I said she visits farms and outlying villages.'

'Yes. Her cart was heavy and I think the excise man would have relieved her of some of her load.'

Macnab's eyes flickered and Gregory could see his concern.

'If he'd looked under the cloths he'd have found something to make him happy.' Again Macnab made no comment. 'Though, perhaps he's a man who is keen on omelettes.' Gregory's sarcastic laugh echoed round the room.

Macnab said admiringly, 'You were always a good liar, Rory, and how much more convincing now, when the untruth comes from the mouth of a church minister.'

'Steady on, Jock. That makes my little white lie sound black.' He bit his lip. Relating the incident had made it sound less amusing. But he remembered scenes with his father when he'd brazenly taken the opposite stand. Why? Was he naturally confrontational? But Macnab was looking relieved.

'I'm beginning to think they are laughter lines etched on your face after all.'

'I fear not.'

'Then it's to be regretted. Do you remember the bumboat in Plymouth?' Jock chuckled enjoying recall of the past.

'Bumboat?' Gregory frowned as though it was a long ago event forgotten without trace.

'Aye, you handed your precious rum ration to Byres after the women had gone and said, 'Here, Byres this might raise your spirits and your …. for the next boy, I mean girl, you fancy. And do you remember he never said a word in his defence? Though, from then on you could count him amongst your foes, as much as the Frenchies. You were a brave lad, or perhaps foolhardy, seeing as at that point you hadn't got the Admiral's protection.'

Gregory smiled ruefully. 'Yes, it was a boy's jest that drew an adult-sized anger. Vincent Byres was not one of those I missed when I changed ship. You were different.' Yes, Macnab had been a loss. He'd become the serious Oxford scholar when Macnab was no longer the accomplice.

'Mind, the men whispered about you when you found your books and then your religion.' Jock eyed Gregory with a quizzical smile. Gregory made no reply, and the good natured Scotsman gave

Gregory a hearty slap on the back. 'But becoming the swot pleased the Admiral. You made him smile, Rory and that was unheard of. Anyone would have thought he was the original dour Scotsman.'

'In place of you then, Jock you couldn't be serious for five minutes. And now here we're sharing the same hearth and laughing together. I am more content than I have been for many moons.'

Jock looked gratified. 'Aye, lad, your coming is something to celebrate. Stay awhile. You mustn't depart before we've made new memories to be laughed over.'

They did nothing memorable that day. They walked in featureless country. Northward, hills spread as far as the eye could see, vast miles of land that rose and fell like ocean waves. Silence, nothing moved: no birds, no animals. Gregory followed his companion without question as their feet trod the thin, sparse vegetation. Tussocks of Juncus reeds clogged the ill-drained land, the rush standing black, like dark wreaths amongst scattered rock tombs. A bird skull, caught in a narrow cleft, was washed clean, the eye sockets gaping at the trespassing feet.

Onward, upward, 'Where are we going?' Gregory gasped out his question at last as he caught up with the older man. Jock's lithe, taut legs put Gregory's sedentary body to shame. The muscles in his legs ached painfully, his feet were wet from the streams they had waded and a blister on his right foot marked every step.

'Do we need a destination?' Jock moved back down the hill to stand beside his flagging companion. His eyes mocked the younger man, but he knelt down by the stream they had just crossed, cupped his hands together and gulped the water. Gregory needed no second bidding. Slowly he bent his aching legs and his hands sought the welcome refreshment. It was very cold, it caught his breath and he choked. He drank long and gratefully. He guessed it would be some time before his hard taskmaster allowed another such stop.

Did they need a destination? Jock had asked. Was it necessary to know where you were going, or did you just follow the ups and downs and arrive eventually, two puny figures that hardly caused a ripple in the vast wilderness?

'I need something to aim for.' Gregory stood up and looked Jock squarely in the face. 'At this moment I need to find my way out of this maze; it is claustrophobic even though we can see for miles. I want to get back to four walls and a roof over my head.'

Jock turned round. Gregory followed, and in less than a quarter of a mile they were down on a worn track, the wilderness had been left behind.

'You old devil,' Gregory said. 'I really thought you were trying to get me lost.' He surveyed the green drove road that led back down into the warm sun. It looked easy-going, his muscles and blister nagged. 'You led me on a wild goose chase, though I suspect even a goose wouldn't find its way up there.'

'I wanted to show you Scotland. It lay over the next ridge.'

'Oh. I'm sorry, Jock.'

The Scot shook his head. 'No need to be, Scotsmen throughout the centuries have faced the other way. Their eyes fixed on their neighbours' goods and chattels. Didn't you know, grass is always greener on the other side.'

'Why did I doubt you?'

'Because, lad, you lack trust, in your terms, faith.'
'I...I just need to know the right path.'

18

Gregory slept the sleep of the blessed. When he woke he lay cocooned in the dark bed. He listened for noise. There was none. Jock never slept two nights in the same bed, the border blood coursing his veins. He would have gone by first light. Already he'd be crossing the Scottish border to his home. If he called any place home.

Gregory put out his hand and felt the space beside him, there was a residual warmth. The Scot had not long gone. He pulled the cover over his head and smelt the comfort of human presence. His old friend was a solace that was immediate. Yet he would not follow him. His companionship came only at invitation.

There was no repeat of the previous morning feast; the hearth was cold and the ashes still rested where they had fallen. Gregory stretched as he dropped down from the bed and peered through the small window. It faced south and through it he could see the sun. Here the sun seemed to shine every day. At Thorneyburn it was reluctant to show its face.

The aches and pains of yesterday had gone. Two months here, he thought, and I would be fit, more able to face life's problems. He thought of his cold empty rectory; it offered little of the comfort of this mean peasant dwelling. And the cottage of the Dodds family, likewise poor and cramped, yet it too had had the warmth of simple love. Pray God, it would do so again. Their ray of sunshine had gone but out here in this wilderness it was easy to believe Jessie was gone somewhere just across the border.

Plying her trade he thought of Kitty. She had not returned. Like her father, it would seem she was averse to continued occupancy. Was her cart now empty, a picture of innocence to any traveller she met on the road? No alibi or lies needed. She seemed as far away as the little girl lost to view. And Cecilia was she tending her vegetable patch at this very moment? He shrugged his shoulders; for now his life stretched only as far as the ramparts constructed by the Romans.

The fort entrance lay to the south. No need to climb his way out. Ever conventional, he took the flattened way that ran between the three-feet-high worked stones making the gateway. Once there had been sentries, today there were no eyes to watch his movements. He scrambled down the slope to the stream that gurgled happily in its valley. He'd watched Kitty and Jessie hand in hand go down to fetch its water, filling the ewer with ice-cold liquid that had tasted like nectar from the Gods. Already he'd happy memories here.

'What hindered you?' Jock was in the lee of the bank. A small fire, sheltered from the wind fried the fish that had come just minutes from the stream. Pink flesh appeared as the skin split into deep brown lesions. The smell caught in the overhang and invaded Gregory's nostrils; he was very hungry.

He didn't speak until he'd devoured two trout and then he watched as another unsuspecting swimmer darted before Jock's quick eyes. The man bent below the overhanging rock and slowly and deliberately began to tickle the fish under the chin. Gregory watched as his expert fingers gently soothed, and then with a quick flick of the wrist his victim was on the bank. There was no contest. Like his attraction to women he had a way with fish.

Gregory grinned. 'You live like a king. Ham yesterday, trout today, so what feast is in store for tomorrow?'

'Why think beyond today? Only when tomorrow comes will we find the answer. You ken as well as Rabbie Burns, 'The best laid plans o' mice an' men gang aft a-gley.''

'You're right. I should live for the day.' Gregory's sigh was genuine contentment.

They did not move from the stream banks. Jock taught him how to tickle fish and when they had gathered a pile on the shingle sides he fetched salt from the house and rubbed it into the warm flesh. Then they carried them up to a flimsy shed that nestled behind the house and the fish were stacked onto crude wooden slats. Finally they carried large empty ewers down to the water's edge and Gregory listened to the gurgle of the liquid and thought there was no sound like flowing water. As the sun set, Jock scythed unruly grass from around the shed. Their day had been spent within the confines of the fort ramparts where watchful sentries had guarded from surprise attack. Had life been so bad here for the Roman army?

But there had been watching, hostile eyes. Gregory looked out up to the hill ridge that encircled their camp. Another world lay out there beyond this man-made safe haven. Jock joined him as he gazed eastward.

'I should be on my way.' Gregory's voice was reluctant.

'Where are you headed?'

'Hethpool.' The father's amusement was as keen as the daughter's had been.

'Then you are out of your way coming up here. Though, I'm glad you did, laddie. I used to tease you that we were traditional enemies, but it's not true; this borderland of England and Scotland has no real barriers. Here men have the same brogue, the same needs, the same dreams.'

Gregory questioned. 'Your cattle are my cattle?' The troubles were a still-raw memory.

'Yes and why not?' Jock grinned up into his face. 'We share common blood, though sometimes it was achieved at knifepoint. It was not good to be a lassie here in the troubled times. If you were sensible you found yourself a big strong man to defend you. Or at least one who could wield a sword.' Gregory looked at Jock's strong arms and thought he would be useful in a fight; height was not everything. The younger man had stature yet no one would be queuing up to be on his side.

'And what takes you there?'

'Oak trees.' He guessed his companion's scorn.

Jock's laugh was unbelieving.' That is a strange quest. Oh, Rory, when will you ever grow up? Now if you had said you sought a woman, I would think it a natural calling. Not some trees.' Jock's amusement was loud and long.

'They are allegorical.' Gregory retorted. Years of study divided the two men. What mattered that the other could land fish and find his path through hostile country.

'Allegorical is a big word, a foreign language in these parts.' Jocks brogue grew with his amusement. 'Ye ken, you're a troubled laddie still. I think what you're trying to say is that you seek answers yet. But, Rory, often they are under your very nose. You cannot out distance troubles.'

Gregory ignored the comment. 'The Admiral said to me, "go and plant acorns lad, throw them into ditches and one day they'll build a new fleet for England." As you know I've always been obedient.'

'Well, perhaps by the time they have grown we shall need a new fleet. You know as well as I do, the ones we have lie unused.' Jock sounded unconvinced.

Gregory made no reply and Jock chuckled. 'If you ask me, your trees are just an excuse to leave behind your doubts and questionings. I see a change in you, lad. Go find a woman, that is where happiness lies.'

'So, Jock, was that always the answer for you?' It was Gregory's turn to sound condemning.

'Don't do what I do, do what I say.' Jock was smiling. 'You're right, this is my woman now.' He threw his arms wide and pointed to the landscape around them.

'Beauty, peace, it doesn't answer back. Unfortunately, the ideal woman can't be tickled and landed like a trout.'

'Surely you could have learned the art if anyone could.'

'Take my word for it fish are less slippery creatures.' Jock shook his head.

'So, Gregory you have a road to travel, and that is the one you must take.' Jock gesticulated to the flat green path that left the eastern side of the fort and disappeared into the distance. 'That is the Devil's Causeway. That is the road for you.' There was a strange smile on his face.

He jumped down from the embankment and turned to look up at Gregory. 'That is my road also, but I need no companion.'

Gregory called after him, anger in his voice. 'I hope I find that God prevails in this unlikely land.'

Gregory could not believe the effect his old friend's departure had on his mood. He'd watched the man until the figure was lost to sight. Now the solitude threatened to engulf him. He'd alienated his friend just when it seemed they had achieved their old rapport.

What rapport? Their friendship had been stormy, natural in the confines of a ship. With a stab of anger he remembered the time when they had ceased to be shipmates.

After days of stalemate in the Spanish blockade, they were bored. The storm lasted three days and by the end they did not need to step foot on land to find actual enemies. Byres and Macnab were unlikely cronies and it was Gregory who bore the brunt of their idling tongues.

Jock was moody. He'd taken Gregory's rum ration without a word of thanks and as he downed the last mouthful, he'd stared up at the lad who now towered over him with a look of disdain.

'Who are you looking down your nose at? My Tweed blood is as good as your Tyne blood any day of the week. You've been smug having the Admiral as protector, well that's no more the case laddie, from now on you're on your own. We can both hear the dog's howls lying beside his dead master.' He laughed and Gregory hastily turned away so that the man would not see his tears.

Jock persisted. 'What think you of our young friend, Byres? Now he no longer has his books to hide behind. Is he man enough to follow the natural ways of men? I'm not so sure and I don't think he is.'

Byres, his smooth face creased into a sneer, poured another rum ration for the man. 'Master Felton is out to please everybody. He sits on the fence, this lad. That can be a bit uncomfortable for the parts that matter.'

Macnab roared his approval. 'So that could be his problem.' And with that the two men had seized him. He'd struggled, but it was two against one and he'd stood his britches about his ankles.

'So!' said Jock admiringly, 'some woman or man will know he means business once he knows which one he wants to chase.'

They'd sailed from Menorca, their precious cargo homeward bound at last. But homesick Collingwood lay in a wooden box. The Admiral's stand-in-family Gregory and Bounce stood beside him as they pulled away from the shore.

Gregory dry eyed stared ahead. Within a day he'd lost two father figures, the Admiral and Jock Macnab. He faced an uncertain future.

Where was Macnab going at this time of day, ever restless, ever unpredictable?

Rory ate his solitary meal of fish purloined from the newly-filled store. It tasted of salt and it stuck in his teeth. The shared feast on the river bank was just a memory. Would he see Macnab again? Would he meet him on the Devil's road? How apt that his journey followed such a path.

The Devil came to him in the dark of night. He listened to the footsteps. They were light and fleet. But Gregory was waiting. He knew what form his tormentor would take.

19

Gregory sat at the dying embers of the fire. The box bed lay empty. He had no desire to seek its semblance of comfort. He feared the recess and its unmitigated dark. The light had not entirely disappeared from beyond the window when he heard the cart wheels cross the stone way into the fort. He poked the fire and added another log to the grate so that there was a spurt of flame as Kitty walked through the door.

'Gregory.' The shaft of orange light showed her quick smile of pleasure as she saw that the room was already occupied. 'So, man you have made the fire and the kettle sings, just the greeting for a weary traveller.' She threw off her cloak and held out her hands to the flame.

'Home sweet home and look what I've brought for its comfort.' She picked up a bundle she'd jettisoned with her outer garment and handed it to Gregory. He felt the soft luxury of a velveteen cushion and almost dropped it in his surprise, so out of place was it in this Spartan room.

It was a beautiful cushion, empress purple with gold swirls of silk. It would not have looked out of place in Buckingham Palace. It had not come from there; he knew only too well its original home.

'Where did you get this?'

'I found it.'

Gregory laughed his disbelief. 'I think you need a better story.'

She peered at him in the near dark; the last light had gone, the dying embers of the fire throwing gentle light on both their faces. Her eyes sparkled mischievously, his were cold and questioning.

'I like pretty things.' Her smile was ingenuous. Gregory looked accusing. 'So, Hepzibah will not miss it. She has others. This room needs some comfort.' Kitty picked up the cushion and placed it on the stool vacated by Gregory and sat down on her new possession. The sigh from the cushion equalled the girl's murmur of satisfaction.

'But it was part of the furnishing of Hepzibah's room. I imagine she will be far from pleased when she discovers her loss.' Gregory sounded pedantic, at a loss to find a plausible excuse for the girl's act.

Kitty frowned at him. 'What a spoilsport you are, Rory. You'll not tell her I took it?'

Gregory's laugh was filled with exasperation. 'Don't think, Kitty Macnab, I'm your accomplice in your every wrongdoing. Did your mother never teach you the difference between right and wrong?'

'My mother died when I was eight. My father... I'm not sure what his message would have been if His Majesty's Navy had not guaranteed his continuous absence. I've learnt if you see something lying under a rock, hanging from a tree, nestling on someone else's settle, that you take it. Otherwise when you return it will not be there.' She looked and sounded the naughty child.

How old was she, eighteen, nineteen, old enough to know right from wrong? But now was not the time to deliver a sermon. He saw a child, not much older than Jessie, and one that had not had the fortune to have a Mrs Dodds for mother. Would he have been different if his mother had not died giving him birth? Life was a cruel gamble when the dice were loaded.

They sat either side of the fire, taking it in turn to feed the flames. Kitty seemed literally attached to the cushion and, hidden under her skirt, Gregory was able to forget the offending object. When the girl did finally seek the box bed the cushion went with her and became her pillow. In the early morning it was the first object Gregory saw as he woke from an uncomfortable and interrupted sleep by the blackened fire. Kitty was holding it in her hands and gazing about the room a look of uncertainty on her face.

'Where shall I put it?'

She would like his doll's house. He saw her on her knees moving the furniture, seating the figures, shaking the rugs. The eager girl in front of him was a million miles away from the voluptuous girl who delivered morning dew.

He felt a new liking for the daughter of his old shipmate. What matter the questionable character flaws? The wretched cushion fitted neither bastle nor Roman fort.

And Kitty was no longer his temptress.

When he'd heard the girl's cart, he'd felt a throbbing expectation that he knew was devil sent. He waited breathless for her hand on the latch; but in came a naughty small girl who'd confessed her theft and he'd seen her for what she was, Kitty Macnab, a wilfull child lacking supervision in her formative years. He was willful for the same reason. He sighed with satisfaction. His first steps had traced the Devil's Causeway even though he hadn't left the safety of the Roman camp, and he hadn't stumbled.

He tickled a trout for her and then another. It felt the achievement of his life. They sat beside the stream and Gregory watched her surprise; she made no effort to hide her pleasure at his success.

'Did Jock teach you?'

'Yes. He saw I wouldn't survive long in this place. A town lad cast adrift in hostile country.'

'Hostile?' She looked surprised. 'I never think of it like that.' She sounded affronted.

'It has become less so.'

'I'm glad. Jock wouldn't like it if you didn't feel at home with us. He's always thought of you as a son.' Her face was earnest, 'So that makes us brother and sister, doesn't it?' She caught hold of his hand then grabbing two sticks from the ground she thrust one into his curled fingers.

'Let's see which one will go further down the stream. I never had a brother to play with and I want to beat him now.'

'We'll see about that. Remember, I'm well practised in all things moving on water. You should be quaking in your shoes already.'

'That, I'll never do. I know I've a steady hand and a good eye.'

'But that will not count here.'

'No.' She grinned up at him. Everything in this life is down to luck. It's best to hope you are not standing under the tree when it's hit by lightning.'

'Then it would've been God's will that you'd chosen that spot.' Gregory felt the need to remember his belief.

He followed her downstream where the course of the water straightened, but dropped steeply. A series of rocks made obvious obstacles. She crouched low, looked long and deep into the water then released her stick. It swam sweetly avoiding the obvious pitfalls and was lost to view. There was a look of satisfaction on Kitty's face, but as Gregory crouched beside her she grabbed his arm and pointed.

'Aim toward that rock and it will glance off the edge and carry on downstream.'

He did as told and watched his stick follow hers. 'Thank you for the help.'

She smiled. 'I have practised many times on my own. I would not want unfair advantage. Come on, let's find our sticks. I think they'll be equal; tomorrow the contest will start in earnest and you'll be on your own.'

'But, I have to go.'

She waded into the water and he followed. The water's chill made him gasp, but as it swirled about his toes he felt again a surge of happiness. Did he really have to go or could he wait another day? He knew the answer was no. Kitty was not his sister. Her smooth skin glistened as her feet splashed the water into a surge of droplets, like tears of happiness weeping down her leg. She began to shower him with fast and furious scoops. It hit his shirt, as breathtaking as a well-aimed fist and he gasped like a winged bird. Then he too bent and returned the fire. In minutes they were soaked. They tired at the same time and he stood shivering from the unexpected bath. A bird called overhead, but all he could hear was the sound of water and laughter and water. The water was an innocent plaything, but he was too old for childish games and so was Kitty.

He turned and walked back toward the cottage.

'Wait, Rory. We must seek the sticks and see which one of us has won.' She sounded the disappointed child.

'Oh please wait, Rory.' He could hear her splashing through the stream and she'd caught up with him by the time he'd climbed the rampart bank. 'Guess who won?' Her eyes sparkled with fun. She held a stick behind her back.

'So do you expect me to believe you?' Gregory raised his eyebrows. 'I wasn't born yesterday, you know.'

Kitty scowled at him. 'It was yours that went the furthest. I wouldn't lie about such a thing. You are the champion.' She began to clap her hands in a gesture to mark his success. Gregory bowed his head in acknowledgement. She slipped her hand into his. 'Of course you'll never know the real answer, Rory. Were you the actual winner or was it because I wanted you to be?'

'Kitty, I've had enough of your games. It grows tiresome.' Gregory looked and sounded annoyed. 'I must be on my way. I have dallied too long.'

'But you can't go. I have another treasure to show you.'

'It must wait for another time.'

'It's as good as my new cushion.'

'Then you should return it to its rightful owner.' His voice was curt.

'I am the owner. It was given to me.' Her lips pouted. 'What a bad opinion you have of me. I thought you were my friend.'

'I am.'

'Then you must admire my book.'

'Book?' Gregory hesitated. It was the last thing he would expect the girl to covet.

'Yes. It's Walter Scott's latest novel'.

Gregory's laugh was incredulous.

He trailed her indoors and watched as her wet footprints led to the corner bed and from under the bottom of the pallet she lifted out a book. She handed it to him and a look of pride crossed her face. 'It's a good story. Have you read Ivanhoe?'

'Yes, I have.' He had bought it from a bookshop in London. His last purchase before he came north and he'd read it through the long first winter. Scott told a gripping story of good men and bad, with a hero and heroine and plenty of action. 'Have you read it, Kitty?'

'Not yet, but when I've time I will.'

'Who gave it to you?'

'You do not know him.'

'No.' Gregory's reply was sharp and the girl looked at him, her expression one of disappointment.

'Vous ne le connais pas, mais, il arrive et il va.' Her accent was good. He looked at her in amazement.

'You speak French?'

'Un peu.' She laughed.

Gregory held out his hand for the book. By now he was speechless. Who had given Kitty a present of newly published novel and taught her a smattering of French?

Kitty put the novel behind her back. Her face told him she was into a new game using book instead of floating stick to goad him. He stood inches from her; her lips pouted and her eyes flirted. She took a step back and then another. The bed blocked any further retreat. He stopped inches from her. There was the moorland smell of heather and fresh clean air. Her perfume was hypnotic. He breathed in heavily. He towered above her but her eyes, peat-brown, did not waver. He exhaled long and noisily and closed his eyes.

In a fleet movement she ducked below his outstretched arm and was across the room almost to the door before he caught her. She squealed with imaginary pain as his hands closed around her wrists, and they stood, the door this time blocking her escape. His hand hardened against her soft flesh and he heard her sharp intake of breath but he squeezed harder and with a yelp she dropped the book. It fell with a loud bang on the floor. She shot out her hand to retrieve her treasure but he already had the book high above his head, and even on her tiptoes it was beyond her reach. She laughed up into his face. It was not the look of a sister. He looked down at her; she could put up a fight, a fight to the finish and he was a poor opponent. He was out of his depth.

'Give it to me back. It's mine.'

'Is it? I doubt that very much.'

One-handed he opened the flyleaf. The inscription was in English;

"This book belongs to Vincent Byres."

20

Gregory stopped only to gather his cloak and satchel and then he was striding out along his chosen route, one he should have taken two days ago. The Devil's Causeway stretched as far as the eye could see. It looked smooth and green, a pathway that appeared level and flat and an easy route. Its name suggested otherwise. He'd left without another word to the girl. Questions crowded his brain but he knew Kitty would furnish no answers and if she did would he believe a single word of it?

Vincent Byres! That was a name from the past, and one that he would rather not remember. He pictured the blond, slim man who'd been his tormenter from the time of the Plymouth incident. It haunted him yet, like a stealthy companion always just behind his shoulder never in step so that he could not look it in the eye. Byres had been the instigator of Gregory's nightmares.

He stumbled as his foot hit a rock, grass-hidden in the track. He swore. The obstruction brought him full square back into the present. He looked back. There was nothing. The view was the same behind and ahead. Kitty's home was nowhere to be seen. The landscape was uninterrupted as though the house had been only of his imagination. He swore again and kicked the stone with his foot. He knew only too well the mean cottage with its fancy cushion and Scott novel was as real as the obstruction in the path. It was no illusion.

This land played fast and loose: miles and miles of vast never-ending loneliness with hidden pitfalls for the unwary. Was he destined to tramp here through its claustrophobic nothingness for the rest of time, with guilt and suspicion his unwanted companions?

How had Kitty come by the book? By foul means if he knew the girl at all. She did not know the difference between truth and lie, the novel as easily acquired as the coveted cushion of Hepzibah Hunter.

Yet, he thought of their easy carefree game by the stream and her desire not to have an unfair advantage over him. She was not all bad. So how else could Kitty have come by the book? Even now he was prepared to give her the benefit of the doubt.

Of course, he halted and said out loud in his relief, she got it from Jock. Nothing more natural that when the shipmates parted company the book had been exchanged and Macnab had brought it north; a simple explanation. Father had passed it on to daughter.

Gregory thought of his pleasure when he'd read the story; how much more would it appeal to Kitty, with its chivalry and romance, just as he could understand the appeal of the plush velvet cushion to the girl, whose life was stark and without comfort. Real life was very different from the fantasy of fiction. There was a sermon in that if he ever had a congregation to go home to. Home? It held no comfort. He thought of Cecilia, the natural home-maker who had need of none of the make-believe of Scott's story.

Was his whole life not based on make-believe? He shuddered and pulled his cloak more tightly about him, his thoughts an unwelcome companion. Questioning brought only more questions. And the first fact to stare him in the face was that his explanation about Kitty's possession of the book could not be. Ivanhoe had been published only the previous year and Macnab had been back in his homeland for many more years than that. Vincent Byres' hands had been on that book only recently.

The dislike of his old protagonist stuck in his throat like a regurgitated meal; it tasted foul, a mixture of fried trout and spring water and decaying lettuce, his border diet. What if the odious man now walked its paths? What nonsense, it could not be. His surprise at meeting up with Jock had been palpable and yet this was Jock's natural homeland. What possible reason could have brought the effete Officer Vincent to the uncultivated north, with or without Mr Walter Scott's latest masterpiece? It was beyond belief.

He should have questioned Kitty, forced her to give an honest reply. Why hadn't he done so? Away from the disturbing closeness of the girl he could not understand why he hadn't been more forceful. His weakness was shaming. He looked back. He'd covered only a short distance: the fact that he could no longer see his departure point was entirely due to the fickleness of the terrain. A few positive strides and he could find the answer to the mystery. Cecilia Howick would have railed at his lack of backbone. He could hear her contempt; direct questions brought answers. He turned back the way he had come.

Cecilia wiped the sweat from her eyes and leaned on her spade. She looked down at the exposed brown earth; it showed a rich soil. In her garden it gave a healthy yield but cabbages and potatoes were no longer the crop. Here in the Thorneyburn churchyard it was bodies: the harvest to be gathered not on this earth, but in Heaven. She was sexton now by dreadful necessity.

Cecilia had watched Martin Dodds dig the grave of Jessie's

younger brother, his anger and sorrow delving into the earth in fast, furious movements.

As he climbed unsteadily from the hole, he'd seized her hand with his soiled palms and his words were hard wrung.

'The Reverend is a good man I should not have driven him away with my anger. I pray for his and God's forgiveness.' Oh, she'd not known that Gregory's efforts at comfort had been so rebuffed. Poor Gregory, he'd have taken it badly.

Cecilia sank the spade once more into the space. This one was larger but her arms muscled by the extra digging, the line in the churchyard testament to that, no longer felt the physical pain of her toil. Martin Dodds had dug his last hole, Cecilia dug his grave. She looked at the lengthening line. Age was no barrier, the disease had taken young and old. Fear grew with each disturbance, who would be next? Somehow she knew it would not be her. God did not want the likes of her, feisty and uncompromising. He would have taken Gregory Felton, a good man though he did not know it. She whispered her gratitude that he had gone from this destroying place. She looked up to the moorland. She hoped by now he had discovered that not everything perished in this land, though it was getting harder to cling on to that belief.

Angrily she brushed a tear from her cheek, it showed her physical weakness. It was wrong to think thus. She was a gardener and in a new year there would be a new cycle of growth. She prayed that before that new season's awakening there would be no more wastage, that frail old plants would not succumb at the end of their allotted season. It seemed to her that her father had begun to wither.

Last night, she'd lifted the book for their bedtime reading, though her eyes were heavy. It was Gregory's copy of 'Ivanhoe' and thankfully she'd become lost in the tale of the doughty Rebecca and her selfless acts. But Thomas Howick heard few of the words and she knew she was reading out loud to herself. Had she imagined a flush on his elderly cheek? She hoped he would hear the end of the story.

Gregory picked up the offending book and idly flicked its pages. It hadn't been returned to its safe hiding place under the mattress, Kitty had left it carelessly on the table as though she no longer felt its worth. He looked about the empty room. She'd gone. He couldn't voice his questions. His retraced steps had been a waste of time. He was thwarted and he felt a mounting anger. He wanted to know the truth.

There was only one way to find the answer and that was to follow her. She could not have got far. He strode from the cottage and looked about him. This was wide open country and one could see for miles. It was no different from standing on deck scanning the horizon for an elusive enemy. He felt a sudden mixture of excitement and purpose that he had not known in days. One only had to use one's skill, one's knowledge. He remembered the track Jock had led him on, there'd been purpose in the man's step until Gregory had called halt. He turned north and walked. This was a deviation from his path but he needed to know.

He reached the stark rocks ringed with dark rushes. The first time the country had appeared featureless, but soon there were little signs that he'd noted and stored in his memory as though he knew he would tread that way again. His pace was brisk in spite of the rough going and as he breathed the upland air he felt a growing feeling of exhilaration. He'd always enjoyed the chase even when it had been the day-to-day routine of the Mediterranean Blockade. Pitting one's wits against one's quarry was satisfying, especially when their local knowledge was superior to one's own.

It didn't matter. She was there, a mile ahead, bobbing up and down like a ship on water as her feet followed the up and down nature of the land. Kitty did not look back. Her purpose lay somewhere out in the empty borderland that was no-man's-land between England and Scotland.

Along a narrow flat valley with banks that rose steeply on either side they tracked a burn. When they reached its head the girl veered eastward before picking up a stream that flowed north. They had crossed the watershed and soon they were in the valley of a river as big as the North Tyne and the Rede though in its early course. He had heard of the Coquet but it was his first sighting. It flowed with purpose, as intent as the girl to reach its destination. Like her it had no distractions, nothing to keep it from its allotted course.

Gregory paused for breath. With the change of direction he was leaving the light behind him. It would soon be dark. He breathed in the gathering dusk and there was a different smell. It was the aroma of night and of people. The peat smoke warned him of habitation even before he saw the building. They'd reached Kitty's destination.

Light, smoking chimney, noise and laughter cut the silence as abruptly as coming upon enemy ship in the middle of an empty sea. Gregory could almost hear the frantic order to man the guns, the adrenalin rising as the crew prepared for battle. Ahead of him

Kitty had quickened her pace. He followed suit. He needed to know some answers and the only way was to ask questions. He looked at the isolated building that throbbed with life. What did it hold for Kitty?

21

The noise was pulsating. It was as though the entire population of the moorland, like its myriad streams, flowed naturally into the collecting basin that was the inn. Gregory hesitated for just a moment before he trod the path down into the reservoir of human flesh. Carts huddled in untidy shapes, horses stamped their impatience, shadowy figures stood about the yard.

Inside it smelt like an animal pen. After a hard day's work there was only one liquid the men were interested in and it was not water. Momentarily overcome by the fug, Gregory sensed that he was very little different from the rest. It had been several days since the luxury of his rectory bathroom. His unshaven face sported a good growth of stubble, surely he could pass for any one of the mob that crowded the room?

But of course he could not; here noses were not fine-tuned but eyes were. They watched as he crossed the threshold and stood hesitant by the door. Light was subdued, just a few rush lamps in earthenware pots, but it was enough to show that there was a stranger in their midst.

He looked about him. Kitty was nowhere to be seen. If she'd entered the room she'd already disappeared. In truth he hadn't seen her go into the building. He himself had paused before he joined the gathered crowd; hit by the reluctance that had held him back from entering the Black Cock after Caleb Hunter. As then, he knew what his reception would be - a man of the church was not a man of the people. Silence sounds loud in a throng. He fingered his unshaven chin. He'd left his old persona behind. No-one here would place him in a pulpit.

He peered into the gloom, he'd followed Kitty for miles only to lose her finally amongst her own. Had she headed for the place through custom or for some special purpose? Was there someone here she had come to meet? This was no church convention; every ruffian in Christendom had found his way to the meeting place.

Here was below decks. But these were unfamiliar shipmates. The silence threw his resolve. A dozen pair of alien eyes turned on the intruder. He stood, the young lad on board ship met by a sea of strangers. It had taken time to turn them into friends, ones like Jock Macnab.

These men were the old seadog's own people, rough dressed, rough shaven, but Gregory knew that appearances often lied.

'What brings ye to Slymefoot?'

Gregory almost laughed aloud. Slymefoot - he could not have thought of a better name for this cauldron of low-life ingredients.

'What man do ye seek?' The nearest one of God's misfits addressed him and his voice echoed their doubt. Any one of half a dozen drinking men could have repeated the challenge. Gregory had been comfortable with his looks, yet there wasn't a man there that saw only an outsider in their midst.

Gregory considered his reply. He knew that when he opened his mouth he would confirm their doubt. Surely there could be only one name that would be his password to acceptance.

'Jock Macnab. I wonder is he here?'

'Jock? What is your mission?' A man, if anything rougher and darker and more unkempt than the rest thrust his way to the head of the group. His attitude said this would have to be good. 'What manner of business do you have with him?'

'He was a shipmate of mine.'

'Shipmate?' The man used the word as though it were an oath. Disbelief was like a drowning wave.

'Did ye no hear tell that Jock was lost at sea? The man roared his laughter.

'Aye.' One of his companions theatrically began to wipe his eyes. ''Tis a sad end when a man goes to meet his maker, wallowing in a vat of rum. There can be no worse fate. Do ye open your mouth or keep it tight shut?'

There was a murmur of derision. Gregory could feel his anger rising like bile from his stomach. Jock hadn't been the ready password into the throng that he'd imagined. He bit his lip, and immediately they sensed his weakness, a detail seized and noted and stored away for future use. A collective memory aided survival in such a land. He'd been so sure that Jock would be his introduction into their midst instead it had made the new arrival the butt of their hostility.

Outside, the night dark awaited him and with it the lonely hillside.

'Tell Jock Rory was asking for him.' He turned on his heel and seized the door latch.

'Rory, did you say?' The leader of the group showed his surprise. Rough hands seized his arm. And now there was fear in his throat. He was a drowning man.

'Why didn't you say so, man? What keeps you on the threshold?' The obvious spokesman of the pack pulled him into their midst.

'John Armstrong.' He held out an unkempt hand; the grip felt like a vice. Gregory knew he'd not want to feel that hand other than in friendship.

With the offering of names came sudden light. More tallow candles appeared from nowhere and eyes that had peered with suspicion now reflected acceptance. Gregory took the drink thrust into his hands as a man who did not question where the rescue lifeline came from.

'So you're a Newcastle man.' John Armstrong stated his knowledge of Gregory. His tone was half accusing.

Surprised Gregory could only reply, 'Yes, Are you acquainted with it?'

The man snorted. 'Aye, but I'm glad to say, no well. I go there once a year to pay ma rent and stock up with winter provisions.'

Gregory thought is that where he gets his liquid needs? He guessed not. It was not the smell of ale but whisky that came from the man's breath. He glanced around the mean dark room. It could have but one function, a hard drinking place for hard men. Ale might flow above the counter but there would be another drink for those in the know. However it was achieved, this place would have no licence for the hard stuff.

'Aye, it's worth going now and then to Newcastle.' As he spoke, the burly man eyed Gregory, as a farmer might appraise a prize beast. 'I like the girls. They're more refined and they don't smell of lanolin.'

There was an appreciative laugh from beside him. 'Aye, but the rain washes off our lasses when they raise their skirts on a wet hillside.'

'Here's to long fleeces.' A younger man raised his drink and the next few minutes held a ribald discussion of country superiority over city womenfolk.

Gregory listened to the banter but his thoughts raced. What more did they know of him? How did they know he came from Newcastle? How was his name accepted without question in such a place as this? Did they know his calling?

'I'll give you city girls are better.' A Scotsman standing beside him voiced his preference. 'But the women of Edinburgh beat those from the south, man. In Auld Reekie the wind helps raise their skirts. It means you can give two hands to your ale.'

No, they did not know he was a man of religion. Their earthy talk reassured. There would have been natural reserve, a holding back of their baser instincts in the presence of the church. Gregory let their banter waft over him. With thoughts concentrated on earthly pursuits their interest for the stranger was only half-hearted. He would guess they were conservative, God-fearing men for all of their bravado. These men would respect little, but that did not include their maker. With a hidden smile Gregory thought these men before God were as naked and vulnerable as the females they conjured in their thoughts.

'So what say you, man? Would it be the lasses of Newcastle or Edinburgh from your experience?' All eyes were on him

Gregory stared back at them. At a guess he could alienate half the room with the choice of the English town and the other half with the Scots. Most had probably never set foot in either, but loyalty did not cross borders.

'Come on, man, you must have a preference.'

Faces were not pulpit high looking up to accepted knowledge but eye level and they awaited the answer of the experienced sailor with assuredly a woman in every port. He needed the judgement of Solomon. He laughed.

'There's a saying in Spain. All cats are the same in the dark. The same can be said about women.'

There was a roar of agreement; John Armstrong slapped him on the back,

'You speak truth, though there's nae need to go to Spain to find that out. If we put out the candles here, you wouldn't know if it were Prudence or some other comely wench.'

He pointed to a woman that hovered in the background. She had produced the candles and was the source of the ale. She would be called ugly in city and country alike. It was as though her skin had been yellowed by the burning tallow and creased as the fat wrinkled down into the saucer; she was as short and as plump as the spent candle, its early light long used up. She smiled at the jest and her teeth were yellow, survivors and gaps in equal measure.

'In the dark Prudence can hold her own with any lass, Prudence or..?' Armstrong paused to name a rival. He'd sense enough to know there were fathers and husbands and even brothers in the room. He'd survived to middle age knowing there were things best left unsaid.

'You minding your words, man?' The younger man standing beside him grinned. 'Can it be said that John Armstrong begins to talk like a woman?'

'Aye, Rob Shiel, I've heeded their mouths as well. They can talk more sense than a man. Besides I would hesitate to name such as your Jean in such a conversation. I know you are a jealous man.'

There was an instant howl of anger from Shiel and the rest of the assembled men laughed. The man's eyes blazed, though he knew that Armstrong was goading him,

'Aye, Jean will be waiting for me.' He turned towards the door and there was renewed mirth.

The incoming night air caused candles to flutter and it mingled with the stale smell of drink on breath. As Shiel took his leave, it ushered in a newcomer. It was Kitty who walked into the alehouse.

'So, Armstrong, here's your comparison, Prudence or Kitty?' Shiel threw the remark over his shoulder as a final rejoinder.

Kitty looked about her, struck by the sudden quiet of the usually boisterous alehouse. She looked confused, yet anyone questioning her appearance would note she had been thus before she ever set foot inside.

'Prudence or me? What is he talking about?' There was a note of impatience in her voice as she moved towards the huddle of men beside the table of ale.

'Well now, Kitty. Our good friend here says all women are the same in the dark. Would you not say shame on him? Here is no man of discernment.' There was a low murmur of assent, the listeners once more questioning the intruder in their midst.

'Rory!' The girl's gasp of astonishment as Armstrong pointed to the stranger echoed in the silence. She stared at him and a deep flush suffused her weather-beaten face. 'W…What are you doing here? How did you find this place?' The girl stared at him open-mouthed. Gregory noted the blush and her obvious confusion and he was not the only one. Armstrong saw her reaction and a delighted grin spread across his face.

'This calls for the experiment, I think.' As he spoke his hand crushed down onto the nearest candle beside him and the flame spluttered and died. He did likewise with a second. 'Here girl come stand beside Prudence. We shall see if our fine friend really does get confused in the dark.'

There was a roar of delight from the rest of the room and willing hands obliterated the remaining lights. The alehouse became the colour of night.

'Now sir, make your choice. You who say all women are the same under the bedclothes.'

There was no sound. No chink of light, no shadow. It was below deck in the mid night hours when men slept silenced by their dreams of women. Gregory, like a sleep-walker, moved forward, his hands outstretched. Out there in the blackness of night Kitty was no dream.

22

The moon had not cheated in the Slymefoot game of chance. There had been no collusion in the result, no stray beam to show the prize worth winning in the foolish contest for men who worked hard and took any bet that came their way. Kitty had not giggled, Prudence had made no protest and strangest of all Gregory had played his part.

His hands had been as eager as his feet as he stepped unseeing into the blackness and the thick mass of Kitty's hair entwined in his fingers, the net catching the helpless fish. He clung on to her as though the girl was the last catch in the ocean. He could feel the blush that suffused Kitty's face for the second time that evening and his cheeks flamed in the dark. His heart pounded. He cursed the rush light that returned his discomfort to the assembled men.

'So, man, you see in the dark. Perhaps a blindfold would make a fairer contest.' Armstrong's hand struggled with the kerchief at his neck and Gregory raised his hands in protest.

It was Kitty who took charge of the scene.

'Enough of the games, Rory, my father waits and will wonder at our delay. He will think some harm has come to us. We will bid you goodnight, Mister Armstrong.' The fun ceased as quickly as it had begun, their exit hardly noted; too much hard drinking time had been wasted.

He followed her, a mere player in the entertainment. It was a game, harmless, of the moment, like shipboard tig when there had been some youthful energy left after a hard day at sea and the lads had chased each other in the moment of release. The night air enhanced that feeling.

The alehouse had been claustrophobic. Now the intimidating hovel was behind them. Instead, the Coquet lay illuminated by the moonlight; Kitty headed uphill beside a small stream. 'We follow the Rowhope Burn out of the valley. It's a good guide day or night.'

The land rose abruptly and soon the alehouse was a dark smudge below them. Kitty stopped for the out-of breath Gregory to catch her up. She giggled as, panting, he reached her side.

'We'll make a hill man of you yet so that you are not always groping in the dark.' She was gleeful. 'Just imagine if you had got Prudence. What would you have done with her?' She laughed up into his face and Gregory echoed her.

'Yes, I was a little anxious. I thought you might stoop down to her height. Then it truly would have been an unlucky dip.'

'Why would I have done that?' Her voice teased.

'I know you like to play games.'

'Not when the dice are loaded. I always take what is offered.'

Gregory retorted. 'It would have been more of a contest if one of the other men had been involved as well. There were some handsome young farmers in the gathering.' He thought of the reason Kitty had gone to the alehouse in the first place. It hadn't been to encounter him.

'You put yourself down, Rory. You stood out in their midst. I am happy with my fairground prize. It's as good as any that I have won at Stagshaw Bank.'

The silence hung between them.

'So, Gregory, do you think you have won the prize on the top shelf?' The moon reflected in her playful eyes as she raised her face questioningly to him. He did not answer.

'Oh, Rory, you've no sense of fun.' She sounded petulant. 'It was only a game. However, I do expect one kiss as a reward.' She leaned towards him and he hesitated. Out here on the open hillside he felt less brave. In the inky black of the drinkers' hovel he'd felt only desire for the girl.

She stood now inches from him, as close as then, her flushed cheeks expectant. If he put out his hand he would feel her colour. It was only a forfeit. Her cheek was cool and soft and involuntarily he put his hands on her arms. She moved and their lips met. He tasted heather and mountain air and the Rowhope Burn. Abruptly he drew away from her. But in that moment he knew he had become part of her landscape. It was no longer a barren land for him.

'We shall walk together on this stretch of the way over the Barrow Law before dropping into the next valley.' She had become the country again and with the naming she was making him part of it too. 'Then we shall have to go alone. It will be single file after that.'

'It's a cruel land that brings together and then parts so uncaringly.' Gregory increased his step to keep up with his companion.

'So meetings and separations are as fickle as the rise and fall of the contours?' She was ahead again. 'Out here, one lives for the moment.' It was a truth that he found not unattractive.

He quickened his pace and his fingers tightened about hers. Her hand lay still and compliant as the smooth hill grass under their feet. The moon showed no obstacles as they dropped down into the next strip of light that trickled down the hillside in a gurgling, jumping dash of water.

'This is the Barrowburn.' Her charting of their walk punctuated the companionable silence. He was the explorer being led obediently by his native guide. She moved up the hillside for a few yards and then her practised eyes found the spot where the obstructing stream narrowed. It was her turn to tighten her fingers round his. 'Ready, steady, go!' Their jump was high and long as though an air current lifted them above the stream and they landed flat on the ground on the other side, laughing and giggling in a floundering of arms and legs. Gregory could feel her flesh. Their lips made contact. He could have lain there for ever.

She pulled him to his feet and he staggered like a drunken man but he knew that it was not the drink that intoxicated him. He'd drunk for most of his life, well versed in its effects, but he was the beginner in this feeling of physical headiness.

They climbed again, their hands still clasped as shadowy walls blocked their way. It was a sheepfold. They skirted it and then they were dropping, down and down in a steep erratic descent. The stream that barred their way was broad and a natural obstacle. She let go of his hand and he felt bereft.

'You're on your own here, Rory every man for himself!' She pulled up her skirts and strode off into the churning waters and he followed. His eyes were no longer on her but on the water swirling about his boots. She reached the other bank and turned to watch him, shouting. 'The Usway Burn can be a devil in winter, now it's over its spring flood.'

He stood beside her, his feet wet, but he felt no discomfort.

She pointed back up the stream. 'Always remember to cross a stream facing up the valley so that you can see the amount of water coming down; the force of water can buckle the knees from behind. It's not a good idea to turn your back on what could turn out to be a surprise enemy.'

'You make a good teacher.' His head and feet followed her every step. Up down, up down, they criss-crossed the hills and streams in a dizzying ascent and descent. He knew now he was lost, walking into oblivion. And he knew he was entering the unknown and treading a dangerous path.

They were climbing again. It was the steepest slope, seemingly almost vertical and his breath came quickly, but it was excitement as much as the exertion. She stopped abruptly and he leaned towards her. Gently she pushed him away.

'You will soon have dry feet.'

'It does not signify. I am no soft southerner.'

She laughed. 'Feet first! Dry ones are the aim of every hill user. Not long now. We will soon be home.' He looked about him. Her words sounded empty. A faint glimmer ahead showed the first light of day, but there was nothing to be seen - wild open country lay in all directions.

Gregory felt a sudden tinge of doubt. Was this some ruse devised by Kitty to counter his Slymefoot game? For a brief second he thought has this been a giant tease, leading him off into hills only to desert him when he had completely lost his bearings? Had her naming of the physical features been a lifeline to help him find his own way back, just as she had shown him the trick in the stick race at the Roman fort? Was it a mix of cruel bravado and wanting to help? He knew already that Kitty was quite capable of such a prank. He let go of her hand; his palms sweated and he wiped them against his cloak. He wanted her to know he could stand on his own two feet.

'Don't get lost now, Rory.'

He could hear water, though still he could see nothing. He breathed in deeply.

'I do not smell peat. There is no hearth close by.'

'You're learning.' Her voice sounded her approval. 'We shall make you one of us yet.' She seized back his hand. One moment they were on a flat empty hillside the next they were descending into a steep, deep cleugh. The cleft in the land was sudden and steep. Her fingers gripped his as he strove to keep upright. Rocks and hidden vegetation battled to check their feet. But he followed blindly.

'Watch the glidders,' Kitty warned, as the small pebbles of scree made their descent suddenly steeper and more hazardous. In a final skid they touched flat land. They were surrounded by buildings.

'Welcome to Wholehope.'

A shower of the glidders dislodged by their feet resounded against the walls.

23

The buildings lay on a narrow haugh in a crook of the burn. Every inch of flat land had been utilised. To the south the site was overhung by a small crag, whilst to the west, rose the almost perpendicular slope that they had descended the previous night. From the north-east a fast flowing stream showed the steep angle of its young valley and from its upper regions a loud noise revealed a small but busy linn.

Gregory turned full circle and took in at a single glance the place where the girl had led him. Wholehope. He smiled at the name. It spoke of promise, so very different from Slymefoot where he'd stepped, so hesitatingly, over the threshold. He turned and strode back the few feet into the low stone building with turf-covered ridged roof that had been their resting place; exhausted theirs had been like the sleep that knew no waking.

The air had helped to clear his head. He looked about him. A low fire curled up through the hole in the roof that acted as chimney. There was the welcoming smell of burning peat.

He remembered breathing in the night air when Kitty had stopped so abruptly on the open hillside and he'd noted there was no smell to denote nearby habitation. And just when he thought he was learning the signs of the land she had thrown another surprise at him - a hidden world in the middle of nowhere.

Kitty must have lit the fire before disappearing. There was a kettle that hummed companionably, the vapour trailing the smoke of the fire to the roof. He seized a cloth to cover the heated handle and poured the boiling water into a cup: it was without a handle, but just the kind of pretty thing that would have made it hard for the girl to throw away. Blue printed roses and tulips ornamented its curving sides. It had already been filled with crushed leaves. The nettle tea was hot and pungent.

Though the space was cramped there were small touches of comfort. A good, olive-green, glass bottle graced the rough table. He picked it up and buried his nose in the rim. Its contents were to be expected. The whisky filled his nostrils like smelling salts and he choked, though it could hardly be in surprise.

'So the streams run whisky here in this Garden of Eden?' He raised his eyebrows as Kitty came into the shack.

She laughed. 'Of course, they could do no other when they rise so close to the Scots border. Even the ewes milk is flavoured.' The girl moved to a primitive cupboard and from its confines she took a small leather pouch. The cheese inside was strong smelling. 'Here try it. The taste is like no other.'

Kitty broke off a hunk, sank to her knees beside him and with a smile placed it on his lips; obediently he ate. Her hand hovered and he smelt only her skin.

'So the whisky from Scotland does not stop at the border?' He needed to distract his mind from her close presence.

She laughed. 'That would be against nature, would it not?'

'Yes, we cannot fight nature.' He smiled unsteadily at her and on pretence of stretching his stiffened joints rose to his feet. Kitty put out a hand to help.

'Nature is a hard master.' She pursed her lips. 'It is almost as hard as your God. Just when you think you have reached the top of the hill, there is another slope for you to climb and always there are swamps and narrow gullies and jutting rocks to ensure that the going is never easy.'

Gregory laughed. 'So is that why you come to hide away in a hidden valley?'

'That would be defeatist. No, we cannot better nature or God but we can fight the taxman. He's only a fellow human and he has been put on this earth for us to defy.' She tossed her head. 'During the Napoleonic Wars the tax levied on spirits in England rose four-fold. Is it right that a few miles away in Scotland a gallon of whisky is nine shillings and three pence cheaper than it is here? That goes against nature.'

Gregory raised his eyebrows in surprise, 'That is a lot of money.'

'Yes.' Her face relaxed. 'You see then that I work for charity.' Her smile was cheeky. It was the first time that her illicit trade had been mentioned between them and Gregory shook his head.

'You are incorrigible.' But his voice held no censure. He broke off another piece of the cheese and almost shyly he handed it to her. 'As you say, it's very good.'

'So I speak the truth?'

'Sometimes!' He grinned.

'And now?'

'Yes.'

'Then I am happy.' She smiled coyly as a child.

'Are you?'

'Rory, you know I am. And you?'

'Happy?' He repeated the word as though he would explore its meaning. It had not been a word in his vocabulary. His conclusion took him by surprise. 'I believe I am.'

She laughed. 'What took you so long? Happiness is immediate it does not wait for deliberation.'

'No, you are right. Questions always make more questions.' Her dark eyes were only feet from his. 'So ask me again.' He sank to his knees beside her.

She smiled up into his face, 'Oh, Rory, sometimes I think you are the boy.'

'That I'm not.' He caught hold of her skirt involuntarily in a gesture of annoyance, roused by her jibe. She made no protest, her hair cascading about her face and on to his shoulders. He seized a dark tress and his fingers were entwined as in the dark of Slymefoot and this time he knew exactly what he wanted.

He kissed her long and hard. It was not the first illicit fumbling of the alehouse or her stolen prize on the hillside but the knowledge that this embrace could go on forever. Here within these crude stone walls of the animal shieling, nature was lip-close.

He wrapped her in his arms and he could feel her tremble, a spasm that showed her need and he cried out in his. He had waited for this moment all his life. She responded to his fervour and he kissed her over and over again. Breathless, he tousled her thick, luxuriant hair and then his hands were down on to her body and her breasts felt warm and soft through her rough homespun blouse. Her skirt was high to her waist. The earth floor was their mattress. He entered her and he cried his delight. Yes, this moment would last forever.

Time needed no counting. Thoughts needed no contemplation.

Bodies needed no feeding. No questions were necessary, why or how or where? There was succour there in that refuge that Rory knew would sustain them not just through that day, but through whatever lay ahead. Was it the next hour, the next week? When finally he raised his head he saw the shadow of the open door had lengthened across their bed. She stood in the doorway, a vision that filled the space. She had been down to the stream and her wet hair fell in ringlets about her bare shoulders. He watched her as she moved across the earthen floor to him and he pulled her down to his level. They lay together as one.

'How blessed is this cleugh just wide enough for us to lie side by side. I love our summer shieling.'

She made no reply and he brushed the hair away from her face seeking to see the agreement in her eyes, that she too had found her heaven. Her eyelids were closed but a smile hovered about her lips and he kissed the upturned corner of her mouth. She clung to him and again he felt the security of their shelter.

He lay back and stared up at the roof. From the chinks of light through the turf cover a splash of water fell on to his arm. Nature was not far away, it had begun to rain. He pulled her to him as though he would shelter her from the elements and once more they made love, the outside world just feet away from their animal byre.

She lay curled up in a foetal position in a deep sleep. He watched her, this feral girl at home by her hearth, and he felt a happiness he had never known. Here there was no need for shutters to shut out his despair; even the leaking roof made him know his new freedom.

She could feel his gaze and she was awake at once. A quick shadow of alarm crossed her face as she sensed the presence of someone. Then it seemed to Gregory that she realised who was beside her for there was a happy smile of recognition. She was on her feet and reluctantly he rose too. Only then did he feel the hardness of their bed. His legs and back felt as though they had tramped forever. He stretched painfully, and she laughed.

'It was a hard bed, Rory. You are too used to your comfort.'

'Yes.' He smiled apologetically. She moved with ease as she busied herself at the hearth. In minutes she had the smouldering fire leaping with flame and the kettle singing. She poured the scalding water into the pretty cup he had used earlier. Then carefully she placed it on to a matching saucer.

'Rory, you used only the cup before. That is not done in the best circles.'

He laughed. 'There is no end to the comforts of this high class establishment. I hope the price is not too high.'

'Oh, you can afford it, reverend sir.'

Her tone was loving, playful, and he sought to pull her down to his level again as she handed him her prized possession. Startled, the girl lost her grip and the cup went flying. It landed between them and broke into pieces, scalding tea splattering in all directions. There was a shocked silence.

'Oh, how could I have been so clumsy? I will get you another. I promise.'

The girl shrugged her shoulders, 'There is no need. I have another,' and moving to the cupboard she produced its replica. 'Besides it is impossible to replace.'

He made no reply, stopping the question that formed on his lips. He knew already that one did not enquire about the provenance of her few precious belongings. He looked at the girl and felt his regret at the accident. She'd made no complaint but he thought of the care with which she had carried the object over difficult terrain to her hidden home, only for it to be smashed by his clumsiness. How could he have been so careless? But he knew the answer. It had been her calling him reverend that had caused his disquiet. He needed no recalling of the outside world. That it followed you however many miles you retreated from it was not something he cared to remember.

She put her hand on his lip. 'You are too upset, Rory, over something small.'

Unsettled, Gregory walked to the door. She followed and put a restraining hand on his arm. 'We are better indoors on such a day. There is nothing out there for us.' He peered outside and saw the sense of her words. A low encircling mist had descended into the valley almost to the door and the other buildings were menacing shapes crowded into the narrow defile.

'Tis a clagg. They come suddenly on these hill tops and are neither good for man nor beast.' He followed her back into the room. 'It cannot get us in here. T'is a poor shelter I know, Gregory but the best I can offer.' She peered at him as though suddenly she saw it through his more sophisticated eyes.'

'No. Do not say that. To me it feels like home.' He felt the immediate protection of the bare walls and rude roof. But there was a trace of annoyance in his voice as he said. 'My name is Rory. Do not call me other.'

'It suits you. And you belong here with a name like that.' Her smile was child-like. 'It is Rory from now on. No more Gregory.

He, poor man, is left wandering somewhere out in the mist. It is his fate to disappear down into a deep cleft and never be heard of again.'

'Aye.' He joined in her amusement at his sad demise. 'He'll not be missed.'

'No, not by me.' Her eyes searched his face. 'The poor man was always looking over his shoulder, little wonder he didn't see the ravine ahead.'

'So we'll waste no time in mourning him, the foolish fellow.' He sighed theatrically. 'It is sad that no-one will give him another thought. But he goes and Rory comes.' He smiled and bent to kiss her but he saw not the girl's dark beauty but the intelligent face of Cecilia Howick. He brushed it quickly from his mind. Cecilia, there was a name that belonged in this place as poorly as his former name of Gregory.

He closed his eyes to dispel the unwanted images and kissed the wide, generous mouth but it was the thin disapproving one of Cecilia Howick that he felt. He opened his eyes and with a trembling hand traced Kitty's thick parted lips.

'Say my name and you will christen me.' He wanted rid of his disquiet. Her voice would make it go away.

'Rory, Rory, Rory. You are thrice welcome in place of Gregory.' Kitty took hold of both his hands and she noted his tremor. She comforted, 'The Cheviot defiles are deep; already there is no trace of your former self.'

There was a noise outside. They both instantly stiffened and Rory raised his eyebrows. 'What is that?'

Kitty cocked her ear and the sound came again.

'He is out there.' She crossed herself, this time slowly and deliberately.

'Who?'

'Why your old self. Rory, you have not wished him totally gone. He has come back to haunt us.' She feigned her terror. 'Rory....'

'Rory!' The door opened and the dark figure of a man stood outlined against the grey mist. They squinted into the sudden light. Jock Macnab strode into the room. He looked from his daughter to his friend and a strange smile crossed his lined face.

'Rory! I thought to find you here. News travels fast in these hills.'

Rory staggered to his feet. 'Macnab!' The girl's father! He waited for the man's anger at finding him with his daughter. What had he done?

Jock was beaming. 'So lad, I hear you've earned yourself an added nickname. It's Black Rory from now on.'

24

Jock surveyed the couple, his face a strange mixture of astonishment and pleasure as though he'd travelled the world and now he'd seen everything. Gregory felt his colour rise. There could be no other explanation for his presence in that unexpected place than the one that the older man now so clearly and correctly surmised.

'So, look what the mist has brought us. We weren't expecting you.' Kitty was the first to recover. 'You must have smelt the brew.'

She poured a drink for her father into another tulip-decorated cup, was about to hand it to the newcomer then thought better of it. Seizing a saucer she placed the drink upon it and with mock ceremony gave it to Jock.

'We should mind our manners, father.'

A blue Willow pattern saucer. The combination was jarring. Rory noted the ill match and felt an inexplicable irritation. It was as though the new arrival had come to remind them that not everything in this life fitted. And surely three was one too many. The crowded space had become a hovel that no manner of decoration could disguise. But it had been he who had caused the unlikely marrying of the cup with the saucer. His ardour for the girl had broken the match.

Jock, unaware of such trivia, seated himself on a stool by the fire.

'So you've earned yourself a nickname, lad.' He looked at the ill-at-ease Rory and there was the old twinkle in his eye. 'Black

Rory, would you believe?'

'What a christening.' Kitty chuckled gleefully. 'You've achieved the name remarkably quickly when on the surface you are all that is pure and white.' Her shoulders shook with laughter and she wiped the tears from her eyes. 'John Armstrong must be a discerning man. He's looked deep into your soul and found someone other than the one that shows his face to the world.'

Gregory made no reply and Jock interjected. 'I think daughter, the black refers to the fact that our friend here can see in the dark. It does not concern his character.' He chuckled his appreciation. 'From what I hear it was no contest at Slymefoot between you and Prudence. Who would choose the other girl? Only one who is blind, deaf and dumb.'

Kitty scowled at her father. 'So, it was a poor selection was it? At least there was choice. Usually when groping in the dark one finds just one pliant body.' Her good mood had gone. 'Just maybe it was God's hand on his.' Kitty placed her hand on the younger man's arm. Rory jumped.

'Leave God out of this.' Protested Rory. 'We find our own salvation. The mind is its own place, it can make its own heaven or hell.' There was a long and awkward silence. 'Or so the poet Milton wrote.'

'So, Rory do we have heaven or hell here?' The girl's voice held a new note. 'I think you will discover that there are both.' Her eyes flickered, 'perhaps you should go.' Her voice faltered. 'But wait for the clagg to clear.'

She put out a restraining hand. 'Then why wait for that? If you can see in the dark, you can see your way through mist.' She was the temptress. He looked away. Did she really want him to leave? Her eyes told a different story from her lips. Her body had paired them like cup and saucer, she the base, he the ill-matched vessel. He could not leave and she knew it.

It was as dark outside as it was in. He had no desire to get lost out there. Here he was amongst friends, secure. Only relationships had changed. Yesterday Gregory would have welcomed a long banter between him and Jock, remembering the old times; the Scot was nothing if not good company. The trouble was he had a daughter and because of her he had become Black Rory. He felt the name change and all that it portended.

Gregory moved back to the cast-iron grate that cradled a small but healthy fire where the kettle hummed companionably. He sat himself down opposite Jock and smiled.

'I think you'd agree, Jock, there is no contest between staying and going. The outside has no appeal for me today.'

His words left open the option he would leave tomorrow or at the latest the day after. This was only a detour on his longer journey. In this hidden valley he could see no tall upstanding trees and that was what he had set out to find.

Kitty laughed delightedly, her temper restored, 'So I've beaten the hill mist just as I defeated Prudence.' Her words and eyes goaded. She bent towards him and helplessly he caught hold of her as she threw a defiant look at her father. He pulled her down to his level on the stool. He could feel her fire. He stopped breathing. There was nothing beyond this moment. He cared nothing for Jock, just feet away; nothing for the valley hidden from the outside world, or for that world manifested in the Slymefoot den and his rectory at Thorneyburn. It lay far off, somewhere on another planet. He kissed her long and hard.

Above it he heard Jock swear and shuffle to the door. He struggled to his feet and Kitty called after him. 'Remember now you are Rory.'

Her father laughed, 'Aye that'll be right. I can show Wholehope to Rory, never to Gregory.'

'So Rory it is.' He followed the man who had named him thus at the age of twelve. It felt a familiar garment. They walked into the fog. It was a wet mist and the rain pierced his shirt. Outside was reality.

'So what is this place? What do you do here, Jock?' But already he knew the answer. He could hear the plop, plop of water as it fell into an empty bucket by the door and the stream rushing in a mighty roar down the valley slope. Water was everywhere and because of it another liquid flowed. He looked at the shapes that clung to the valley side, the mist was clearing and now they were solid buildings with stout doors. Four in all, precarious they straddled the valley sides.

'Do ye really want to ken?' But the Scotsman seized his arm with the question and with the production of a great key from his jacket, they gained entrance to the nearest of the stone buildings, the entrance directly opposite the living quarters. They ducked their heads under the low door jamb.

The room was larger, the floor cobbled and sloping. No windows alleviated the gloom and Rory could smell the rotting vegetation. He looked to his companion. There was a gleam in the eye of the older man.

'What a perfume, it's the best in the land.' He seized a great wooden spade leaning against the wall and began to rake the floor in swift turning movements, flinging the substance into the air and catching it as it descended to the ground.

'Tis an easy crop to tend. No sun or rain needed just an occasional turning after the initial soaking.' He looked smug. 'I can come and go as I please. The barley can be left to its own germination. It matters not who does the turning. Kitty did it for me yesterday. Perhaps it could be you tomorrow?'

Rory raised his eyebrows in a gesture of wait and see. He had smelled the decaying vegetation on the girl on her return to the living quarters. Then it had smelled of the earth and it had excited him. Now Rory wrinkled his nose and Jock laughed.

'There's nothing to beat the smell of malt. I can smell it now. The plume will not be long. And there's nothing to beat your good home-made stuff, especially as they tax the malt as well as the whisky. They drive us to it, man.' The Scot shook his head sadly as he gave one final turn of the spade and then they were out of the door and scrambling at the back of the building towards a distinctive circular shape.

'The kiln awaits its firing.' Jock pointed to the blackened hole. Stacks of peat heaped in the limited space crouched like witches, a huddled group of jet black crones. 'You'll no quarrel with this smell when the match is put to it. It's the peat-reek that gives the malt its taste.' He was a man talking of the woman he loved.

'Tis dried crisp, never scorched- scorched sugar would turn to caramel.' His hand moved lovingly along the metal pipe that ran from the kiln and disappeared through a wall. Rory followed him round into the last of the buildings.

'Welcome to Wholehope Distillery.' Jock chuckled. 'I do not say that to many.' He looked to Rory for his reaction and involuntarily Rory gasped as his eye took in the Scot's illicit works. Here in this room lay the meaning of Wholehope; a forbidden secret of a hidden valley.

It was the hub of the operation, a confusion of equipment of different shapes and sizes and functions.

'This clever little gem is the still small but beautiful and, because of that, it will give the best spirit. And this pewter neck links it into the worm-tub beside it.' The latter was fixed firmly to the wall. 'The worm is a great weight when filled with water.' Macnab was a teacher on his favourite subject.

Strange, alien shapes and names, Rory stared at the upright spiral of copper tube. Beside it ready stacked on the floor were cans, a funnel, a pewter siphon, a poker, fire shovel and rake; a line of tubs on the far wall awaited the filling. It was easy to imagine the noise, the heat, the confusion, but most of all the smell.

'Mashing, fermentation and several distillations, all can be done here.' Jock's eyes gleamed; he could be the passionate man given the cause. Kitty was her father's daughter. Excitement constricted his chest. Rory could feel the girl's presence though she'd not followed them: her allure was as hypnotic as the moonshine.

The two men stood together on the level ledge that held the whisky-making plant. It dropped steeply down to the shelf of land that carried the flowing water so necessary for the process of the distillery. Above them towered the hills.

'Everything we need is here in this place - abundant water, endless peat.' Jock sounded smug.

'What of the barley? How do you get that?' There was no space even to grow a crop of hay in the narrow cleugh that was Wholehope.

Jock pointed up the thin defile where a narrow track was being worn between the rocks and bracken. 'Pack animals and any number of willing farmers provide our raw material.'

Rory thought of the characters he had seen just a few hours ago in the alehouse, as dark and hidden and secretive as the Wholehope cleugh. Like his companion, they were the land, tough, isolated and fearless, a law unto themselves. Normal rules meant nothing in such a lawless place they were there only to be broken. These tough hill men answered to no one.

'You make it sound so natural.' Rory sought to veil his disquiet.

'God has provided the materials. It's not blasphemy to say so.' His look was as near to being apologetic as Jock could summon. 'All we have to do is take advantage of them. We would be foolish not to.'

'Like I said before, leave God out of this.' Rory stifled his annoyance.

'As you wish, at the end of the day I answer for myself!' Jock nodded abruptly. 'We make our own destiny.'

'Destiny?' Rory said it as though it was a word he cared not to think of. 'Life here is real and now. Destiny is a far off country.' He looked up at the hillside. He could see nothing beyond the steep slope except the grey impasse that was the sky. Wholehope was here and now, even Slymefoot was another world.

He closed his eyes and he was back in the black hole that was the smuggler's haunt. He'd walked into its hostility and suspicion, a lone stranger seeking, seeking what? Into that darkness he'd stumbled blind, his hands outstretched, his future at the end of his groping finger tips. Were they devil led?

He shivered. The rain had stopped but the mist still lingered keeping him captive in this unlikely place. He could almost feel its restraining hold. Was he prisoner or free to go? And then where? He did not know the answer. He had been led here, but surely of his own free will. Here to this wilderness? Why?

Keep God out of this, he'd protested, yet both Jock and Kitty felt the need to include a higher being. Were father and daughter his deceivers or his rescuers? He dismissed the thought with a visible shake of his head.

'Jock, I would know the answer I seek, it is a puzzle.'

His companion grinned. 'It depends what it is. I am not one to philosophise.'

Rory shrugged his shoulders. 'Oh, no, I've left the unanswerable questions behind me it's time to ask questions that do have an answer.'

'That's a relief. Sometimes you are beyond me, Rory. But it was always so, even when we were shipmates.' He laughed, 'I remember thinking when that boatload of doxies came on board that you really did think they were our cousins and our aunts.'

He ignored the jibe. 'Why did I enter Slymefoot an unwanted stranger and leave a friend?'

'Because of my daughter, of course I'm relieved to know that now at least you know what a girl is for.'

'How can you speak of your daughter so?' Rory rounded angrily on the man and Jock shrugged his shoulders.

'I sought to lighten your mood.' He looked at his young companion. 'You take life too seriously.'

'Perhaps, but we digress, man. I would talk now of the Slymefoot whisky house. For that is what it is. They served me ale but do not think I could not smell the favourite perfume of these parts.' He sounded his exasperation. 'It was before the advent of Kitty. I walked into that place and I was amongst enemies.'

Jock said nothing and Rory continued, his words spilling out like the stream at their feet. 'I mentioned your name, thinking it to be my salvation. It was not. Only when I mentioned my own name did the atmosphere change.'

He sounded his incomprehension. 'It was the magic name of Rory that loosed their tongues, brought the whisky and the camaraderie. Its effect was almost magic. Why had they heard of Rory?' He sounded his disbelief.

'I had told them of you. Is that not enough?'

'No. It is all the stranger. Why me?'

'I needed a name and yours was as good as any.' Jock laughed, though it held no amusement. 'I did n'ae think you would ever come by. In a game of chance what were the odds?'

His eyes showed his disbelief. 'All I needed, Rory, was a strong man behind me.' He surveyed his tall companion, 'Absent you could fit the bill, they would never see the unlikely Latin scholar. Really all I wanted was a name, a figure, a wealthy patron from Newcastle involved in the Wholehope project with me. I wanted to keep them out. Armstrong is a big man in these hills and muscles in where he is nae wanted.'

Rory shook his head. 'So what's in a name?' and he laughed,

relieved at the explanation. 'They were not to know the strong man behind you was less than impressive.' He flexed his puny arms and Macnab grinned.

'There'll be muscle on you before we're finished with you. So, Rory,' the Scot spread his own strong arms. 'This laddie is yours. This is Black Rory's Still. '

25

Cecilia stood looking out into the mist that had crept down from the hills. The landscape was a blank canvas. Her world had retracted to her doorstep and now into her very home.

Smallpox bridged every barrier and it had reached Greystead. She had watched her father from the first sign of fever through agonizing days that ended only when the scabs had totally masked his features. Quietly he accepted his approaching end, after all to him it was just a new beginning.

She felt nothing but anger, her father taken before she could do without him. She shed no tears, female helplessness had never been a part of her.

It was the mist that penetrated her resolve as it wrapped itself around the rectory, obliterating all else. She thought of nearby Thorneyburn. Its doors bolted the rooms dark and empty. She sighed, and peered into the swirling white; there was one shape she would like to see right now above all others, the tall, spindly form of Gregory.

If only he would come. He had lost a friend, she a father and he would have comforting words, for he too was a man of God. But there the similarity with the Reverend Howick ended. Gregory would be angry like her, struggling to hide his natural feeling under what was expected. The younger man was a long way off her father's quiet, undemanding faith and right now she knew that she was closer to Gregory's turmoil.

He'd been near to violence at Jessie's death. It was his

questioning, his doubt that she wanted now, so that together they could walk through the obscuring mist, debating and arguing this way and that to emerge out on the other side with some sort of answer. But he was not there. She was on her own.

She retreated, back into her silent house. Sitting down at the piano she realised music held no comfort. What now? She did not know. Her father was gone and with him the roof over her head. This room would soon be devoid of her belongings. Cruel indeed when she had spent her nightly prayers asking for guidance to be the dutiful daughter, to accept that her life lay within the rectory's four walls. Now she was free to go wherever she liked, but where? She didn't want to leave; these wild open moorlands had become her home.

The mist cleared as quickly as it had come and with it came the obvious fact that another day without Gregory stretched before her. How long ago was it that she had sent him off? To look for oak trees? Her incredulous laugh echoed in the quiet room.

Had he been gone, two weeks, three? She had lost all track of time. Time was measured in bodies not days and it had seemed long, Jessie and her father, the child's brother and uncle and now her own father. She'd become gravedigger. Tomorrow she would turn the soil more lovingly than that of her garden and Thomas Howick would enrich the earth in his small allotted spot.

She turned again to the window. The figure strode through the burn. She saw the water splash up the side of his boots almost to the top. The man was tall but there the similarity with Gregory ended. He was well-built, his strong muscular shoulders revealing that he could pick up a sheep as easily as a lesser mortal could grapple with a forkful of hay. Her heart sank: Caleb had not been on her list of hoped-for callers, but he was better than nothing. She opened the front door and went outside.

'Miss Howick. I trust...' He saw her pale face and her still upright stance and he stopped in mid sentence; even Caleb Hunter could be lost for words. She smoothed her apron but did not offer her hand in greeting.

'Mr Hunter. You come too late if it is my father you seek.' Her voice shook.

'My sympathy, Miss Howick!' He took a step back. She looked at his muddy boots. They had not seen polish in weeks. But there was no fear for her scrubbed hall; he would not be venturing over the step. His fear of upsetting convention now she was a lone woman held nothing to his fear of contagion.

'He'll be buried tomorrow.' Her voice sounded her resolve for she'd no wish for Caleb Hunter to help her father on his track to heaven. The thought of his large, nail-bitten hands anywhere near her slight, aesthetic father filled her with a distaste that almost made her shudder. She waited for his excuse.

'I'm off tomorrow in search of a new ram. It will take the day.'
'No doubt.'
'Tis over Coquetdale way. I'll be off at the crack of dawn.'
'Wild country - it will be a sturdy beast from those parts. They are survivors up there.'

She should send him packing, she'd no interest in the stud for his flock, but she stood. Neither did she wish to return to the house, heavy with the knowledge that this man's voice would be the last she would hear that day.

'It's even lonelier than here.' She spread her arms to indicate the hills that encircled the rectory. 'Up there are more sheep than people; you'll have a solitary ride.'

'Aye, that's no hardship. Give me Jed, that's all I want. My dog talks more sense than any man.'

'Then I'll detain you no further, Mr Hunter.'

Surprised at her ready dismissal, he took a step closer and his eyes narrowed as he peered down at Cecilia. 'There's no knowing who I might meet on my travels. Is Gregory Felton home yet?' He sneered the name. 'They say the drove roads are filled with travellers and vagabonds, all those who call no place home.'

She faced him. 'Indeed, Mr Hunter, not everyone is fortunate enough to have the comforts of your mother's hearth to return to. Most would be too uncouth to sit on her fine furnishings.'

'Aye, just riff-raff or...' He scowled, 'or some folk who would ape our superior taste. One of mam's brocade cushions was taken. She hasn't forgiven Kitty. Wait till she comes round these parts again with her easy smile and easier fingers.'

'Kitty?'

'Aye.' His eyes narrowed, 'A wild girl, who is no better than she might be. As I say I'll be glad to have my dog to fend off such folk. ' He paused and then looking straight at Cecilia. 'They even say there are runaway parsons up there that have taken to the hills.'

Cecilia stared back at him. His face had darkened an obvious blood vessel at the side of his nose throbbed red. The effrontery of the man!

'Whom do you have in mind?' Her voice was steely. She strove to keep any emotion from her face.

'Why, Reverend Felton of course. They say the church is locked; there's not been a service for Sabbaths.'

'As of here. All the nearby churches are closed, even the URC as you well know. Contagion spreads as easily as unfounded gossip. You should be careful, Mr Hunter. She took a step towards him and he took two back.

She laughed. Caleb was so very predictable. It was like working a puppet on a single string.

'The Reverend Felton has important business concerning Admiral Collingwood.'

'Admirals do not hold sway in hill country. It's ruffians and cut throats that control the land. It takes a brave man or a foolhardy fellow to step off the known paths.' He laughed his contempt. 'I know where to go and where not to.'

'So please do not let me detain you any further from your everyday round. It pays to be unadventurous.'

Caleb narrowed his eyes. He stared at her, a mixture of expressions crossing his face. 'Are you saying I've got no spirit?'

'Of course not, everyone knows you look after your mother.' She smiled.

'All I'm saying, Miss Howick, you'd best keep your doors bolted, now you're by yourself and vulnerable. There's no knowing who might come to your isolated home. Remember there are thieves and worse. A lone woman is never safe.'

'Like I said your mother is a lucky woman.'

'It is not her I think of.' He took a step towards her and she could smell his whisky breath. He leered down at her. 'C-Cecilia with your father gone, you need a man.'

It was her turn to take two steps back and he followed. She was trapped against the door. She could feel his agitated breaths on her cheek. His face was inches from hers. Fury flooded her cheeks red. She gathered every last drop of spittle in her dry mouth and spat. It landed on his parted lips and she heard his gasp of horror. It was as telling as the end of a sharp sword on flesh.

Furiously he wiped his mouth with the back of his hand, grabbed a filthy kerchief from his pocket and stumbled to the stream. She did not watch the rest of his ablutions. She slammed the door behind her and drew across the bolt. She leaned against the stout frame and then sank to the floor, her head in her hands. She did not know whether to laugh or cry.

26

He was in harbour, the deepest, the safest, the most natural haven he had ever found, the buffeting of his journeying there a distant memory. They lay side by side, on the one piece of land by the Wholehope burn where there was space enough for them to stretch full length. Their feet dangled over the side as a gentle spray of water tumbled down the slope.

Out of sight, this hidden place was their own little paradise; not even a bird violated their space. The Garden of Eden had been thus. He thought of their love making, passionate, uncontrolled and then gentle and leisurely. Now, it was again just the two of them in this secluded place. Macnab had gone in the night. In his heady state Rory neither questioned nor surmised where Kitty's father had disappeared, only too aware of the beautiful girl that lay beside him and the knowledge that he shared her with no other.

'No eye to watch, and no tongue to wound us

All earth forgot, and all heaven around us.'

He murmured the poem that so closely reflected their reality. Here on this bare hillside he was as close to happiness as he had ever been. What now the questioning, the indecision? No tongue could wound them here.

They lay just inches apart, the distance ordained by the terrain. He was content, awareness of each other enough in their rocky bed. The land held them. Their mattress was the hill grass, the sun their covering, soft and warm like a lamb's fleece. Her eyes were closed. He could see the gentle swell of her breasts under her smock. He had felt their hardness and their soft, smooth curve. The girl was as changeable as the hill weather. Asleep the bubbling stream that was Kitty Linn had reached its level plain.

What was she thinking? He raised himself on to his elbow and the action brought her within a finger's space but again he was content to keep apart. Her closeness was enough to give his whole body a suffusion of heat. She felt his gaze and she opened her eyes.

'Rory.' Again he saw the relief flood her face when she realized who lay beside her. A smile at once mischievous and happy parted her lips. To hear his name spoken by her was enough to make his heart sing. She sounded like the youthful, turbulent, free-running burn. She pouted and it was the old Kitty.

'I am idle but I cannot move.' She lifted her hands and felt her wrists and she frowned. 'No fetters to be seen but I feel them. You hold me, Rory, as securely as any rope. It's tight.' Again there was the pout. 'Ow, it hurts' With a grimace she flexed her wrists. 'How are you so strong? It is not just physical prowess.'

'You have a good imagination.' He laughed and she arched her hands together, her fingers entwined, her thumbs linked and pointed upwards.

'Here's the church,

Here's the steeple,

Look inside you'll see the people'.

She opened her hands and gently waggled her entwined fingers, proxy for the imagined congregation. She was a child reciting the childish rhyme, but her voice held a reverence that belied her twinkling eyes.

'They say St. Cuthbert carried his portable altar with him when he tracked these hills. You, Rory carry your goodness with you. I can feel its power.' She sat up abruptly and looked down at him, a wistful smile on her face. 'I hope it is catching.'

Rory smiled his assurance. 'It is there if you want it.' His voice carried his conviction and her half-teasing, half-serious words brought the seal to his pleasure.

Could it really be that his presence here had been God-sent? He thought back to the four walls of his rectory, his loneliness, his inability to see God's purpose in his northern journey, and then the sudden visitation of the beautiful girl with all the temptation she brought with her. He had been weak in his immediate fascination for the unknown visitor. He had followed blindly, easily persuaded by the well-meaning, but uncomprehending Cecilia, to go find the answers he sought. He had sinned when tempted, but was that not God's purpose? His and the girl's salvation were surely linked.

A cloud passed over the sun and they both looked heavenward. Kitty scrambled to her feet.

'I have work to do.' The childlike expression on her face had gone. The full lips were drawn in a purposeful line, but there was a pleading note in her voice as she clambered back up the slope to the buildings. 'I can feel the rope slackening, Rory. See you hold on firm however hard I pull against your restraint.'

He followed her to the buildings, clustered behind them they had been no part of their view, now they dominated the confined space. She made for the malt house, agile and sure footed as a mountain goat. He watched her swaying hips; was she happy child or temptress, the simple symbol of summer-lit hills or the darker treacherous shape of winter when it was foolhardy to venture further? So she wanted his restraining halter to keep her on the straight path. Was she saying she needed him? The distillery buildings crowded his vision and he could not see beyond.

Two giant wooden implements leaned against the wall awaiting use. Deftly and easily she began to turn the decomposing barley. Rising, falling, rising falling like life in its ups and downs. He gazed hypnotised, good, bad, good, bad, tossing, falling like a game of chance. He leant against the shoddy walls of the illicit building, the idle spade close to his grasp. She had need of him. He seized the other tool and began to turn the stinking crop. Her bending hips just feet in front of him made him dizzy. He closed his eyes and saw the steady working shape of Cecilia in her garden. It calmed his agitation.

The day was full and silent. There was no need for words. They had no refreshment but the cool clear water of the burn. At last when the sun had disappeared behind the western hill Kitty called a halt. Sweat coated her brow and she smelt of toil. Without a word to Rory she ran back down to the stream and lifted her skirt above her head. He saw the childlike breasts of the girl and her rounded belly as she splashed in the shallow depths. He followed without hesitation. The water was clear and very cold and he cried out as it washed over him. Together they ran giggling up the slope to the hovel. They were girl and boy; she was the playmate he had never had.

She kissed him gently as she handed him the steaming dish of rabbit from the fire and he devoured it as hungrily as he had taken her in the night. At the last mouthful he sighed contentedly and handed back the tortoiseshell bowl with its speckled black sides.

Empty it revealed its cream interior.

'It's a pretty piece.'

'Yes, it's old. It belonged to my mother's mother. I do have family heirlooms like other girls, you know.' She picked up a jug from the crude dresser. 'My grandmother loved this. It is even older than her. I would not part with them for all the tea in China. To me they are priceless.'

Rory smiled, 'You have a love of beautiful things.' And he felt a stab of guilt. He'd been quick to condemn her possessions, had questioned too easily their provenance. They were family treasures that she harboured in this hovel, kept as lovingly as Hepzibah Hunter collecting her out-of-place possessions in her fortress home.

How quickly and wrongly he jumped to conclusions. Kitty must have seen the older woman's cushion, commented on it and a gratified Hepzibah presented it to the girl. But what of the Walter Scott novel hidden by Kitty under her mattress? How had she come by that? The book that clearly stated it was the property of Vincent Byres.

The question and the need to know the answer had made him turn back from his mission to find Collingwood's oaks. He had been drawn on a pointless diversion through the dark cauldron that was Slymefoot, here finally to Wholehope. And still he had not put his query in to words. Was there, as with the china, a legitimate answer for how the book had come into her possession? As he voiced the question, his reason told him it could not be.

'How is it you have a book belonging to an old shipmate of your father and of mine?'

Kitty frowned, 'Why do you want to know?' She was peeved like a child caught in the act. He forced a smile.

'Your grandmother cannot have given it to you.'

'Why not?' She was at once defensive. 'She could read as well as you.'

'She would have to be very accomplished to read this book. It is a new novel and she is dead some few years I think.' He sounded pompous and she gave him a withering look.

'I was given it by my friend, Vincent.'

'V...Vincent Byres?' He could hardly speak the name.

'Aye, that is he. Why not? You are not the only gentleman I know. You see us as uncouth, but John Armstrong reads Scott. In fact he has spoken with him.' She looked to impress. 'Scott comes from the borders and uses our stories.' Her voice wheedled, 'Would it not be fine, Rory, to have him tell ours?' Her good mood had returned as quickly as it had gone.

'You've not answered my question. What of Vincent Byres?' The spoken name conjured the sneering face of the man and the old animosity of years sounded in his voice. In this unlikely place he'd come back to haunt him. Kitty grinned.

'A fine man indeed, with his blond curls and his soft hands. Not a man for these parts.'

'Is he to be found in these parts?'

'Why, aye, man.' She looked him straight in the eye. 'With a mission similar to yours, Rory. He comes amongst us to keep us on the straight and narrow.' She was now openly laughing.

His colour rose she was enjoying his discomfort. 'He's not a man of God, but the next best thing,' she was taunting him, 'Excise Man to his Majesty!'

He let out an exclamation of disbelief. It was beyond the imagination of Walter Scott. His old adversary, even when both were fighting the French, Rory had ever looked upon the man as his enemy. And now he had come north, once more in his country's employ, to the troubled borderland and by a trick of fate the two men were on opposite sides.

'And Byres likes his whisky however he comes by it, either in the pound or drunk companionably at the illicit fireside. You only just missed him that day you came to Bremenium. He left by the back door. It's his favourite exit.'

Gregory looked at her. Vincent Byres within feet of him, his mouth staining a glass provided by Kitty and her father.

Kitty laughed. 'Wouldn't he like to know that you are Black Rory and the name behind an illicit whisky still?'

Rory ignored the jibe. 'Does Byres know of the still's existence?' He heard his voice tighten.

'Of course not, do you take us for fools?' She raised her eyebrows in wonder and he felt immediate relief. He was beginning to learn that she spoke her version of the truth. Yet he felt his unease.

He saw the self-satisfied man out of his depth so often in the world of shipboard life now floundering in this alien land. As ever, Byres was the ferret after the rabbit. He felt his inbred dislike of the man. He clenched his fists. Yet this land could defy Byres as easily as he and Macnab had defied him in the past and here were cleughs and claggs in plenty to thwart his game.

Here was a game indeed. Byres would never find Wholehope. He felt the old recklessness sweep over him.

'Macnab said that Byres was not a friend of yours.'

'No. That he was not.' His words were emphatic. The name invaded the place. He strode to the door. The moon was up. Its searchlight gaze beamed down into their hidden cleugh exposing the buildings to any ones' gaze if they cared to look. And then a cloud obscured the revelation and shadows long and dark merged into the hillside. Here was a game of cat and mouse and it was a game he had always played.

'He is a friend of mine.' Kitty stood beside him. She sounded petulant. Without the moon the black was intense, country dark and he could not see her. He could smell her freshness, her burn-washed smock, natural perfume.

'You do not choose your friends wisely.'

'Perhaps not, but then choice is a luxury in these parts. You say yes when you really mean no.' She sighed.

'You say yes?' Rory could feel his anger, his jealousy? He knew now he was a jealous man. And with Byres? He shuddered.

Her laugh was cold. 'Aye, there's a lot between yes and no. I say yes to a drink. Why not? What is a glass of whisky between friends? And then when he is comfortable by the fire and his eyes close, I help him towards a much deeper sleep. A draught for the gauger keeps him always one step away.'

'For Byers, no place is far enough.' Rory squeezed her to him. She was warm and compliant. The moon reappeared, though he needed no light to find her. His arms tightened about her. The soft silver light transformed her hair into a halo.

27

The fire burned with a red hot glow that made Gregory think of his cautionary sermons about hell. But that was where any similarity ceased. The devil finds work for idle hands and there were none at Wholehope. The day was long and exhausting and at night when the toil had finished they sank to their bed in a stupor of fatigue. He had never worked so hard in his life or felt so content.

Their activity concentrated at the far end of the row of buildings where the circular kiln with its bow front projected into the kiln house through a fire hole. The kiln house, snug to the crag that towered above it, cowered with low roof so that the temperature built to a crescendo. The peat turfs that Rory fed on to the fire stoked their sweat so that it ran as freely as the cleugh burn. He worked shirtless, Kitty in her chemise. Temptation was finger close.

They hauled the rotting barley to the kiln spreading it on a wire floor above the continuously rising peat smoke and then, when it was ready for fermentation, they bruised it with rollers. The yeast acted upon the sugar to turn it into crude alcohol, taking three to four days.

He was an eager pupil, keen to learn from both his teachers, for Jock had now returned. With his coming, Kitty was at arm's length, and he felt her withdrawal. Father and daughter formed an impressive team. Rory did as he was told, the menial jobs his tasks. He kept his head down and worked. He wanted to prove to Kitty that he was not as the soft-handed Byres, out to spoil their labours. That she noted was not obvious; she'd no time to heed his presence except for the shortest of breaks for a bowl of crowdie. At night, after their barley and vegetable cake, she implanted a quick kiss on his forehead and he went to his slumbers. Macnab got between the girl and him metaphorically and literally in the confined space. But the man would disappear again as soon as he had come. He could wait.

Wholehope had become his world. It limited his eyes to ground level or only as high as the stoking kiln. It suited him. His thoughts roamed no further than the next peat turf. When the heap had diminished he was forced to expand his horizon.

He climbed out of their valley. The tortuous path that he'd noted when they first scrambled down into the cleugh led him up back into the world that had ceased to exist. He had cart and peat cutter and new strong arms that witnessed his recent labour.

The hilltop achieved and he felt a strange sense of nakedness. Above was the sky and beyond in every direction the vast empty hills, but below Wholehope shouted its presence in the snake of buildings that clung to the valley sides. A feeling of panic seized him as he gazed down on to the rough stone shacks. How had he been so easily led into thinking they were hidden to the world? He breathed in and the smell of burning peat fuelled his fear. His blind faith in the thought that it was entirely hidden now made him shake his head in disbelief. He was easily fooled. But then why would Byres or any of his cronies come to this remote place? They stalked the drove roads and places like Slymefoot where the whisky runners congregated.

He shivered, glad he had put on his shirt; away from the heat of the kiln and the trapped stillness of the valley the wind brought reality.

The rounded blade of the cutter sank into the boggy hillside and he felt the ground yield beneath him. Foot on blade, pressure, lifting, foot on blade, pressure, lifting; the movement was rhythmic, comforting. Vertical cut, and squelch, horizontal and lift and squelch. The sods piled on the cart in a dark shape that mirrored the Cheviot summit away on the skyline, a hazy blue that had less form than his man-made hill.

Nothing to see, just soft blue distant hills and grey and white clouds that mountained the skyline in contorted peaks, cutting down to size the rounded slope under his feet. A fresh breeze ruffled the tufted grass, the only moving thing in a vast empty landscape. He knew he was holding his breath as if even that slight movement would upset the calm. Silence was interrupted by the soft squeal of blade into peat.

There was no one to see the mole-like activity of Kitty and father below ground in the hidden still. His distillery, his secret; he was part of the underground reality whether it was hidden or not. He looked at the bare patch of hillside where he had dug the peat. He had left a sign for anyone who would venture here, but of course they would not come.

The noise was sudden, unexpected and it sounded an army. He spun round and it was. He was the negligent sentry on duty, he hadn't covered his back. He stood transfixed. Ponies and figures browed the hill and turned in his direction.

Peat cutting was no crime, he would bluff it out; enemy on the skyline and they needed to be outwitted. He waited for the assault. A man and a boy and three animals, laden with panniers of barley bore down on him. With a reckless feeling of disappointment, he recognised Rob Shiel from Slymefoot.

The man raised his hand in greeting but wasted no words and Rory watched as the arrivals found the cleugh entrance and disappeared in a swaying, noisy line down into Wholehope. The path was narrow and steep and needed the innate sense and knowledge of beast and driver. From above, Rory watched as the sure-footed animals negotiated the treacherous incline. Shouts of encouragement and more fulsome imprecations as feet slipped on the loose stones broke the morning silence.

The outside world had invaded their valley and Rory thrust the cutter into the yielding peat, the resulting squeal drowning his exclamation of anger. He resented the intrusion. It could have been a posse of excise men for the violation he felt. They were vulnerable, he and his whisky runner. He mopped his sweating brow, how could he have thought otherwise?

Kitty's grandmother's cups welcomed the newcomers. The girl was all smiles and she had brushed her hair. The world had come to Kitty Linn and she responded as though it were an everyday occurrence.

Rob Shiel was not very much older than the girl and if he'd ignored Rory he was overly friendly with his hostess as she ran out to greet them. Once the load of barley had been dispatched to the malting house the visitors crowded the living quarters and the newly lit fire soon competed with the kiln heat. Rory eyed the rough hands on the fine china and felt again his resentment at the intrusion. What nonsense. He remembered Shiel had a wife and had scuttled back to her at the goading of Armstrong.

'Good to see you, Rob, isn't it, Rory?' She smiled from one to the other. 'Thanks to Rob we have more barley and thanks to you we have the fuel.' Her words made both complicit in the whisky-making process. Rory stood by the door, but it offered no escape; her hidden bonds tied him to the scene.

Shiel sat at the grate, on the stool that had become Rory's, holding the precious china bowl filled to the brim with her freshly made crowdie. The man was content as he spooned in the oatmeal and warm water. Now it appeared he was less inclined to hurry back to his waiting wife.

'So then, Rob, what news, it's not enough to bring just the barley?' The girl fixed her large dark eyes on their visitor awaiting his words as avidly as their hungry kiln took in fuel.

'Nothing of note.' The man shook his head and the girl didn't bother to hide her disappointment.

'Surely you've heard something at the alehouse, gossip there is the wattle in the walls.'

The man shook his head so that a lock of his lank hair fell across his face and playfully Kitty reached across and brushed it out of his eyes.

'Does Jeanie no cut your hair for you? Where are my scissors?' Rory bit his lip. The girl's flirting was almost more than he could bear. He thought back to the scene at Slymehouse when local strongman Armstrong had staged his little joke. He'd known instinctively that Kitty would play her part, knew already she was the local tease.

He looked to Macnab. Could he not tame his own daughter? His friend sat on the low hearthside stool the other side of the fire, a pipe in his hand, its bulbous white bowl crammed with a hefty pinch of tobacco. So the ponies had brought more than just the barley. He'd not seen Jock with a pipe at his lips before. All life's needs came to hidden Wholehope. There was a contented smile on the older man's face.

A pall of smoke wafted across the room and Kitty breathed in loudly and exhaled equally noisily.

'What news, Rob?' Her voice was goading, almost bullying. 'I starve if I'm not fed the food of fact. No, not even that, rumour will do.'

Rob Shiel laughed. 'Let me see. They do say,' he paused and turned to look at Rory, for the first time acknowledging his presence.

'They do say that a well-known girl of these parts has taken up with a stranger and....' He drew his hand across his throat, 'and that John Armstrong is not best pleased.' Kitty tossed her head and her eyes flashed but her words were cool.

'So we have an acquaintance of father at Wholehope. It's no more tha..'

Jock interrupted, 'It's to be remembered that the stranger employs us, daughter.' He put out his hand and gave the girl a playful smack across her buttocks.

Shiel was amused. 'So Jock, you're taming your daughter, and not before time. It's to be seen that your girl runs wild. A good spanking is never out of the way.' The two men laughed. Kitty's face flamed and Rory could not hold his silence.

'There is never cause to lay hand on another.' He sounded the preacher and the visitor raised his eyebrows.

'Tis moral teaching as well as clout that comes with your partner, Jock.'

'Aye man. You can tell John Armstrong there is nowt to fear. It's a good partnership we have here; a working partnership.' He nodded at Rory and then turned his attention back to his visitor. 'Betimes man, before ye gang you'll take another pipe and a bit more crack.' Rory felt himself excluded.

'Aye,' The young man grinned at Kitty. 'I almost forgot. There's a happening the day after tomorrow.'

Kitty smoothed her hair and sounded almost casual but her eyes showed her irritation. 'So Rob Shiel, who is the tease? It's good you remembered.' She drew her hand across her throat as the man had done to her. 'Now, I don't have all day to waste' She made for the door, head high; something had displeased her.

The man threw his final remark. 'Armstrong said to be sure to be there.'

28

Cecilia sat on the gilt couch, her plain dress looking homespun and out of place. She felt it. Hepzibah Hunter dressed in a fine purple silk could have been awaiting an audience with the King. Cecilia thought what would he have made of her, this out-of-place woman in her out-of-place home? But there she was wrong. The building fitted the landscape and had done so for centuries. It was human interference that mocked its function. The woman was trying to ape something that she and her house were not. She stole a glance at her hostess.

Hepzibah was eating cake, her small fingers lightly holding the fragile porcelain plate. Contentment was written all over her face and why not? She'd accomplished, through her own endeavours, what in the face of it would appear impossible.

Cecilia and Gregory had laughed at her, oh so righteous in their condemnation. But this woman had the last laugh, she was happy with her lot. She'd created the world she wanted where she wanted. Incarceration in her fortified home had been no problem. What matter what went on beyond her door, smallpox could reach the gate but her door was stout and firm against all intruders.

'Miss Howick, I am truly gratified youse saw fit to accept our Caleb's invitation. We could not leave you alone and grieving.' She eyed the girl's plain black dress, so drab beside her lustrous skirt. 'Though I forbid him to ask you until the infection had past. One cannot be too careful.' Cecilia could feel the woman's eyes on her unblemished face. It is to be hoped the Reverend Howick has taken the infection to the grave, were her unspoken words. Had Caleb hinted to her of his near contamination? She thought not. Cecilia remembered her almost obsessive searching of her own face in the bedroom mirror, in the days following his death. It was out of character. Then nothing had been normal.

'Thank you, you are very kind. I've had plenty to do since my father's death.' Cecilia smiled, but she saw again the cruel and ugly disfigurement on his pallid skin. She'd never cared what appearance she gave to the world, and there was no reason to start now, but she'd feared the scourge of smallpox. What matter? Now she was alone and there was no-one to care about her looks.

As if Mrs Hunter could read her thoughts, she said, 'What news of the Reverend Felton?'

'There is none though I'm sure he will return very soon now.'

'What makes you say that?' Her tone and words voiced her disbelief.

'The hill country lacks your comfort.' Cecilia waved her hand at the room. 'The Reverend Felton likes his own fireside.'

'That isn't what I've heard. It's strange, would you not think that he roams through Redesdale and now beyond to Coquetdale, if the stories are true, and thinks himself a home-loving man? It's to be wondered why such a man would answer the call of the wild.' She peered at Cecilia. 'I thought you, Miss Howick, if anyone, would have news of him.' Mrs Hunter frowned. Her disappointment was palpable. Then her face lit up.

'And so Cecilia, what with you when soon, you too, will have no roof over your head though, through nae fault of youse? Not like some I could mention.'

Cecilia put down her cup and saucer on the mahogany side table, placed for such an eventuality, and took the time to assemble her reply. 'No rectory roof of course, my home, as you correctly state, went with my father.'

'So do the hills call you too?' She was disbelieving.

'No, that they do not. I have a wider world to choose from now that I'm no longer rectory housekeeper.'

'Housekeeper! No doubt you will return to London for such a position?' Hepzibah sounded her scorn.

'The capital has many advantages but it's not for me and neither do I wish to devote myself to a house and its running.' There was an edge of annoyance in the girl's voice at the woman's condescension.

'But from next week I shall have a new roof over my head.' Cecilia announced her news in a note of triumph.

At that moment Caleb Hunter came into the room and his mother turned to him, horror written all over her face. 'Son, Miss Howick is to leave us. You must dissuade her. You are tardy with your words offering her something I am sure she would jump at. Oh, son, you have not removed your clogs.'

Cecilia stared from the woman, a porcelain-figure to the stout, red-faced farmer standing on his mother's fine rug. His feet were clad in home-made wooden shoes; thick knitted socks shaped his legs and on his head was his wide-brimmed hat. Underneath it his small eyes darted from one woman to the other as he tried to make sense of his mother's words.

'What, woman? Are you saying I should remove my clogs when I propose to Miss Howick?'

Cecilia smothered her rising incredulity, smoothed the material of her mourning dress and said, 'It is good to joke, Caleb. I've been too long on my own with my sad thoughts, I knew when I accepted your kind invitation I would find topics to amuse me.'

'Joke?' Mrs Hunter looked from the girl to the man and her forehead puckered. 'Young lady, you do not know serious words when you hear them.'

'Indeed I do. It is my turn to be serious. I've considered my position and I know now I cannot leave this area. Here is my home.'

'Ah.' The woman let out an exclamation of satisfaction. 'There, son, I told ye so.'

Cecilia smiled gently. She'd recovered her composure and now she was enjoying herself. 'I've had quite enough of house keeping, as I said. I have decided to become a teacher.' She announced her momentous decision with a flurry. The moving expressions on the face of her hostess were like season change.

'I have taken Martin Dodds' old cottage and from there I shall run my school.'

She brushed back her hair from her sloping forehead allowing her words to sink in. The distance between eyebrow and hairline denoted brains, so they said, and she knew she had the required amount. She'd been mentally starved for long enough and now here was the opportunity she must seize without a second thought. They could not fail to hear the excitement in her voice, but would they understand her needs? She thought not!

Only Gregory would have a hundred per cent sympathy with her, when he heard her news. Yes, for too long she had been both mentally and bodily starved. The school would feed the first requirement, the second was more of a problem and the answer did not lie here. Startled at her thoughts she looked to her hostess, thankful the woman could not read her mind and her farmer son could never comprehend. He was not the man she needed.

Mrs Hunter was a mixture of emotions. 'You are to be a schoolmarm.' She raised her eyebrows in disbelief. 'You'll tire of that soon enough.' She folded her arms across her bosom and a smug look crossed her face. 'Your black dress will be fit for the school room. When your mourning is over you'll be ready to wear the white. Now then, Caleb, 'tis time to take Miss Howick home.'

Cecilia smiled her acceptance. That she faced a journey alone with the son in the family pony and trap filled her with disquiet. Would he take her words as final? She allowed him to help her up onto the seat and she arranged her skirt slowly and deliberately as Hepzibah watched from the bastle door. She looked puny against its massive wooden frame. She waved her hand in an imperious gesture as the animal began to trot.

It was a fine evening. Hunter was silent. He'd made no comment at her news, leaving it to his mother to jumble her thoughts and reactions. Cecilia gazed ahead. She'd not wanted to come in the first place and had protested when Caleb had appeared that morning and insisted she go back with him there and then. He'd got a nerve after his last visit to Greystead. But hadn't a salmon been specially cooked for her? His mother would be so disappointed. He'd said nothing the whole way, now she knew the reason for his nervous state. Had he intended to propose to her on the return journey? She breathed a sigh of relief that her news had taken the wind out of his sails.

The analogy brought Gregory back into her thoughts. They were passing the end of the track that led to Thorneyburn and she looked away. That house stood empty and silent and soon Greystead would be likewise abandoned. As if her driver could read her mind, he slowed the horse and pointed back up the lane.

''Tis a godless place hereabouts. Two churches built and two shut before you could count to ten. Mind you, it has always been so.'

'How do you mean?' Cecilia did not hide her irritation.

The man did not reply but checked the horse with a heartfelt thump across its shanks. They came to a halt beside a large mound where the Tarset stream met the North Tyne and Hunter pointed to the tumbled ruins on its top.

'Times past it was here that the local folk were forced to come for their spiritual comfort.'

Gecilia looked at the grassy mounds. Hunter was bursting to reveal some revelation that backed his bigotry. She sat still, her lips pursed. He needed no invitation.

'It was a local man, Hector Charlton who took it on himself to ride to St Cuthbert's Church in Bellingham where he stole wine and 800 wafers. He brought them back to Tarset mound and gave mass to the assembled reivers.'

Cecilia laughed. 'Those days have long gone.'

'Aye, perhaps, but some say they are come again. You do not believe me?' Caleb frowned. 'There's nothing new under the sun. Do you know why he was forced to steal the Communion bread and wine?'

'No' Cecilia sounded tired.

'Because the great Cardinal Wolsey had closed the Tynedale churches.' He paused for impact. 'And why? Because in these parts both clergy and parishioners were equally wicked.'

Cecilia could feel her temper rising at the man's glee. 'My father and the Reverend Felton are good men.'

'Aye, your father, right enough, others say different about Felton.'

29

Rory climbed out of the valley. The cleft in the hillside was claustrophobic and it was with a feeling of release that his head appeared above the cleugh and he felt the wind that scoured the exposed hilltop. Below ground it hardly registered, above it was more a gale.

He stood and felt the full force on his outstretched arms and the torpor of the last hours was blown away. He thrust the sharp blade of the peat cutter into the ground, heard the reassuring squelch of the released clod and his spirits rose. He worked all morning and the resulting stack threatened to become a mountain rather than the squat bee-hive shaped kyles appearing around the kiln as the result of his labours.

'So, are you planning to move the whole hillside?' It sounded as though she chided. He did not turn to greet her but bent lower to lift the peat brick, his back arching as bridge from one side of the cut to the other. She waited and then when he made no answer. 'Here, you must be in need of this.'

He straightened what were his needs? His world had narrowed to basics. He took the jug of water that she offered without comment and drank fiercely the water cascading down the creases of his mouth and on to his chest. Empty, he handed it back and she took it also without a word. She turned to go back down below ground and he watched her go. It was the first time he had seen her that day.

Gregory had slept in the kiln house, leaving the living quarters to the girl and her father. There was an atmosphere. Even after the departure of Rob Shiel he felt the crowding and he'd made his excuses, saying it was his turn to feed the fire. He'd risen late after a fitful night and as Jock and Kitty came into the distillery he'd left. Neither looked as though they'd slept and the girl's wide eyes stared from a pale face. No easy words slipped from her tongue.

He'd grown used to her teasing, the kind of shipboard banter once enjoyed with her father. Kitty took nothing seriously. Even the sound of his new name on her lips sounded playful. He considered the fact that like everything else in life he was to her a joke. Rob Shiel had been the butt of her banter, was no one immune? John Armstrong was different; she had taken the message from him with a slight frown though she had made no answer. Jock Macnab, no, she did not tease her father. So at least she had respect for age and strength.

Now there was no easy smile; had she minded so much his night retreat to the kiln house. He thought not. Why hadn't she followed him? He had waited in vain.

'Kitty,' he called after the retreating figure. He called again, the wind carrying his thanks. Her head reappeared, like a startled rabbit from its hole and her smile was hesitant.

'The water was good. Thank you. I needed that.'

'You have earned it.' She stood half in and half out of her burrow. He felt his chagrin, he had been churlish. How quickly he'd stood on his high horse; sulked might be a better term. But it was more than that; he was jealous and it was devouring him. Their lovemaking had not been repeated. He'd expected the girl to come to him leaving Macnab to his own devices, but she had remained with her father.

Was she afraid of the small Scot? For the first time that likelihood filtered into his thoughts. He thought back to Jock's arrival at Wholehope. Had he been surprised, pleased, or annoyed when he saw Rory with his daughter? Then he'd been too obsessed with the girl to notice anything other than her. They'd only just risen from their coupling. Surely it had been obvious to the man that he had interrupted something momentous?

Gregory wanted her now. He moved to stand above her and she stared up at him, a strange look on her face. He saw then that she had been crying. The red about her eyes was not the result of the buffeting wind but the rough wiping of hand across face. Dried rivulets of tears stained her cheeks and then he remembered his disturbed night.

He'd woken with a start and, going out into the dark to relieve himself, he'd heard them. There were angry words, raised voices, a man's and then a woman's in higher key. Kitty and her father were quarrelling. Although he could not hear their sense, he knew the girl to be frenzied, her deep voice high pitched.

He looked down at her. So the quarrel between father and daughter had brought angry tears. The girl was quiet now, unnaturally subdued.

'Kitty, you work too hard, you are weary. You work as two people.'

'Of course not.' Her emphatic answer cut through his words.

'But you know what I say is true.'

'So, Reverend Rory,' she looked up at him and there was the fleeting half-teasing smile, 'you cannot refuse my request.' She scrambled back out of the hole to stand beside him. He felt her presence. He said,

'Kitty I'm willing to take your place alongside your father.'

His reply brought a mirthless laugh. 'No, never there!' Then her face relaxed as she saw his reaction to the rebuff.

'Rory, you are too impressed with your new muscle power.' She wrapped her fingers round his arm and squeezed it. The mocking could never be far away. 'But it takes a lifetime to develop such power and you don't have that time.'

He winced improbably she had read his thoughts. If it hadn't been for the red eyes he would have told her his plan, then and there, that tomorrow he was going. He'd leave once his self-appointed task of piling the peat to furnace the illicit still was done. The situation was incongruous. Once he'd served his servile purpose he could leave with impunity. He knew now he was no more to her than all of the others; farmers, shepherds, excise men, whisky runners, all part of her easy-come, easy-go life. She had led him on and had so quickly tired. If only she had followed him to the kiln, but, no she had stayed with her father. Gregory/ Rory stood, his hands on his hips, looking down at her. He was deep in the pit he had dug for himself.

'Will you take me to the Happening?'

Her words cut across his racing thoughts and stupidly he repeated them.

'Will I take you to the Happening?'

'Yes, please, dear Rory.'

He did not want to hear the pleading in her voice. He said, roughly, 'Yet another whim. So what is this Happening? Is it as sinister as it sounds?' His misgivings showed on his face and in spite of her unsure mood she giggled.

'No that it is not! The Happening is a rite of spring, to say good bye to winter.'

'Then I have no place in it.'

'Let us say it is your Easter, come late to the hills when winter storm and snow are well behind us, everything happens here later than in other places.'

He looked dubious. 'It is harmless fun, a celebration, Rory.' She was pleading now

'Where is it be?'

'Slymefoot, where else?'

He laughed. 'There is nothing harmless about that place.'

'On a summer evening, Rob Shiel brings his fiddle and we dance, oh how we dance, Rory!' Her voice wheedled and she seized his hands and spun him round in an abandoned jig, round and round, gathering speed so that he ended in a dizzy heap on the earth. She kept her feet, looking down at him with a look of triumph and her eyes flashed purpose. 'There I promise to dance you off your feet, Rory, and on to your back.'

They left together, he and Kitty. A young couple going to a dance and her preparation had been time consuming.

The girl had washed her blouse, taken his grubby shirt from his back, soaked them in the burn and hung them out to dry. There was no repeat shared bathing in the burn. They went separately. Her hair had been brushed so that Rory thought that it would spark into fire. It shone lustrous and silky. She produced a small box of rouge and her cheeks glowed her expectation. Lastly from nowhere she produced a scarlet red skirt and she twirled before him to hear his admiration.

She was ready and they climbed out of the valley. She, still in her strange mood that he could not fathom, he set-faced and his shoulders braced. He gave no backward glance, though he knew he would not return to Wholehope. His weakness had led him there, now he must find resolve to escape.

Slymefoot looked different in the light. It was a balmy May evening, and a blackbird sang its song above the greetings called from the converging men and women. At the first sighting, Kitty took his hand as though to proclaim that this was her young man. He stopped himself from pulling it away - she still roused him.

He fingered his beard and sideburns. They were his necessary cover. He wanted no sighting now. He feared any last minute recognition before his return to his other life. His other life? He closed his mind it was a million miles away.

He had changed, visually at least. Did his hirsute state make him look older? He'd no way of telling but he knew he felt the opposite. His body was taut and firm, his muscles responding to the heavy work and the miles trod. He'd never felt so well not since his active days on board ship. And tonight the place was different. The atmosphere had changed.

The alehouse door stood open in greeting and the violin strings issued their invitation. He squeezed Kitty's hand and she looked up at him and smiled her temptation. She'd promised to lay him on his back. He bit his lip, how she loved to lead him on. It could never be, though every bone in his body fought against his reason. She was a witch, a temptress, who had enticed him to an unchristian happening. This girl's hold over him was pagan.

The small room was crowded with young folk, pretty, eager girls, reluctant young men keener to get hold of their ale than girls' waists. Rory put his arm round Kitty and felt her warm flesh beneath her blouse as they were dragged into a rowdy Scots reel. The speed of the violin matched the whirling feet and at the end of the dance both Rory and the girl were gasping for breath. Now he understood why Macnab had declined to accompany them and Armstrong was nowhere to be seen. In the tight confusion there was no space for standing out. He began to relax. Kitty's happening had no sinister undercurrents. It was exactly as she had said; an excuse to bid farewell to the restrictions of winter and welcome the brief summer freedom. The strings played the message of release, the laughter and noise told that it had been received loud and clear.

Another frantic dance, another collapse into his arms at the end by the awakened girl and Rory's final suspicion and distrust melted away. They stood close recovering their breath and her heart beat against his. When the music started again it was he who led her into the skirmish and when the violin breathed its last their breath was no longer hard won; they had absorbed the rhythm of the dance.

Rob Shiel acknowledged them with his bow as he wiped the sweat from his brow. Then once more he placed the instrument under his chin and pulled the bow across the strings in a long, low wail. The music was a lament, a sad melody that penetrated the noise and the pleasure of the dancers. Rory, breath-close to the girl, felt her shiver at the plaintive hill tune; he heard the harsh, wild, empty land crying its sadness and he felt its torment. He glanced down at Kitty and saw a tear roll down her rouged cheek. He pulled her to him, disturbed by her distress. She squeezed his arm and mouthed,

'Let us get some air. It's stifling in here.'

Outside, it was still as light as day and dawn was not far off. The moon was not needed to show the girl her path back to Wholehope. Though she would walk alone the going would be easy. And what of him, his path must lead in the opposite direction.

Couples were dancing on the limited grassy sward around the inn, whilst others sought the dark shapes of its peat kyles to hide their couplings. Rory averted his eyes. His girl was only fingertips away and he could feel his chest constrict and his breathing become as erratic as their earlier frenzied dancing.

The night had only just begun. Again, eager hands pushed him into place as figures moved together for an eight-some reel. Most of the flat land above the Coquet valley was taken up by the alehouse but this was no obstacle for those intent on enjoying themselves. The couples took to the drove road that passed but feet from its door.

There was much giggling and banter at the improvised dance floor. Feet apart from the girl now, Rory faced his partner, hemmed in on either side by two hefty hill men, their beer breath only slightly lessened by the fresh air. They eyed him silently and then, as the first couple began to move, lost interest, fixing their befuddled thoughts on the dance steps. He was impelled across the divide to Kitty, their hands met and he felt again the unpredictable girl. Almost shyly she sought his hand and together they moved up the line of the set, their feet in harmony, though he'd never learned the steps.

They danced the ageless movements not once but twice, though they could no longer hear the violin. Finally, the ale beckoned their fellow dancers and they were left alone.

The girl seized his hand and pulled him away from the alehouse. The boulder was huge, nature, not giant had found its resting place. They stood dwarfed beside it, its granite strength bearing their weight as though they were butterflies on a pebble. Her body was soft against the rock and his practiced hands felt her yield. Her breasts were full, her belly round and plump as though she had put on her summer body in place of her winter frame. His desire answered the change. He wanted her more than he had ever wanted her.

The horseman was just feet away, down below them on the well-worn track, and the animal's hooves resounded in the evening still. Gregory could feel the newcomer's eyes on his back. Kitty moved away from under him. He swore softly under his breath. He'd been saved from his baser instincts for this girl was still under his skin. He caught her arm. She said over his shoulder,

'So then, Vincent, you have come to our celebrations.' She squeezed Rory's hand in a warning gesture as her voice took on the teasing tone he'd come to know so well.

Rory tensed as the man's reply moved him effortlessly from Cheviot hillside to the deck of a frigate in the port of Plymouth.

'Kitty Macnab,'tis a fine night, or should I say day?' Byres sounded his confusion. Rory felt the years fall away and his hand tightened on the girl.

Her eyes were wary as she quipped, 'Too fine an evening for an excise man to be working.'

'Who said anything about work? We have nights off, like any man. There is no law to say an excise man can't take a pint of ale. Besides, a bit of crack with a woman, as you would say, is more a need sometimes than a man's drink.' His silvered tones sounded his loneliness and Rory thought if he didn't know him better he could feel sorry for the man, but he knew him only too well; the man's needs would not stop at a bit of crack. The northern expression sounded false on the southern tongue and Rory knew his dislike of the man had not diminished in the ensuing years.

Byres had come to Slymefoot. Had he come just for ale? He thought of the beer running freely when they'd left the alehouse, but by now could it be something stronger? Was the man's real intention to catch the locals red-handed? He knew him of old.

Kitty seemed to have similar thoughts for she moved closer to Byres and Rory whispered, 'Keep him out as long as possible,' as he turned back towards the building.

He heard her say. 'So, Vincent, the air is as sweet as a nut. You have come for a chat, have you? Then I'm your girl.' Rory stiffened but her tone held no promise.

The door was closed, but there was no guard and it yielded easily to his hand. The smell of the room had changed it was as telling as the smoke of peat. Shiel stood with his violin under one arm, a drink in the other. His cheeks were flame red and there was a contented smile on his face.

'S-so, Black Rory,' his speech slurred, 'I've no need to light the candles for my fiddle playing, can you play a tune for us in the dark?'

'No, never that,' Rory shook his head at the suggestion, 'It's not the fiddle-player that needs changing but the drinks before the gauger comes through that door.' Shiel swore an oath and relinquished his violin. They moved with the speed of the Highland fling, signal, whisky removed, ale returned.

He went outside in search of the girl and her unwelcome companion. There was no sign of them. The jealousy came throbbing back. Where had they gone? Then he saw them, the girl's red skirt vibrant against the pale waning moon. They had moved up the hillside away from the alehouse, Kitty the temptress once more filling her role.

He strode towards them and as he did so a loud call came wafting through the night air, and then as if by signal the call was taken up in a raucous chorus that flooded around the hillside.

Kitty turned an excited face to the approaching Rory. 'Welcome to the happening of the birds. Tonight there is choice for birds and humans alike. Which mate to take?'

She smiled a dazzling smile at Rory and then at Byres who stood irresolute beside her, torn between girl and alehouse. He was less than pleased to see the approach of another man. And the girl was excited. Rory saw the change as she preened before her two companions.

'This is how we should choose our mates.' Kitty giggled and pointed to the flat piece of land that sprawled the other side of the Coquet. Rory followed her gaze and gasped. The ground was covered in moving shapes, a noisy, throbbing mass of prancing, preening birds.

'The mating rites of the Black Grouse, and they have chosen Slymefoot for the yearly ritual. It is called a lek.' Her voice rose in excitement. 'This is surely a night to remember. Not one of the birds leaves unsatisfied.' She flounced her red skirt as she spoke and tossed her head as though in imitation of the birds.

Uneasy, Rory turned away from the girl. Byres moved nearer as he sensed her mood. She giggled into his face. 'Look at the males strutting their finery. Anyone would think they're human.'

The males were very obvious, their bright colours eclipsing the drab grey hens that moved slowly through their ranks. The cocks, large beautiful birds with glossy blue-black plummage broken by white wing bars and bright red bulges above the eyes knew their worth. Necks and chests were swollen in justifiable pride and as they sought to outdo the opposition, the red marks erected above their eyes. Rory let out a whistle of admiration.

Kitty said excitedly. 'Look at their lyre-shaped tail. The males strutted, wafting their tails imperiously then dropping their wide wings before the chosen female, slowly emitting a loud, crowing call.

'The males are showy, the hens are drab.' Gregory bent to Kitty and whispered. 'You're wrongly dressed in your red skirt. You should be colourless and unremarkable.'

'Yes in the bird world it's the males that attract.' She laughed up at him. 'So is there a handsome, strutting male hidden inside you, Rory?'

'There could be.' He caught hold of her arm and Byres at once moved nearer to the girl on her other side. The excise man peered at Rory as he grabbed her free hand. With a quick petulant flounce the girl released herself from their grasp.

'Gentlemen, like the male Black Grouse in their yearly lek you'll have to prove your worth. Watch the birds, they can teach you a thing or two.'

The resplendent males were hopping up and down before their opponents in a mock display of force, moving ever nearer the centre as they gained the upper hand. The greyhens moved with them, each tilting their tails and bodies at the courting males. Every movement had a meaning.

'Look, now she knows which one she fancies.' Kitty giggled as one of the females had obviously made up her mind. It was decision time, and impressed at last, she selected her mate crouching down before him.

Kitty greeted the submission with a snort of disdain. 'It all looks so straightforward, but of course it isn't. There's no lifetime commitment they're a promiscuous lot right enough.'

There was a bitter ring to the girl's comment. Then she shrugged.

'So why not? Life is for the moment, and the birds know how to seize it. At the lek, the males get numerous matings. I don't suppose they bother to keep count.'

She looked from Rory to Byres, slowly and deliberately as though she too would make a choice and then turning her back on Rory she moved to stand before the bemused excise man. Slowly, she began to imitate the female grouse strutting before her chosen partner. With a roar of approval the swaggering man responded, hesitantly, then eagerly imitating the dance of the male grouse; fanning out his arms in an extravagant drooping in response to the elaborate movements of Kitty.

Rory turned away he'd had more than enough of the evening entertainment. He saw his place in the night spectacle, he saw Kitty for what she was-wanton and no better than the cavorting birds.

'Rory, are you no longer in the game?' Kitty was at once beside him. She preened close to his face, pouting at his display of distaste. 'Come on. Rory, do you not like the game of chance? Anyone can be the winner, will it be you or Vincent? She breathed as Byres, the other male in her ritual charade, pushed his aroused body between them. Once more her back was to Rory and then abruptly she turned and there was her laughing face just inches from his.

He stood stiffly not wanting to join in her game. She giggled noisily as she strained to kiss his closed lips and there was a furious exclamation from Byres as he ceased his dance in mid flight. Abruptly Kitty turned towards the alehouse. She called over her shoulder, 'Come on both of you, the choice is too limited here. In the true lek there is infinite choice.'

She burst into the inn, a loud and disruptive figure as she intended and there was immediate silence at her entrance and that of the two men. Shiel stopped his fiddle playing and Armstrong who had arrived bringing his pipes, trailed to silence.

'John,' Kitty flounced up to the older man and, seizing his arms, began to re-enact the grouse display. Armstrong looked first surprised and then delighted and there was a great cheer, as the girl did the same to the violin player.

By now Kitty's fun was infectious, she shouted, 'Come on, the birds' lek is so much more exciting than this,' as theatrically, she moved between her chosen males, Byres, Shiel, Armstrong, and finally Rory. She stopped before him, her eyes danced and then slowly and deliberately she turned her back on him, as she had done outside. He stood, his face aflame at the very public rejection, and then his shame was immediately replaced by fury as the girl stopped in front of Byres and slowly and deliberately stooped low to the ground.

There was a murmur of disapproval that swelled to resentment as the intruder Byres sank to floor level beside her. As he rested on his haunches, a foolish smile on his face Kitty jumped to her feet and turned to Armstrong.

'John, have you got the special drink for my choice of mate tonight? Of course you have and I know where you keep it.' She disappeared from the main body of the building and there was silence.

Byres laughed delightedly, 'T..that's my girl, you know I have a taste for peat-flavoured whisky.' He stayed supine on the ground as he waited for his promised prize. They stared at the ridiculous figure with ill-concealed contempt and Rory thought Kitty has lost her reason. The bemused man peered up at Rory and a frown crossed his face. 'So, my spurned rival, I don't believe we've been introduced.' He struggled clumsily to his feet and swayed as his legs sought to steady his body. Rory took a step back and felt a hat placed on his head, a wide-brimmed shepherd's headgear that fell across his brow and left his face half hidden. He murmured his thanks to Rob as he retreated further into the shadows.

Byres smirked. 'So we have here a grouse that does not seek to parade his assets. Kitty,' the girl had come back into the room, 'Kitty does my defeated rival not have a name?' The gauger thrust his head forward into Rory's bearded face and held out his hand.

Rory waited for the look of recognition from the excise man. He could see his old enemy only too clearly. The blonde hair had darkened to corn, but his face was still clean shaven and unlined, though pinched into ferret-features. Rory fingered the deep crease from his own nose to mouth and thought that is the difference between us, Byres is still the uncomplicated man who sleeps easy in his bed.

'He's a friend of mine.' Kitty smiled up at Rory and their companion snorted his amusement.

'That was very clear even from my spot on the road. A close friend one might say. So, you really are a rival?' Byres was agile. With a speed that took them by surprise he lunged at Rory and then seizing the girl kissed her long and hard on her lips. Rory reeled, recovered his feet and with fury seized his adversary by his coat tails and dragged him off the protesting girl.

'Yes you could say we are close friends, too close for your comfort.'

Rory swung a fist at Byres and the silence sensed there was to be further entertainment. Byres dodged expertly, well practised, and although Rory made no contact there was fury written all over his adversary's face. Kitty put a restraining hand on Rory's arm.

'Leave be, he meant no harm.'

'Byres always means harm.' Rory's caustic comment was out before he could stop himself and Byres' brow furrowed!

'Have we met before? I thought you extraneous to these parts.' He peered at Rory and there was a half look of recognition!

Rory said, 'You use big words, too big for the likes of me,' and he fingered his shepherd hat. Byres turned away.

'You're too good for these hills, Kitty. The lek here is too limited for the likes of you. You should go seek a wider world.' And Byres looked scathingly at Rory. 'Life's losers pick a fight for nothing. They usually have something to hide.' He took a step nearer and a flash of interest crossed his face.

30

Dust flew in all directions. The small window, open on the latch for its escape, cleared the room, though not before a beam of sunlight highlighted its route and focused on the newly scrubbed floor. Cecilia watched it dry before her eyes. Her companion surveyed the results of their hard work with equal satisfaction. Cecilia, leaning back on her ankles, looked up at the older woman, a quizzical look on her face.

'Should the desks have their backs to the window or face it? Or do you think the goings-on in the village would be too much of a distraction for my industrious scholars?'

Maria Dodds shook her head. 'Indeed, they'll be slow thinkers if they wait for a happening outside to take their attention.' She removed her apron and sighed. 'It would have been different with our Jessie. She wouldn't have noticed if Napoleon himself had strutted down the street, so lost was she in her books.'

'Yes.' It was Cecilia's turn to sigh at the thought of the girl who would have been her star pupil. 'I miss her sorely, as you do, Maria. No one will ever replace her. But her memory lives. The cruel disease that took her from us is the reason I'm in a position to start the school. God moves in a mysterious way.' She was matter of fact acceptance for she knew that both she and the girl's mother were close to tears. It was better when they were scrubbing floors, there was little energy left for sorrow.

Maria Dodds said, 'What would we do without you, miss? You are God-sent indeed. You've not left us to our misery.'

Cecilia shook her head, 'Remember the school will help us all, it will fill my empty days. It cuts both ways.'

Her companion nodded, but made no reply. Cecilia stole a glance at the woman and admired her resilience. Life threw misfortune at her as though she was a coconut shy and yet she stood and took it all. She had not seen one tear fall from Maria Dodds' eyes as family were felled, one by one. Together she and this brave woman would see that the remainder of the children would grow big and strong and equipped to take whatever life threw at them. The woman felt her gaze and sniffed.

'It's to be hoped there will be no Latin on the timetable.' Her voice trembled and Cecilia looked at her with concern. They had been too long idle.

She laughed, 'Strictly reading, writing and arithmetic.'

'That is proper. The children here have no need for subjects that are way beyond them. It was wrong of the Reverend Felton to fill our Jessie's head with such nonsense.'

'Oh, no.' Cecilia took hold of the woman's hand as the tears began to fall down her care-worn cheeks. 'Your Jessie loved it. She soaked it up and asked for more.' Cecilia's words held no comfort for the mother and she sobbed. Cecilia let her grief run its course.

'It was wrong of the Reverend to try to raise her above her roots.' The woman blew her nose and stared defiantly at her companion.

'He never sought that. He just wanted Jessie to have the luck he'd had. Gregory Felton had seen the wider world and he wanted Jessie to have the chance to see it too. All right, Latin might be an unlikely subject for you and me, but it would have made Jessie a scholar.' Her mother made no answer.

Cecilia smiled, 'You know, Maria, although the rector has travelled the world, he is not worldly wise. His feet do not tramp the same land that our down-to-earth feet tread.' She thought of him away in the hills.

'There's to be no Latin, then.'

'And now there will be no doll's house.'

'Doll's house?' Maria looked puzzled.

'The rector had started to build one for Jessie, a beautiful Spanish one.' She thought of the unlikely house chosen by Gregory. 'No he's not down to earth, he's filled with something beyond the everyday necessities of life. Only he could have chosen a white house.'

Maria stared at her and Cecilia continued her defence. 'You see, a special toy, or a dead language, are to Gregory Felton as necessary as bread and cheese are to the likes of us.'

''Twas a kind thought, but where would we have put it?' The practical woman looked about the room, the same size as her cottage next door and there was doubt written all over her face. 'Still, it was well meant, as you say.' Maria sniffed again but her face softened. Then she muttered, 'So, why has he left us?'

Cecilia looked down on the floor. It had dried in smears. It could do with another session of knees on floor and another bucket of soapy water but they had done enough for one day. Both women were tired.

'He has gone seeking oaks grown from an Admiral's acorns. I told you he is not like other men.' She laughed and there was pleasure in her words.

'At—at a time like this?' Maria Dodd's brow furrowed and

Cecilia felt immediate remorse. She'd sought to comfort but her words showed a lack of feeling for the bereft and bewildered mother. She'd sought too eagerly to place Gregory out of the woman's displeasure.

'It was necessary to close the church. Father did the same at Greystead, anywhere where people might congregate. It was I who told the Reverend Felton to take the journey. He was not needed here.'

'Not needed here?' Maria repeated the words indignantly.

'My father stood in his place.' Cecilia was again defensive.

'And he took a fine service but who buried him? They had to send to Bellingham for a minister. It was my Jimmy who took the message.'

Cecilia brushed the hair from her eyes in a weary gesture. She had been upset that it had been left to a stranger to bury her father. Gregory would have spoken from the heart, if only he had been there.

'So where are these oak trees?' Mrs Dodds could hardly hide the scorn in her voice. 'They must surely be on the moon.'

'He will come back. But it was a quest he'd set himself and I understand that.'

'Do you?' The woman's query told that she did not. 'Aye, he was keen to get away all right. He had itchy feet from the beginning.' She sounded scornful.

'Did he?'

'Aye, that he did. When I found those long black hairs on his desk it unsettled him even more. He would stand and look out of his study window up into the hills.'

'Long black hairs?' It was Cecilia's turn to repeat.

'I told him the old local ploy to tie them around his wrist and then he would dream of his true love.' She looked Cecilia straight in the eye. 'I believe he has gone after a woman. Excuse me for saying so, Miss Howick.'

Miss Howick at home in the quiet rectory sat with a sheet of paper on her knee. She had planned to write out the syllabus for the first term but her eyes were unseeing. Miss Howick, prospective school teacher, could think only of a skein of black hair, of a doll's house, of a long-dead language, of sprouting acorns. The tangled images flashed through her head in a distorted jumble. She gazed into space, her hands idle. This way, that way, her thoughts raced and gradually she threaded them into the unpleasant answer. Gregory sought intangibles but could it be that reality held the true reason. Had he gone seeking after a woman?

She repeated Mrs Dodds' words over and over in her brain many times and still she made no sense of them. The woman's comments showed country ignorance and superstition. The very thought of Gregory wrapping some hairs around his wrist overnight should have made her laugh a disbelieving denial but that she had not done. A niggling doubt told her that Gregory Felton was quite capable of such an act. And her earlier defence of her friend had actually made the woman's accusation sound more than feasible.

The Reverend Felton was not a man with feet fixed firmly on the ground, she had freely admitted it to his bewildered housekeeper. The two women had discussed Gregory's continued absence and suddenly here was the answer.

How long had he been gone? So much had happened; events that would take a lifetime had been crowded into a few short weeks. She had lost all track of time. Why had Gregory not returned? How long did it take to view a stand of trees however tall, however straight, even though they had been planted by a man revered not only by the viewer but by half the nation?

A stab of concern made her put down her idle pen; her brain could not function. What if he had had an accident? Lay now on some hidden track that even shepherds and drovers did not frequent. She paced the floor, feeling her helplessness. She hadn't questioned his route. She'd waved him goodbye. His behaviour had been strange, the unquiet man filled with anger and a helplessness that now reflected her present state. His feet pointed resolutely to the hills. She'd watched him out of sight, a mixture of emotions. He disappeared from her view, but that had not been his last sighting.

It had been young Jimmy Dodds who had seen him those many weeks ago. Out snaring rabbits early morning, he had come across the curled-up figure of the rector lying beside the burn just half a mile from his home. He could have spent the night snug and dry in his own bed instead of exposed to the elements. The lad related his find when he dropped off one of his victims and she had hidden her concern. Asking the important question, she discovered that Jimmy had seen him rise, drink from the stream then set off up the track that led to the hills.

Gregory had been in a strange mood, tormented by Jessie's death and then Martin Dodd's rebuttal. The church, his usual succour, she surmised held little comfort. Had the black hairs around his wrist influenced the easily-led man? She let out an exclamation of anger, how could her thoughts lead her to such a conclusion? It was beyond fancy to one who could gut a rabbit, cut off its head and enjoy the flesh with no false sentiment for its scampering amongst the heather just hours before.

She strode out of the scullery door into the back garden of the rectory to the large tree that skirted the garden. Her occupancy of the house was ended, forced to fly the nest; at twenty five she was an old fledgling. The pigeon's nest, once full, now held a solitary occupant. The bird did not fly off at her approach. It could not. It sat perfectly still, its eyes facing ahead, conditioned by usage as though the string that tied its feet restricted its peripheral vision. It could do nothing else. Cecilia looked the bird in the eye and its plight made her blink. She had seldom cried even as a child and now she felt even more the pointlessness of tears. Weakness was not a chink in her armour. But for tied bird read 'tied unmarried daughter' and now there was not a single bond to keep her in her nest.

She was free to go where she liked. She put out her hand and touched the warm breast. Its eyes did not flicker. She stood on tiptoe and seized the compliant bird. Maria Dodds had taught her the local habit of tying young pigeons' feet together in the nest, so that they could not escape. There they sat until it was their turn for the pot. She flexed her fingers and moved her hand up the neck. The dying breath squeezed into the summer quiet.

The carcase lay still in her hand. The pigeon could not fledge, but what of her? No! Gregory had trapped her as surely as she had ended the bird's chance of flight. And for what end?

So it was a woman who lay behind Gregory's absence. It was now as clear as the nose on her face; she couldn't believe how blind she'd been. Young Jessie had spoken of a woman, a goddess in the eyes of the girl. Her words had tumbled in an excited outpouring and a protesting Cecilia had told her to slow down for she could not make head nor tail of Gregory's and Jessie's adventure. When, finally, she learned that Venus was carved on a stone she had given the story not another thought. But there was a woman, now she knew, and one with a name she had heard: not as exotic as Venus but Kitty had a certain ring about it. The story had had a second airing that day at the Hunter's. And the absent Kitty had dominated the table talk.

Hardly noting the young plump flesh, Cecilia ate the pigeon together with the cabbage from her garden picked before its prime. The other vegetables would go to waste though she would return to harvest them as often as she could until the arrival of the new incumbent. She hoped he would have a family so that her hard work in the garden would not be in vain; but how much more important were loved ones for the sanity of the man. Her father had been happy here; lesser folk would find it hard.

What did the place mean to her? She frowned at the empty chair opposite. She'd been the dutiful daughter. Then Gregory had come into her life and she'd seen herself reflected in his impatience. Gregory had escaped, gone off into the hills. Now that her father was dead she could go anywhere, there was nothing to stop her. Instead she had chosen to move just two miles down the road. Why did she remain? She already knew the answer. One day Gregory would return.

31

Wary eyes watched Byres as he stood in the centre of the room, his swaggering stance showing his hardly-concealed pleasure. He knew that all there wished him gone and he savoured their hostility. Their evening would be ruined if he chose to stay and he showed no sign of moving.

'I'm going nowhere just yet,' he said to no one in particular, though he looked gratified to know they had all heard. He turned to Kitty. 'When I do leave you should come with me.'

She laughed, 'So would that be the nudge necessary to get you over the threshold?' She put out a hand to him and he grabbed it.

'So you'll come with me?' His voice was a mixture of surprise and hope. 'I'll have the whisky first. Then we'll go.'

'Why not?'

She turned to Rory and said, 'Our friend needs a helping hand back over the threshold, though a kick in the arse might be just as satisfying.'

Byres frowned at her, trying to work out whether he liked her comment or not. His non reaction showed it was beyond him.

'What more can a man want than a whisky in one hand and Kitty Macnab in the other?' He looked from the girl to the drink and a slow satisfied smile edged his lips.

Rory was just inches from him. His hands itched to be about Byres' neck. He stood, anger in his throat, but he had no wish for open confrontation and recognition. Not now. The man's senses, briefly alerted, were dulled by the whisky. Byres had failed to see his shipmate of over a decade ago.

In contrast, every fibre in Rory's body was alive and pounding. It had nothing to do with Byres. It was the girl who stood beside him who threatened to upset his resolve. Hadn't he kept off the drink, knowing he would need a clear head to find the route home? Kitty would go one way, he the other, Thorneyburn his destination. But the girl's reckless behaviour, openly flirting with Byres and foolishly giving him whisky had left him befuddled. Then brazenly she had laughed at Byres, making Rory her accomplice.

Byres' proprietary arm circled Kitty's waist. She looked small and vulnerable and very beautiful, only inches away from trouble, and she was in her element. How could he let her go with Byres?

Yet what could he do? Byres, a brave man indeed or foolish, without any obvious back up, stood amongst barely concealed, hostility, but he'd the law on his side and that in the end stood for everything. Kitty and her father had chosen to flaunt the law of the land. It was not his business. She was old enough to do as she pleased. It was time surely to turn his back on them and all that they stood for. The past and present were crowding his vision.

Kitty gave him a slow meaningful wink. She turned to Byres, a smile on her face,

'So, Vincent, have one more drink on the house, before we hit the road.'

'I thought to drink with your father. Where is he? It must be something important to keep him from his whisky.' He laughed as he turned to Rory, a sneer on his face. 'One might almost suppose Macnab has his own supply of the malt and is not tempted to come for the lesser tipple. We all know Macnab enjoys his dram. But I'll find my old shipmate where ever he hides himself.' His voice was threatening. He touched his nostrils. 'I have a nose for whisky; I can smell it even above the stink of human dross.' As he spoke his eyes pivoted around the room and his words fell into silence. Rory clenched his fists.

'They're all good men here.' Rory spoke quietly, hardly able to contain his anger.

Byres laughed. 'How little you know them. Reiver stock, once a ruffian always, a ruffian.' He leered up into Rory's face. 'So, my friend, where do you fit in?' He frowned. 'You stick out like a sore thumb, the gentleman amongst the peasants.' He eyed Rory with renewed interest.

'Little wonder our beautiful Kitty thought to set her cap at you before she saw sense. Here, girl! Give this man a drink, he's too damned sober. I can't enter a contest with a man who cannot take his drink.' Kitty had a jug of whisky in her hand and a glass. Byres seized them and poured the peat-brown liquid with an unsteady hand. It splashed on the floor as he handed the brimming measure to Rory.

Kitty said soothingly, 'No, Vincent, that one is for you, the special whisky is too good for most folk.' She seized the drink from Rory, her fingers lingering over his, and placed it in Byre's unsteady hand. 'Your drink is on the House, I shall make Rory pay for his.' She turned her wicked eyes on Rory and he saw her intent. Byres said peevishly. 'I'll not drink it, man, until you have downed one.'

Kitty lifted a glass of ale. 'Go on then, Rory.' She said loudly. 'Vincent is right. You need fire in the belly like the rest of us.'

'Rory, did you call him? That name rings a bell?' Byres frowned.

'Could it be a ship's bell?' His face broke into a look of triumph. 'Yes, some long way back, a prissy lad, too good for his own good.' He laughed at the recollection. 'What was his name?' He stroked his forehead and then, as his ramblings furnished nothing further, drank his whisky in a final loving gulp and held out his glass for a refill.

Slowly she took his glass from him and smiled indulgently as Byres let out a loud belch.

It was the last sound he made before he fell crashing to the floor. Rob Shiel picked up his idle violin and played a long triumphant note that accompanied the chorus of cheering and stamping of feet.

'Well, done, lass! What took you so long?' Shiel put down his instrument and held out his hand as the whisky for the rest of them made its long-awaited reappearance. 'It'll taste all the better for the wait. Here's to Kitty. She knows the way to a man's heart.' He caught hold of the girl and kissed her. 'The snooping gauger certainly earned the special draught tonight.' He looked down at the prone Byres. 'Sweet dreams, man! We'll find you a nice heather bed for you to sleep out the rest of the night.'

There was no shortage of willing hands to carry out the excise man. Kitty seized Rory's hand and they followed the departing guest who had come unbidden and had left unresisting. They tied him to his horse and slapped the animal's back as it stumbled off down the track. Kitty laughed delightedly.

'He'll not remember a thing in the morning. Not even Rory, that it was you he remembered. He'll not recall being at the whisky house. Slymefoot can keep a secret as well as anyone.'

'So, come on, Kitty, a big measure for our heroine.' Shiel turned back to the building. Kitty shook her head.

'Rob, you can have my dram tonight! The violinist should be well oiled.'

The man laughed. 'Come now, when did Kitty Macnab ever refuse the moonshine? What ails ye lass? Ye can drink as hard as any man.' He put his hands on her shoulders and peered down into her face.

Kitty pulled away from him and shook her head, 'It's nothing. Perhaps the real moonshine has more appeal this night. Come, Rory, we should make our way home.'

'God's truth, man, you'll no refuse a dram?' Shiel's voice was raised in disbelief. 'Over here, Mac, the girl will have a whisky.' He seized a glass and pushed it into her hand. He stood over her as reluctantly she drank it down.

Rory saw her shudder as though she drank medicine.

'So our Kitty's become soft.' The man sounded incredulous and she scowled at his scorn. With a defiant toss of her head, she seized another from the tray and drank it.

'That's more like yourself.' Shiel looked triumphant.

Her face held no amusement, she was pale and a line of sweat arched her top lip, her hair was matted to her forehead. There in front of him stood Kitty Macnab, whisky runner, whisky maker, whisky drinker. The beautiful Kitty Linn who had painted his dreams had gone.

Then, she had never existed. He'd seen only what he wanted to see a playful, captivating beauty. In reality she was unscrupulous, as at home in this den of iniquity as any of the gathered hill men. He felt a sudden repulsion.

'You do wrong to consume such drink without thought.' He'd become the Byres too-good-fellow, remembered from the past, but instead of her disdain he saw a flash of disquiet cross her face. She caught his arm as she swayed on her feet. Rory's heart sank.

Thorneyburn lay way off in the opposite direction; it was a path he could not take. He must tread the way to Wholehope one more time. Silently he took her hand and, turning their backs on the noisy, inebriated throng, stepped out into the dazzling light that was a northern summer. He looked at the steep dark shape of hillside that loomed before them and was filled with foreboding.

He could feel her mood matched his. There was no repeat of naming landmarks. Hillside, stream, hillside, stream, it was a faceless, desolate landscape that merged into a sea of anonymity. They were rudderless, without chart to find their way. She stopped suddenly almost tripping him up and sat down heavily on a projecting rock. She buried her face in her hands.

Rory said not unkindly. 'It's best to get you home to your father.'

'O, no!' Her exclamation echoed over the hillside. 'I have no wish to return to Wholehope. Take me with you, take me to find the Admiral's oaks.'

Gregory laughed out loud. 'Have you lost your senses? You've had too much to drink.'

'Why then, do you make it your destination?' He could hardly hear her whispered words, and he felt ashamed. Her life had had little room for fanciful, unnecessary goals, chasing oak trees was a luxury she could never have imagined. The thought jolted his complacency; foolish for her, how much more was it for him, a grown man who should have little need of daytime dreams? Why had he run away, spinelessly fled Thorneyburn when everything pointed to the fact that he should have stayed?

With dismay he thought of Cecilia. What must she be thinking of him? Frantically, he sought to dismiss thoughts of the woman who had more common sense in her little finger than he had in his whole being. But her image would not go. He could see Cecilia, her eyes filled with scorn, her lips pursed in a thin line of disapproval.

And what of Kitty? The girl was vulnerable.

'Please, Rory...?' She did not finish her request but she chose that moment to look up at him and her expression was of one who saw in front of her a man to be trusted. That role had been almost unfilled in her short life and now she was looking to him. He found her childlike belief unbearable. What was her need?

What use had been her father? Off at sea in her early childhood, her mother dead. Had she lived with her grandmother? And when she too had died the girl had gathered up the few family keepsakes and come back to join a father she did not know. The man had provided some sort of refuge in the isolated Bremenium and now in the crude buildings that were Wholehope. She deserved better.

He peered down at the girl. She was perched uncomfortably on the rock yet still she made no effort to continue on her homeward journey. He stood patiently, lost in the predicament. What was he to do? She looked compliant but he knew her strong will; he could not make her do what she did not want to do. In her strange mood his unlikely destination had become her goal. It was nonsense for them both.

There was a groan from the girl and he crouched down beside

her and peered into her face. Surely it was not the whisky? Shiel spoke the truth when he said she could hold her drink. It was as natural to her as mother's milk. She looked green, and then she groaned again and vomited at his feet.

He held her head as she retched and then when she had done he cupped his hands in the stream tumbling just inches away and she sipped from his palms like an animal at trough. He saw the colour return to her cheeks. He put his arm about her. She said,

'We are brother and sister are we not, Rory?'

'We are like Hansel and Gretel.' He said, agreeing with her new mood swing, and again he felt the simple pleasure of sitting close to the girl, hearing the gentle breaths that had replaced her frantic words, feeling the warmth of her arm on his.

'Oh, Rory, I would have liked that. You would have been my protector, even when lost in the wood you would have found the way out.'

Rory sighed. 'I think it might very well have been you who saved us both, not me.'

The girl laughed, almost happily. 'So we need each other. That is good.'

She crept closer. 'There are no forests in these parts but I suppose it's a story that could be set anywhere. Like here and now on this hillside. No leaves to keep us warm, but we can snuggle close.'

'Yes, that would be allowed.' Rory grinned. 'You know I always did look upon Jock as a father. He made a good one.'

Kitty made no reply and he felt her stiffen. 'Sorry Kitty, he was a father to me, but that meant that he was not here for you.'

'No.'

'Still, he has made up for that since.'

'I was thirteen when my nana died. I had no one.'

It was Rory's turn to remain silent, how often had he known that feeling, but for a young girl how much worse?

'I knew I had a father somewhere, but it was a bit like looking for your Admiral's oaks. I set off to find him with hope rather than reason. I took with me Nana's teacups, I couldn't turn up empty handed.'

'How long did it take you to find him?'

'Five months. I grew up in that time. By then I had no need of a f-father.' Her voice trailed off and her words hung on the air like a chastisement. Rory circled her with his arms and gradually her head fell forward on his chest and she slept.

Warm sunshine brought Rory to his senses. The sun shone from a cloudless sky and the soft light was almost transparent. Hills were far off on a distant horizon and only the sound of water trickling in its narrow valley brought reality. Beside him Kitty stirred and there was an instant smile.

'Sorry, I can't cook you ham and eggs.' Rory grinned back at her.

'That's the last thing I want.' She pulled a face. 'The water sounds good.'

He repeated his actions of the previous night. Her mouth was soft against his skin, the slurping noises making him laugh.

'It's not very lady-like.'

'That I shall never be.'

'There are ladies, and ladies. For me, you are one.'

'Oh, Rory! You're kind. But you don't always see as clearly as you might. If only you knew!' Her eyes fixed on his face, regret written all over hers. 'I should tell you...'

'Tell me what?'

She looked at him long and hard. And it was his turn to turn away from her gaze. 'Forgive me for taking advantage of you. I should not have been so tempted.' Rory spoke his remorse.

Kitty got to her feet. 'I led you on. You've nothing to blame yourself for. I knew what I was doing.'

Rory bit his lip. Did there need to be blame attached to their love making?

'Come on, brother.' She caught hold of his hand. 'It's time for our early morning bathe. Race you into the water.' With a few deft movements she had removed her clothes and was running naked into the stream. In seconds he'd joined her and their shrieks of pleasure wafted across the slopes as the cold water made them gasp. They splashed, as children in a tub and the clear water careered down their bodies in their abandoned play. They subsided on to the grassy verge in a cascade of giggles.

The sun was their towel and Rory could feel his tingling body, as though it had bathed for the first time. It was a cleansing that had reached his mind. The girl beside him was a special girl. He loved her for the girl he had come to know. Kitty Macnab was every man's dream and no man's reality.

They lay side by side. Neither of them spoke and Rory felt his eyelids close. Still some distance from the crude roof of Wholehope, he knew now he preferred the azure blue of sky. She had said he was blind. Yes, that was his affliction but also his salvation. Why look for problems? That was all he had ever done in the past. Here in this wild open country he felt curiously at home.

He opened his eyes and above them a bird came into his scan.

'They live with danger.' Kitty was watching the brown bird, its behaviour erratic as it saw the intruders. 'And they survive through a mixture of camouflage, bluff and vigilance. The last is the most important. One should always be on one's guard.' They watched the bird as it swooped steeply in a rush of air, causing a loud bleating noise.

'Watch, it is drawing attention to itself. That's what the snipe does to safeguard its young.' She looked toward the thick tussocks of grass by the stream. He watched her as she crept closer to the bank and then gently move aside the sedge. With a satisfied nod of her head, she let it fall back in place and returned to stand looking down at him. 'The nest is there, that's why the mother is alarmed. Four eggs, olive brown and camouflaged by the undergrowth yet how vulnerable they are.' Her face and words showed her concern.

'Nature is cruel.'

'Yes.' Her voice was strained.

'You're fearless, Kitty. I can just imagine you swooping down on your predator drawing attention to yourself.' He raised himself on his elbow and smiled up at her.

She stood against the light. She had put on her shift. It clung to her like a second skin. Her modesty was false, breasts bulged the cloth in hill shape, her waist divided the slopes and then rounded across her stomach. She stroked the cloth taut about her outlined body. Rory stared at her and his eyes focused on the rounded belly. There was no mistaking what he saw. She was with child.

32

Rory recoiled. He sat unseeing. He was back on board the Royal Sovereign, the hag woman pulling open her cloak, revealing the child-filled belly. Repelled, he'd turned and fled to the other end of the ship and there the young, beautiful girl had seduced him. Here was Kitty, a mixture of the pair. He felt a surge of bile.

They'd laughed at him, his shipmates led by Jock Macnab, who as long as there was skirt had been more than willing to lift it. Now the father would be less than amused. Did he know of her condition? Rory remembered the red-eyed girl and the angry voices.

Kitty's eyes were hidden under her skirt as she slipped it over her head. When she emerged there was her little-girl-lost look. He'd learned nothing. In his infatuation he'd lain with this girl, his baser instincts still just below the surface; temptation followed by regret.

He was like any other man. He felt his disgust at himself and the girl. He could forgive neither. But he was not the first. That was only too apparent.

He walked away from her and she cried out.

'Be careful, you're close to the nest.' He looked down at the smooth oval-shaped eggs that lay just inches from his foot, their shells paper thin.

'Kitty, you concern yourself over others. It is you who needs to protect yourself.'

'Camouflage, bluff, vigilance.' She laughed. Do not worry about me. Like the snipe, I can look after myself.' Defiance returned to her face but he showed his exasperation.

'I think it's time for you to return home.'

'Home?' She laughed bitterly. 'Jock Macnab is not whom I need. When have I ever found him to be in the right place at the right time?'

He said somewhat sharply, 'You've no other place to go.'

'No.' Her answer showed she knew the truth of what he said. 'I don't need the learned parson to tell me the obvious.'

He felt her rebuff.

'Come on, let's get you to wholehope.' He said, softening his voice. She would need all the love and care she could get.

She talked non-stop on the way back to Wholehope. The harsh landscape needed none of her defining; instead she talked of the animals that lived there.

'Our old friend the snipe has got it all worked out,' she said admiringly and she began to run a copycat zigzag movement, backward and forward across the grass, her wild abandoned play a painful reminder to Rory that very soon this girl would be forced to grow up.

'That's the snipe's way of leading her enemies from the chicks and sometimes in the greatest danger, she will even pick up the young and fly them out of harm's way, coming back until the nest is empty.' Rory in spite of himself looked impressed and she smiled up at him, 'And of course females have long since evolved to merge into the background, their cryptic colour an almost foolproof camouflage in the dry grass.'

He looked at her. Her skirt was flame colour and her white blouse shone in the sunlight. 'You don't hide yourself away. Is that Kitty Macnab's bluff?'

She ignored him. 'It's the sheep I've the most respect for. Just think they carry their young all through the harshest winter months, giving birth in April so that the lambs have the longest possible time to get on their feet before winter sets in again. They're good mothers. And as for the feral goats, they've adapted to their new situation. It's said they scoop adders up with their horns then trample them under their hooves.'

Kitty stopped for breath and said. 'All this, dear Rory, is my way of saying. I know these hills as well as they do and I, like them, am a survivor. We all of us depend on camouflage, bluff, vigilance.'

Rory said, 'I can see the vigilance and the camouflage part of your theory, but what of the bluff? You hide the truth.' He wanted her words of confession. I am with child and the father is…? He could not voice the question that filled his disquiet. Who was the man?

'You know, the black grouse male neither sits on the nest nor looks after the chicks. It's the female who does it all.' Her tone was bitter. And he knew she'd assumed for herself the female black grouse role; the father would play no part.

Rory considered the possibilities. He'd seen her for the flirt she was. Rob Shiel, the fiddle-playing farmer, could hardly keep his hands off her. He was married but that certainly didn't rule him out. Byres had ogled her and she'd treasured his Scott novel as a valued possession. Rory found it hard to include his name in the list. John Armstrong, as old as her father, but it was obvious he found the girl attractive and he was the power in the land. Hadn't canny Scot, Jock, purposefully brought in his friend Rory as figurehead to keep Armstrong out of his distillery? Anyone of the three was a possibility and none could offer the role that was needed. And what of other eligible contenders? Caleb Hunter was only one.

The tell-tale signs of Wholehope were ahead, obvious to those in the know and he, like it or not, was one of them. Kitty disappeared down the hidden track knowing he would follow.

He stood at the top of the defile, his feet reluctant to move, looking skyward. Huge dark clouds, wind-driven, were approaching from the west and the first spatter of rain blew into his face. There was only one way and that was down. The trap was closing around him; once he took the rock-strewn path, the illicit buildings awaited. Only yesterday he'd resolved never to enter them again.

He wanted to turn back, away from that unlawful place, but now more than ever she needed his support. She must brave the unpredictable man that was her father. Jock would need persuasion to take responsibility for his wilful daughter. A Scots lowlander was ever conservative.

Jock Macnab sat huddled by the hearth, a Toby-jug figure, his limbs in a contorted jumble, his head jutting forward making it look as big as his body. Rory stopped at the door and was filled with a strange feeling that he was seeing his friend for the first time. He looked almost grotesque.

'Where's the girl?' Her father barked the question. He'd been drinking and his words were slurred; by his appearance he appeared to have been at the whisky half the night. Now he sat idle when he should have been attending the still. There was no sign of Kitty, hence the question. Perhaps already she was doing what should have been the man's task. Rory felt a rising annoyance with his friend. The girl was right she already knew she was on her own.

'Where's Kitty?' Jock's voice was wheedling. 'Where's my little girl? She should be looking after her father, not going off. And you, Felton, what do you mean by it, taking my little girl away from her father?'

'She is no longer your little girl. And leave me out of it. I'm not involved in her sorry state.' Rory stood at the door, his angry words spilling out at the pathetic bleating of the father.

An over-elaborate look of surprise crossed Jock's face and then one of disappointment. 'So, Rory, I thought you were my friend.'

'So I am. I am friend to you both. But at this moment it is a father that Kitty needs.'

'Kitty needs a father?' He looked confused, 'Well, by all accounts she's got one. The silly bitch! I never wanted a child.' His words were harsh and they already told he knew his daughter's condition.

'It wasn't your choice,' Rory spat out his anger.

'No, that it was not. I told her to be careful.'

'As do all fathers.' Rory swallowed his impatience.

'Where's the girl got to? I lose my comfort when she goes on her travels. I need my comfort. And I need it right now.' He lumbered to his feet and again Rory saw a grotesque head disfigured by drink.

At that moment Kitty chose to make her entrance, her scarlet skirt lashed to her body by the already sleeting rain. Rory saw no longer the porcelain shepherdess; she was the everyday ware of the hovel. Jock lunged toward her and caught hold of her waist.

'So have you got a kiss for Jock?' He kissed her full on the mouth.

The girl pushed him away, a look of utter distaste covering her face, and he fell backwards.

'You'll no treat a man like that, my girl. You'll do what I want.' And he hit out at her. She cried out as the force of his hand landed her in a heap at Rory's feet. With an exclamation of fury Rory caught at Jock's arm as he swung again at his daughter and the man, befuddled, subsided clumsily on to his fireside stool. He sat blinking at them like a startled owl. But there the resemblance ended. The face was vacant and uncomprehending.

Rory looked from father to daughter. The girl lay at her father's feet, her arm raised in self defence. The man was leering, the girl a strange look of acceptance on her face. And with a slow and sickening realisation Rory saw the reality behind her predicament. He had been the proverbial blind man. Now the truth stared him full in the face. Jock Macnab was father to his daughter's child.

His shocked brain fought to refute the terrible suggestion. No, it could not be. He was going mad. But as the man lunged toward his daughter yet again he saw the reality. This hidden hovel was the bumboat of his nightmares.

Kitty's laugh cut across the silence. It was like nothing he had ever heard, the cry of a trapped animal shouting its last-ditch defiance. She caught hold of her red skirt and tore it from her as she scrambled to her feet and seized her workday brown that hung on the door. With that gesture Kitty put on her female camouflage and her own survival.

The noise of the rain beat on the window, becoming louder by the hour and the rising wind screamed through the hole in the roof. Jock's silence grew with the wearing off of the drink. The place was stultifying. Rory was trapped by circumstance and weather. He could make no quick decision and for that he thanked the elements. Perhaps time and communing with his forgotten God would give the answer. His first resolve was not to let Jock out of his sight.

The three of them worked side by side in the distillery, the heat building so that to Rory it seemed like hell itself. The devil lurked in Wholehope just as he had come to Thorneyburn. Jock worked like a man possessed and, as the drink subsided, Rory sought to see the man that he'd called friend.

The Scot whistled as he fed the peat into the kiln and the red glow reflected on his open face. Rory had to turn away from the well-loved features. Why had he never seen him in his true light? What now the jokes, the devil-may-care attitude to life, the fatherly interest in the awkward boy? It sickened him that the man who had been proxy for his uncaring father had been found wanting with his own flesh and blood.

The girl stood at her father's side as though nothing had happened. They worked as a team. Watching them, Rory considered his lack of perception. He'd been blind but that was hardly surprising. Even now, if he hadn't guessed the truth, there was nothing to hint at it. And still he had not confronted his friend. He'd made no accusation. Was there now 'coward' to add to his shortcomings?

How could he put into words the abhorrent crime? What would become of Kitty? The girl who was now second best? He'd heard the phrase used, had always balked at its unfairness to the innocent victim of incest.

Kitty, in spite of her flirting, was the innocent. Her long dark lashes veiled laughing eyes; her sense of fun interacted with others so that she appeared over- familiar. But he saw the blameless child in her thin supple body, in her hoard of pretty trifles, in her blind belief that she, like the hill animals, was a survivor. Surely her flirting had been born of her shameful secret.

How long had it gone on? He shuddered to think of the young girl come seeking an unknown father. He saw again Jock counting on board the prostitutes of Plymouth, boasting of his natural leanings, and they'd laughed at Byres. In the incestuous confines of the ship there had been both stifled and questionable sexual practices. Now he saw the lonely confined life of the hills manifested in the tragedy of father and daughter.

As they downed tools at the end of the day's work, Rory moved to the man's side. His role was as limpet. But Kitty was already one jump ahead. She opened the door and, in the teeth of the gale, ran next door to the living quarters. Her woman's duties now were to provide a meal.

Rory said, 'I know you are the father of Kitty's child.' He did not raise his voice, he was just inches from Jock's ear. The now sober man started and a quick look of denial crossed his face. 'Do not bother to refute my suggestion, it would be useless and would demean you. Do not disappoint me further, Macnab.'

Jock was a shadow in the corner of the room, where both eating and sleeping were the allotted and allowed functions. The gathering storm had made the peat kiln in the distillery smoke and then finally go out. As they'd run to the hovel, the waters of the Wholehope had raged just feet below. Once inside it had taken both men to shut the door against the wind before Kitty could draw the bolt across. She gave a satisfied laugh that was eerily silent against the power of the wind and her words were lost in a violent gust. Macnab immediately put his head into a large hen of whisky. Rory made no protest.

They hunched silent against the screaming forces of nature that were just the other side of the door. Then what would Jock have found to say in his defence against Rory, his accuser? That these hills were a law unto themselves, he knew that now. And he, the outsider had no right to a voice in its ways. He sat by the blackened grate. The fire had smoked and then gone out; they had no means now of boiling a kettle. He thought of the isolation that worked its way into a man's very soul. He remembered his own furious carving on the rectory shutters- solus, alone -so that he had come close to the point of madness. Isolation distorted reality and in it Man became little better than the animals.

He lay on the hard ground, his thoughts trying to come to terms with the truth that divided the three of them as completely as the storm kept them incarcerated together. He remembered the Reiver Lay of the Minstrel, things never changed. The poem was not about cattle rustling but about feuding and treachery and incest.

And Kitty's was an age-old story: the girl, approaching womanhood, come uninvited into the life of the lonely Scot, a man without purpose or even livelihood since the ending of hostilities with the French. Rory had had the church to turn to. Jock had faced an uncertain future and Kitty had added to his troubles. The whisky-running had followed as naturally as night followed day, and then the inevitable building of the illicit Still.

There was Jock's familiar smell just feet away. He remembered the good times. It had been the cheery Scot who'd nicknamed him Rory and he'd responded to the obvious affection. Again he'd become drawn into the man's life with a new christening; 'Black Rory' had come carelessly into being. He shuddered. Black indeed, he must leave this place, Wholehope was the haunt of evil. And when he went he must take Kitty with him.

He could hear the rushing stream thundering past the building. The small rill that had carved the narrow valley was become a raging torrent. It was as though they were adrift on the sea. He heard again the echo of hurried commands to man the boats, the scurry of feet as they ran on deck. A torrent of water came pouring underneath the door. The flimsy roof shook, a spatter of rain trickled down the walls and the wooden support post groaned.

The storm was heaven sent. Rory felt an overwhelming surge of relief. Here was the answer to his prayer. God was about to destroy what man had so sinfully created.

Macnab in his drunken state shouted, 'Abandon ship.'

33

The dark clouds lay a long way off on the horizon. And by the direction of the wind they would come no closer. The streams of rain that stretched earthward would not water the seeds, she'd hopefully planted in her new garden, even though it was moving to high summer. Cecilia gave the offending weather but brief thought as she watched the dark figure of the horseman wending its way down the drove road that led from the hills. Greenhaugh was his obvious destination.

The man sat idly on his horse as it ambled along the village street frisking the dust of the dirt track. His blond hair reflected the coat of the mare and his fawn coat was the colour of summer-dried grass, as though he'd adopted country camouflage. Now, here in the village, he was tall against the squat dark houses that held none of his superior stature. Cecilia stood behind her small window and watched his progress. Already like the other village women, she'd become the observer of everyday life.

From the man's posture he did not consider himself an every-day occurrence. Where was he headed? The Holly Bush Inn she surmised, popular meeting place of travellers and villagers alike. Where had he come from?

She turned back into the room already losing interest; whoever he was it did not concern her. It was younger feet, skipping along the street that interested her and she could hear the first steps as she opened the door. The two young Dodds were always prompt.

Both were smaller replicas of Jessie, with dark inspecting eyes and unruly hair, but there the resemblance ended. Jimmy always had a cheeky grin on his face and Jane's surprised look had something to do with adenoidal open mouth. Neither had the look of knowledge that had animated their sister's face, long before any facts were delivered. The girl had been a blanket peat bog, saturated even before the rain and waiting to spill over. And Jessie would not have skipped, she would have run. Run as fast as she could down the small vein of the village street away to the heart, away to London.

'Good morning, Miss Howick.' They chorused her name, rote-fashion. On Jessie's lips it had been like the naming of a favourite book. She must stop it. Cecilia stared down at the girl's siblings; they were not her, but they were the next best thing.

'Good morning. How are you today?'

The little girl hesitated. 'My mam said she would give me an apple if I came to lessons.'

Her brother was sarcastic. 'That's no much of a bribe, the stored ones are wizened and grubby by now.'

Cecilia forced herself to laugh. Jessie had been the prize. This season's blemished crop would need much more attention.

'Miss, did you see the gauger riding down the street? My mam says he's a bad man. Could we learn about bad men today? My mam says the French are our enemies.'

'Not anymore.'

Eleven year old Jimmy screwed up his face. 'How can that be? My mam says once a bad apple, always a bad apple. That makes sense; all you can do is throw it away once it's become rotten.'

Cecilia couldn't hide her delight. Here was a different mind from his elder sister but it was enquiring and one to shape. 'My, your mam knows a lot.'

'Aye,' the boy was half way back through the door. 'That's what I said. Our mam can be our teacher just as well as you.'

'Woa, boy where are you off to?' A man's voice sounded his surprise as the fleeing boy collided with his legs and Cecilia saw the bulky form of Caleb Hunter blocking out the light of the small doorway. Behind him another figure formed a double barrier.

The two men filled the room and as they entered her two pupils departed. Cecilia stared at her visitors and her pale face coloured with annoyance.

'You are interrupting my class and I would think for no good reason.' She had become the schoolmarm. 'It's only folk half your size that interest me. I prefer to watch plants grow. It's the nurture that matters.'

Caleb laughed uncertainly. 'Miss Howick, may I introduce Vincent Byres? You'll see, Byres, that Miss Howick speaks her mind. But that's no bad thing. You'll find what you seek.'

Cecilia looked at the stranger. Instinctively, she saw that this seed was suspect. She saw the supercilious mouth and the sharp eyes and she didn't take to the finished product. Likewise, Caleb, of similar growing season but of good local stock had been too cosseted by the grower; a showy bloom, he'd gone early to seed.

Byres ran his long thin fingers through his yellow thatch of hair and his eyes appraised Cecilia. She could tell she'd annoyed him as she returned his stare, as unyielding as his. She didn't have auburn hair for nothing.

'Miss Howick, I am new to these parts, the borders being my

usual hunting ground.' He emphasized the last two words and his eyes narrowed. She heard the unpleasantness of the man. 'Of course, I do not expect to find a whisky smale, not in a place like Greenhaugh.'

'Whisky smale? There you have the better of me. It isn't part of my vocabulary.' Cecilia gave him her haughty look and drew herself up to her full height. The man took in her straight skirt and her tied-back hair, reading the prim appearance of one who lacked humour. Her impassive face revealed nothing of her concealed enjoyment of the exchange.

'Smuggler.' Caleb interrupted.

'Forgive me, madam. It's a word much part of my life.'

'Then, sir, your nose rather than your brain must dominate your activities.'

Byres fingered his nose. 'One could say that is true. Yes, indeed, my nose has always stood me in good stead. I can smell a suspicious matter long before the carcase has begun to rot.'

'There you have the better of me once again.'

Caleb began to fidget. He had brought the smell of the farmyard into the stuffy schoolroom. In contrast his companion was immaculate, a fastidious man Cecilia guessed, one who spent too long at his toilet. She thought it unusual in his occupation, though she'd never met an excise man before. That he stood there now in her schoolroom was a complete mystery. What assistance could she be? Caleb must have thought it possible or he would not have brought him.

'Madame, I am some distance from my usual haunts but sometimes it's necessary to spread the net wide. I seek a man called

Black Rory. He's involved in illicit whisky in the borders.'

Cecilia looked blank. 'You are far off course here, I think.'

'Perhaps,' the man sounded doubtful, then he fingered his nose again and there was a quick flash of amusement. 'Then perhaps the smell of fish brings me to Greenhaugh or rather the ocean that has penetrated this far inland. I am told your new rector was a man of the sea.'

'I believe so.'

'And I believe him to be an old shipmate of mine. It's a strange coincidence but there can only be one Gregory Felton.

'Can there?' Cecilia raised her eyebrows.

'And now he is a man of God.' The man barely tried to hide his delighted amusement. 'I always said he was a goody.... Tell me, Miss Howick, do you believe a man is inherently good, just as a man can be inherently bad? I do believe the latter is easier.'

'We are all hybrids.'

'Partly good, partly evil, I take your meaning, Miss Howick, but it shows how mixed up a man can be when he is not able to live with an outwardly good persona.'

'Perhaps that might be valid for some, but in the instance of the Reverend Felton I've no hesitation in saying he is a truly good man.'

'Ah, how lucky is Gregory with your assessment of him. I would meet with him again.'

Cecilia shook her head, 'He's not here at the present.'

'Neither he is.' Caleb showed his impatience. 'No one knows where he has disappeared to. Swallowed up in the hill clagg some do say. Tis strange just to run off like that.'

'Run off? He has done no such thing.'

Byres laughed. 'Perhaps Gregory goes evangelising, seeking out the sinful.'

'That would be in character.'

'So then, let us hope he comes across Black Rory.' The excise man said the name slowly and distinctly as though he was spelling it out to a simpleton. 'A good man turned bad quickly earns the epithet black. And they say his woman, Kitty, is even more of a bad lot.' He threw his departing comment over his shoulder.

Cecilia felt the thrust of his words as though she had been physically struck. She stared at the man, fighting her rising anger. What a fool! What a blind fool! She could hardly believe how stupid she'd been. How gullible and naïve.

'Wait,' she ran after them into the street, 'you'll find the Reverend Felton somewhere up in the Border region. He went there to find the woman, Kitty.'

Her words followed the two men and echoed round the deserted village. A cloud of dust marked the horsemen's departure. Cecilia grabbed a brush and swept it back into the street. The bristles scratched at the hard surface and activated another cloud; furiously, she repeated her futile action. She stopped, her temper subsiding as quickly as it had come and with it came the knowledge of her ill-timed words.

Jimmy and Jane reappeared from nowhere. Cecilia spoke slowly and deliberately, 'Jimmy, we spoke of the French who were our enemy. Reverend Felton was a brave man who kept them from our shores. Now I believe he is in danger. Tomorrow take a holiday from school and go find him.'

Jimmy was already out of the door. She looked heavenward. The dark clouds that had hung over the hills all morning were coming south west on a veering wind.

34

'No, Macnab.' Kitty screamed above the wind. 'Are you mad? I'll not follow you. We have nowhere to go.' Rory heard the finality in her voice. 'Here we have a roof over our heads.'

The frenzied girl lunged at the addled man as he fought to open the door. Her hands tore at his coat and Rory, going to her aid, pulled Macnab away from the one defence that was keeping them from the fury of the storm. Beyond it, the elements screamed their vengeance.

As the struggling man felt their restraint he subsided into the corner. Kitty huddled in the opposite one, as far away from her father as she could get, her arms hugging her body, her head bowed, so that she was a bundle of old cloths.

'We stay here.' Her muffled voice sounded her resignation, the once reckless girl now bent on survival.

Rory stood as far as he could get from both of his enforced companions. The four walls seemed to move inward with the force of the wind; it had become a prison and the storm could last for days.

The wind shrieked its menace. Rory tried to sound unperturbed, as he shouted above the wind,

'How long do you think the roof will hold?' But his forced laugh was drowned as the prop above their heads groaned ominously. The hurricane was about to overturn their flimsy craft.

Macnab whimpered, once a man for a storm-tossed vessel, now he was with women and children in the boats. Gregory reached out and put a comforting hand on his head.

'I've the height of Atlas if necessary.' He raised both hands above his head as he spoke and felt the weight of the sodden roof. It was a saturated mass like the peat bog surrounding the defile, the water waiting to take any route possible. It hadn't reached that point yet, though the walls were becoming a small waterfall. Rory eyed the growing trickles.

But for now they were safe. Kitty was right. However tenuous a shelter this place offered, it was harbour. Here they would have to ride out the storm, just as they had done once in a sudden squall that had hit their blockade-busting ship off the coast of Menorca. It was then that he had discovered the dark side of Macnab. He remembered his overwhelming sense of loss at the death of the Admiral and Macnab's siding with Byres against him. Miserably he'd gazed at the retreating land as they left port, was the little white house perched on the hillside the last sighting of his lost security? He'd rubbed his eyes, but the little house had disappeared. Within a day he'd lost two father figures, the Admiral and Jock Macnab. There lay before him an uncertain future. He'd strained to catch a last glimpse of the land. The white house, now reduced to doll's house size, floated in the hazy sun.

That voyage home was the last he undertook with the Admiral or Jock Macnab. From Plymouth he took ship for the West Indies. There followed lonely years that led inevitably to Oxford and his calling to the Ministry; and then? Life back at sea as ship's padre had been his goal, the land held nothing. But fate intervened, Napoleon no longer a menace, the fleet idle and he was rudderless; he'd ended up shipwrecked in the foreign port that was Thorneyburn.

In the storm-lashed shack it was dark. His companions had become shapes, piled cargo in a ship's hold. He lay between them. Kitty straightened her legs and eased her body onto the hard ground. Jock watched her and as he looked to follow suit she visibly shrank from him. The three had become as perverse bedfellows as Byres and Jock and Rory in the storm-lashed harbour of Menorca. He felt adrift as he had done then.

Jock had let him down, but now how much more his daughter? It all lay fair and square at the feet of drink. And this, their place of shelter, was dedicated to it.

'Macnab.' He shouted into the dark. 'God is telling you to give up the moonshine.' His words echoed like an Old Testament prophet and were as meaningless.

'Aye, that will be so.' The man's sneer cut into the darkness. 'God's on your side, is he? You're God of wrath come for me and my daughter?' Rory heard his slurred amusement.

'For you, Jock, in his eyes, in my eyes and in those of Kitty, you are the sinner.'

Jock's reply was drowned in the wind but he was on his feet. Rory tensed. The man was as unpredictable as the elements. Did he seek to flee their judgement, even though a more condemning force waited outside?

Instead, 'Forgive me.' The words whispered on a sudden lull in the screaming of the wind. Jock had been ever contrite when the drink had worn off. Now his shame spoke through the whisky.

'Kitty, forgive me.'
'I was a child.'
'And I was a lonely man.'

Rory put out his hand to the man and fumblingly he found that of the girl.

'I-I am friend to you both.' Kitty clung to Rory but Macnab grabbed his hand away.

'I need none of your condescension.' He growled.

Minutes seemed like hours. Rory was hungry. His contest now was between brain and stomach. Yet, still it was his thoughts that hurtled around his head, unrestrained ballast that threatened to lurch and capsize the ship. After the storm what then? The elements could not rage for ever. When at last Macnab, Kitty and himself were free to climb from their hell hole, what then? There was only one way to go for him and now it must include Kitty. The girl's future lay with him. For the man and daughter it was the parting of the ways.

The storm was at its angriest, eddying his thoughts, veering and backing, even nature had lost its way. The defiant wind screamed for retribution as above them the flimsy covering shifted and stirred. The roof lifted and flapped like a giant sail being torn from its mast. He remembered his vain mention of Atlas.

Kitty stirred beside him and he was immediately alert. Then she was on her feet and retching on her empty stomach. Instinctively, like an animal not wanting to soil its bed, she moved to the door and he was immediately alert, his movements stiff and uncoordinated as he staggered to his feet. Desperately she struggled with the wooden bolt as the heaving of her body became ever more frenzied.

'Kitty, no.' She struggled as he fought with her but she was animal-strong. With super human strength she freed the wooden latch and the door swung out into the gale.

It tore off like a piece of matchwood and Kitty and Rory were blown with it, rolling chaff torn from the kyle. The wind shrieked its triumph as it swept into the hovel behind them, wreaking its vengeance on the only standing thing left in its path. With a groan of submission the roof lifted and the wooden beam, its only support, came crashing to the ground. It fell silently and the man below it made no noise of protest. For the last time drink obscured Jock Macnab's dreams.

'Father!' Kitty screamed above the roar of the cascading water as she turned back to the shack. Rory, seizing her arm, slammed her against the wall, his body stilling her flailing limbs. The twelve-foot-high torrent of water rushed past them spurning their flimsy frames, a load of rocks and torn-up bushes from the cleugh side its chosen cargo. They clung to the wall desperate not to add to the flotsam that surged through the buildings of Black Rory's still. Hardly daring to breathe, Rory inched the two of them toward the kiln house. The one standing building, it huddled close to the cliff, its roof still crouched upon its shoulder walls. He could feel the belly of the girl and he felt a new surge of strength in his aching limbs. Whatever else he must save Kitty and her child.

The storm blew itself out in a tepid whimper. An eerie silence coating the devastation. Jock's distillery was no more. Its illicit presence removed from the face of the earth and with it the man who had built it. Macnab's body lay sprawled across the shattered hearth of his hidden home. Rory gazed down at the broken man and knew it to be retribution.

Jock's unseeing eyes gazed into space. His face had a look of regret that Rory had rarely seen in life. He closed Macnab's lids and murmured a prayer over the figure. The moon was down and sullen cloud hung above the defile, a perfect night for illicit running of whisky. But that now would be left to others.

Kitty appeared in the doorway. He watched as the girl picked her way over the wreckage of the half-demolished room to where the crushed body of her father lay.

'We must give him a Christian burial,' she said and then, stepping over the inert form, reached up into the crude cupboard that hung precariously from the one wall left whole. She took out a barley cake; it was wet but still intact. She looked at Rory and a look of triumph crossed her face.

'It's still edible.' She broke it in half and gave him a portion. He took it without protest. It would have been futile. She chewed the unpalatable food with relish and Rory thought, not for the first time, she will win through. If necessary, she'd step over bodies, to get what she wanted. And their path, it led surely back to Thorneyburn? Already, he could feel the security of its well- built walls.

35

The flies swarmed about the displaced boulders and a wagtail sought his breakfast. There was a flash of yellow as the bird darted into the water.

'What's in a name? The bird is an impostor like me; all that yellow and yet he's called the grey wagtail.' Rory sighed. 'No, I was never Rory.'

Kitty smiled up at him. Her face looked pale and thin but she had brushed her hair and her dress, no longer flood-drenched, had dried the pale brown that made her merge into the background.

She looked at him quizzically and then, with her uncanny reading of his moods, said, 'So poor Rory is dead. Gregory is alive again, but not the old Gregory.'

He squeezed her hand, moved by her words. 'Yes, and I, Gregory Felton,' he rolled the name over his tongue, 'shall take with me Kitty Macnab out of this place. Kitty Linn is left behind; we are no longer our other selves.'

Kitty's smile was tremulous. 'But, Gregory, impostor you were not. You are no deceiver. It's not in your nature.' She lifted her head and looked him full in the eye. 'According to Macnab, you never did know whether to show your yellow or your grey side. You strive to achieve only grey, but Gregory, you should know you are the mixture.'

She took hold of his hand; her skin was soft and smooth. He looked down into her eyes. They teased yet.

'Kitty you are my yellow markings. Don't ever let me loose them.' He squeezed her hand as they climbed for the last time out of the cleugh over the storm debris onto a hillside that now lay open to the world. A huge gash exposed their once secret place. He averted his eyes. Others would come to gloat over the small, doomed efforts of man in the face of nature. Retribution they would all agree. And there was Jock's final resting place buried behind the kiln in a natural decline, the river would not reach that level even in spate.

They turned south, Kitty did not look back. They walked into the sun. Both knew to avoid Slymefoot. Up, down, up, down, the summer grass on the uneven terrain slowed their steps. This time Gregory forged ahead, Kitty following. And then there was the drove road; a pale green way that led south and out of the hills. Gregory ran the last few yards and when his feet reached the flat, even track, he felt a huge surge of relief. From here the way was easy. Here folk went about their normal business uninterrupted. They were back in the everyday world.

Cattle were herding south noisy, lumbering, protesting travellers urged forward by strident, impatient men.

Gregory and Kitty watched from a distance. Kitty asked, 'What do you think it takes to be a good drover?'

He eyed the column of cattle. 'It takes muscle power.'

'Yes,' she agreed, 'the beasts are big, but it isn't just brute force he needs. The drover must know the country like the back of his hand and be honest and reliable.'

Gregory said, 'Then you describe yourself.'

Kitty gave Gregory a look that was hard to read. Then a slow, satisfied smile crossed her face before her eyes flashed with amusement.

'Why man, we should be ahead of them, all those brown patches left in our path. Clennell Street is the cattle drovers' favourite road.'

'I hope that's all we have to watch out for, besides, our route does not take us that far. Come let's hurry and overtake them.'

The flat sward felt good beneath his feet. Travel here was legitimate. You didn't need eyes in the back of your head to quest whether it was friend or foe who was gaining ground. The ancient track was as good as the lowland turnpikes, it stretched as far as the eye could see. Figures moved in either direction and Gregory could hardly contain his pleasure.

'The Admiral told me Clennel Street was as broad as the Tyne Bridge. I didn't believe him, now seeing the wide, green road for myself, I know he spoke the truth.'

'I have trod both.'

'Carrying the morning dew?' He sounded his surprise in a whisper and Kitty stopped in her tracks, put her hands on her hips and laughed up at him.

'And who do you think could hear that, perhaps one of the sheep?' He had the grace to look abashed and she said quickly, 'we travel openly on this road, Rrr—Gregory.'

'Yes.' He murmured his pleasure. He stole a glance at her. Her face was set in a determined frown. 'You're brave, Kitty. I know that you face the future with fortitude.'

She laughed at him. 'How quickly you've become the parson. Fortitude, what is that? Is it endurance? I'm good at that.'

'Yes.' It was his turn to frown.

'The future, what is that? To me it can only be the time since I discovered I was with child. I do not look beyond. I agreed to come with you for the child's sake.' He noted the defiance in her voice.

'It's for the best.'

'Aye, but for whom?'

'You have just said, for the child.' He sounded weary.

'Aye. But what of you, Gregory?'

'The present is what matters. You've just said so.' Gregory halted and pointed into the distance.

'Look I see no trees! The Admiral's oaks lie out there away in that direction. They no longer signify.' The treeless skyline brought a wry smile to his face and he shrugged his shoulders. 'They're no longer on my horizon. What matters now are you and your child.'

Kitty did not reply.

'O...of course. I shall never be a rich man, but I can offer a solid roof over our heads and a garden for the child to play in.' He hesitated. 'Or perhaps we might go to Newcastle. I can find employment there.'

'Oh, Gregory, you would hate that.' She put a restraining hand on his arm and stood on tip-toe to kiss him lightly on his cheek. Her dark eyes looked out over the fields. Now, there were walls built to mark out the newly enclosed land. It was chess board ordered. She pointed at the parceled up fields.

'These walls will be a restraining pen for me and the child,' She placed her hands on her belly and sighed, 'when skin and chord can hardly contain one that has mountain water in its blood, perhaps even whisky?' She laughed, her innate humour getting the better of her.

'It's good that you can still laugh, Kitty.'

'There is always something to smile at. It's just the finding.' Kitty added her caution.

'Kitty, I've a good friend, Cecilia, who will be happy to help us.'

'Cecilia, she sounds a good woman. It's a pretty name.'

'Oh no, she's not pretty.'

'Beauty is in the eye of the beholder, is it not? My child will be beautiful in my eyes, though it will have a red, old-man's face.'

'Kitty, you cannot be serious over anything.'

'Yes, food, I could eat a horse. My sickness has gone.' She pointed as a woman riding side-saddle passed within a few feet. Gregory looked anxious.

'I don't know of any eating house nearby. It must be some miles yet.'

'No matter, I know a place, not far from here.'

'Is it respectable or another Slymefoot?' His voice could not hide his doubt.

'That would be no place for a child of mine. It likes good fresh air and natural food.' She spoke as if already the child existed and as she did so she stepped off the path into thicker vegetation as though following the dictate of the infant. Gregory looked dubious. 'Oh, you of little faith.' She called over her shoulder, and with a wry smile he followed her.

She waited for him to catch up. 'This place shall be our stance and, like the cattle, we shall dine free of charge.' Gregory raised his eyebrows.

'So what is your favourite parable, Gregory? Mine is the five loaves and fishes. Sorry I can't provide the bread, but there'll be fish aplenty'

'I'm in your hands.' Gregory held up his, in surrender.

'When flooded rivers drain back, fish get left behind in pools.

They're sitting ducks so to speak.' She opened a gate into a walled field and skirted a crop of hay nearing harvest before they were out on to the other side and she sounded her old self as the unfenced land fell away below them.

'It goes against nature to hem land in by walls and hedges. Now only the birds are free to go where they please.'

They gazed down into a natural little valley that had escaped enclosure. Kitty pointed, 'But nature can be tamed for the good.'

Gregory saw that she spoke the truth; two large pools lay above the river and within them fish floundered and thrashed. With a cry of triumph Kitty waded into one of the shallows, though not before she had armed herself with a stout stick.

He sat and watched her, knowing she did not need his help. He remembered the happy time they'd spent at the Roman fort. She'd treated him like a child, and he in contrast could hardly keep his hands from her. Now his hands rested on his drawn-up knees. Her thickening body arched over the water, her waistline did not exist. Her cascading hair fell across her face and he could only imagine the concentration that creased her brow. Her purpose was food and that was for the child. Whatever passed her lips would be taken as benefit for her unborn.

They devoured a huge trout as soon as it was ready, heated on a flat stone under a fire that she conjured as if by magic. Gregory sat with his back to the hills, leaning against a newly constructed wall, facing the flattening plain that followed the river home. Kitty faced north, her eyes scouring the uplands. Her expression was inscrutable; could she be tamed? Live within walls built by laws?

She said, 'You should never lean against a dry stone wall.

'Why is that, because it might give way?'

'They are the home of adders.'

Gregory moved instantly and Kitty suppressed a giggle. 'That is useless knowledge now. What should I learn, so that I might teach my child?'

'Perhaps it will be how to avoid the traffic on the streets of Newcastle.' That brought her silence. Reluctantly, he looked up into the sky. The sun had still some way to go in its arc and they had made slow progress. If they were to reach Thorneyburn before dark they would have to be on their way. He made no move. The girl lay on the bank, her eyes closed. She looked peaceful and he marvelled at her resilience. She had been through so much and an unknown future lay ahead, yet she accepted all with a faith that was humbling.

'Five more minutes,' he said closing his eyes. The ground jutted into his back and a twig scratched his neck; he thought for the first time of the bed that awaited him in the rectory and he could feel its softness. The girl moved beside him and he sat upright with a guilty start. She laughed.

'There is no need to keep watch, I shall not run off. When drove beasts halted at night they were too tired and hungry to go far. But if the moon rose late after they'd rested, they'd wander. Perhaps you should add to the drover's needs a good sense of hearing.'

'I'll be listening.'

'No need.' She sighed. 'Within a few days, the homing instinct of the animals began to lessen as memory of their old pastures faded.'

Gregory sat hugging his knees. She was just feet away, but he could feel her distance. There was inertia about them both. Theirs was a path into the unknown. He stared out beyond the next stone wall that effectively blocked the way ahead a barrier to a progress that would lead the girl ever further from her roots.

They were being watched. He could sense eyes were noting their every movement. He sought for Kitty's hand and she opened her eyes.

He said, 'There is someone spying on us on the other side of the wall.' He peered at the obstruction, now like Kitty seeing the wall as an unfair aid for the huntsman. Kitty stiffened, the wariness of the trapped animal stilling her body. Then with a loud cry she rushed splashing across the pool, disappeared behind the wall and reappeared with a boy, his ear held tightly by his captor. He was yelping with pain and indignation.

'Please, Reverend Felton, I meant no harm. 'Twas the fish I wanted mister. You'll not take them all?'

Gregory gazed down at the boy, totally lost for words. He'd not been addressed as Reverend in weeks. It sounded oddly clumsy falling off the lips of a would-be poacher, as they themselves had been just minutes before. The guilty connection brought a rueful smile.

'We are acquainted?' The return to his old life had been abrupt and he stared down at the impudent face, trying to put a name to it.

'Why, of course, it's Jimmy Dodds.' He saw the confident eyes of the boy's sister. Jessie had the same awareness but it had always been a quiet acceptance; she'd none of the truculence of her younger brother. But there were her dark eyes and coal black hair that had framed her sallow face seen both from pulpit, and desk.

The brother's attendance at Church had been infrequent; from present evidence the boy was more hunter- gatherer.

Kitty, who'd dropped her hold on the boy when he'd addressed Gregory, said, 'So, Jimmy Dodds. I've left you some fish, there's more there than you can manage. There must be over twenty.'

'I can carry my own weight.' Jimmy said smugly and his eyes gleamed as he looked beyond them to where the stranded fish were thrashing fitfully in what were their final moments.

'You'll never get an easier catch than that. Here, lad, here's my stick, though some don't even need that.' Kitty looked at the stranded fish and there was envy in her voice that now it was another's harvest.

The boy set to the task, the growing bodies littering the bank.

'They look as pathetic as Macnab lying dead,' Kitty said hard-heartedly, a brittle note in her voice. 'He didn't struggle, never even raised an arm to shield his head, just gave up like a stranded trout. That would not be me.'

'I think,' said Gregory gently,' Macnab was a troubled man. He had no will left to fight. It was God's will.'

'God's will!' She let out a snort of derision. 'Do you really believe that the storm was a result of Jock Macnab's sins? So why wasn't I struck down? Why were you allowed to escape his wrath? Have you forgotten your new name of Black Rory?'

As if he could? Gregory shook his head. He'd no answer to the girl's strident questions.

'Come now, Gregory.' Kitty was laughing again. 'Or Black Rory, you surely do not believe that your God knew the truth?'

'Truth?'

'The cunning that was Jock Macnab.'

'Cunning?'

'Wily, lowlander, always one step ahead of his hide. It was some solution he thought up when he learnt of the child. His returned lost friend to become the accepted father?' Her voice shook. 'How easy for the second-hand goods and illegitimate offspring to find such a catch. I only had to lie on my back floundering, so he said, and you would come with fishing line.'

Gregory sank his head in his hands. What a fool he had been.

'I did not know that I was with child when I lay first with you.' Her voice was soft.

He seized her hands he could not trust himself to speak. He remembered the heated words between father and daughter; the girl's sudden aloofness and his jealous reasoning that he was only one amongst many. If only he had known.

The girl said without emotion, 'And now I've submitted as easily as he suggested.' She aped the dead fish. Gregory gritted his teeth, struggling to control his anger. He'd been landed as his old friend had said, as easily as a minnow.

'I'm sorry, Gregory.'

He did not reply. There was none to give.

The boy was back, looking pleased with his catch. He'd had sense enough to stop at ten. Jimmy could hardly contain his delight but if the fish put up little fight in life, in death they were more than a handful. Their scaly skins were slippery and difficult to lift. Jimmy was more than their match. Placing his crude sack on the ground, he shovelled them in without ceremony and then heaved it on to his young back and staggered off the way he had come. At the wall he lowered his burden and then jumping after it disappeared from view.

'That is our way also.' Gregory took her hand. He said with conviction, 'All we have to do is follow the smell. We've no need of a map.'

'I know the way. I too have trod it with a heavy load. The whisky jars could drag one down.'

'No more of that. Your have left your old life behind you.' He strove to keep the anger from his voice.

Kitty smiled and patted her belly. 'Why, aye, I'm of no more interest to a man as zealous as excise man Vincent Byres. He'll not be sending the hot trod after me.' Her eyes gleamed at the mention of the ancient border pursuit of hurriedly gathered posse. She looked back over her shoulder, a pretend look of fear in her eyes.

'If the poor man does come, he'll find nothing more than rotting fish.' Kitty raised her eyes heavenward, 'It's a sad waste of your God's beneficence. I'm sure he intended to feed the five thousand.'

'You know the story?'

'Yes, it could have been set in the Cheviots after a storm. And why not his turning of water into wine, perhaps it was really whisky.' She folded her arms around her waist, as if she felt to embrace an imaginary grey hen, and there was her old look of mischief.

36

The storm had cleared the air. The village had been washed clean and the children, lazy in the heavy atmosphere, came to school the next day bright-eyed and responsive. Cecilia told them about great floods of the past so that by the time they'd gone home Cecilia felt she too had been cleansed.

Even after a day in the classroom she felt fresh and alert. Locking the door behind her, she stepped out into the street. A few desultory puddles lay as though the village wives had emptied their buckets and the houses gleamed in the yellow polish of the sun. She could almost smell the imaginary beeswax of the great communal clean.

That was the nature of storms; they came out of the blue, they worked their wrath and then when they had passed it was as though they had never been. Already it was difficult to recall the shrieking wind under the eaves and the torrential rain that seemed to threaten the roof above her head. And yet at the height of the angry display she'd felt only an exhilaration that had drawn her from her bed to marvel at the flashes of white that made the room as morning. Her euphoria in the cold light of day seemed almost madness.

The children had brought little trophies of the storm: a severed bough from an apple tree, a featherless baby from a blackbird nest, a handful of dislodged sycamore wings. It had been her task to convince that after destruction came the chance to start again. She hadn't even tried to find the platitudes. These children knew better than any, that the only thing to do was step over the fallen, and continue as though it had never happened. What could any of them do for the lifeless chick?

She left the village behind. She'd brought no trophy to the classroom showing. Now she had a child-like need to find some relic of the storm that would impress the children and make their eyes widen with wonder.

Her eyes searched the track. This was the way that led to Thorneyburn. The path was already beginning to grow over in the summer flowering; no feet trod that way now that the church was closed. She could see the tower in the distance and she smiled wryly to herself. What had she expected? To see God's wrath manifested on his unused edifice, the tower rent in two? Would her return with the shattered stones have proved beyond doubt Caleb Hunter's theory that the new building was alien to the land?

The tower broke the skyline, solid and straight. Cecilia felt her relief. Sometimes she questioned her childish thoughts. But then her eyes could be filled with wonder as readily as her charges. She looked up towards the moor. It was flat and featureless as always, there was nothing there to challenge the force of the wind. It had blown its course unhindered over the rounded tops, like water over pebbles. Something was moving. She screwed up her eyes and saw a speck against the pale sky. There was no wind but the object was moving downhill erratically. She watched fascinated as the figure rolled towards her.

Jimmy Dodds was reeling as though he was drunk, a small figure that aped any village man on a Saturday night. Cecilia watched him approach, her frown turning into a smile as she saw he staggered under a heavy load. A large sack slung across his back contained a sizeable trophy. If she had found nothing, Jimmy had certainly come home with the prize, a load that he could hardly manage.

She called out, 'What have you there, Jimmy? Have you found a fallen oak tree?' and laughed at the foolishness of her words. At the height of the wind she'd thought of Gregory and there'd been a spasm of worry, but then she'd considered the impossibility that he would be out in it and she had castigated herself for her nonsense. She should forget the absent man as surely as he had forgotten her. Hadn't she told the children that whatever happened you moved on?

She watched the child still some distance away and then a stab of fear almost took her breath away. She'd sent him out on a mission to find Gregory. Could the boy stagger under the weight of a body? He was tall for his age, a strong village lad, the replacement for his absent father long before the smallpox had removed the man for good. She'd told him to go and find news of her missing friend and bring back…?

The load stank of fish. The boy red-faced and breathless lowered it to the ground at Cecilia's feet and she took a step back. Jimmy grinned at her and began to struggle with the neck of the rough bag.

'I've got one for you, miss, in fact one for every house in the village.'

Cecilia peered into the sack and laughed her relief.

'Where did you get such a catch? I've never seen so many fish in my whole life.'

'There were more, but I couldn't carry them.' The boy grinned, pleased at her amazement.

'It must have taken you hours to catch all that lot.'

A conflicting expression crossed the boy's face. 'The Reverend said it was God's bounty. But I knew that after a storm the fish are left there high and dry.'

Cecilia stared at the boy 'What do you mean... Reverend?'

Jimmy looked sullen. 'I carried them all the way home. He didn't even have a sack.'

'Who didn't?'

'The Reverend Felton, miss.'

'Jimmy, so you've found him?' Cecilia sought to keep her voice steady. 'Tell me clearly where did you see him?'

'He was sitting there eating one of the trout. I wasn't too pleased, thought he might want them all, and me thinking of mam and the bairns waiting for their supper.'

'When was this?'

'Why today, miss. In this heat the fish won't last beyond tomorrow. I best get them home.' The boy bent to the sack. 'I'll leave one at your sink. And I'll cut the head off, if you like.' He smiled up at her.

'Th-thank you, Jimmy, that is kind of you. But first, please tell me of the rector. Was he headed this way?' Cecilia felt relief flow over her. What better trophy of the storm for her than the return of Gregory?

'Not when I first saw them. They were feasting on the fish, like I said; they'd cooked it by the pool because they couldn't carry it. But, later I looked back and they were coming in this direction.'

'They?' Cecilia questioned. 'The Reverend Felton was not alone?'

'Alone?' The boy had the knowing look of his mother written all over his face. 'He was with a lassie.'

'A lady?'

'A beautiful lady. Not from these parts.' He paused then added. 'I do not know her, though I've heard of her. He must know her very well because I saw him kiss her.' Jimmy added the last fact with the relish of a gossiping woman and looked at the recipient of the startling revelation with the interest of one who knew the impact of his words.

Cecilia frowned as she saw the boy's adult awareness of what he'd said. The news would be round the village before the sun had sunk below the horizon.

She strove to gain control of her emotions. The village title-tattle would not be able to add her to the account. She stared down at the boy, her eyes cold though her heart raced. There, at last was the reason for Gregory's extended absence and the truth was hard to take. He was bringing the woman home to Thorneyburn.

She waved dismissively at the sack. 'You'd best be on your way, Jimmy. The fish stink already. You don't want to lose your catch.'

'No.' The boy stooped to pick up the load, almost indifferently now, his mind fixed on his exciting information. 'I've seen the woman, Kitty Macnab in these parts before. Her load is always the moonshine, so they say.' Again, he watched her reaction at his man-of-the-world snippet of gossip.

Cecilia looked at him, disbelief written all over her face. The storm had dredged up dross that had no part in a world lived in one sheltering rectory after another. She stared at Jimmy. Was he speaking the truth? He liked to be heeded, striving to be heard above his noisy siblings. She thought of Jessie. The girl had liked to be noticed too. She remembered the elaborate account of the naked goddess, purposefully intertwined with the meeting of Gregory's old friend's daughter, so that Cecilia had hardly been able to unravel fact from fiction; Kitty Macnab that had been her name, the daughter not the goddess.

Cecilia frowned, 'You say she is a whisky runner?' It was hard to comprehend. Gregory's goddess would seem to have feet of clay. Mirth bubbled in her throat. Did he see her still as the Kitty Linn he'd christened her? The naivety of the man who had sailed the world was beyond belief. The anger that had been simmering at the boy's words rose above her collar in the tell-tale colour that always flooded her face when her emotions were involved. The boy hovered, waiting for the next query.

When there was none, he volunteered, 'Mam says the girl Kitty delivers the grey hens to all the houses in these parts. Some you would hardly believe.' He sounded impressed. 'It's the big houses that get the malt. They can pay up.'

Cecilia's voice was hard. 'Then the excise men should be about their business. One of them was in the village but yesterday.'

She remembered the ill-matched companions. The farmer and the excise man unlikely allies; one could not help but curtail the pleasure of the other. Yes, Caleb and his mother were well aware of Kitty Macnab, they'd talked freely of her. So Caleb ran with the hare and chased with the hounds. He played a difficult game.

'Aye, there was a gauger here, I saw him.' A cunning look crossed the boy's face and he peered over his shoulder as he said confidingly, 'He's an excise man that likes his whisky. They say he doesn't turn in all he finds. Finders, keepers, just like me and the fish. But God looks kindly upon fish, doesn't he miss? He must have known it was Friday today.' The boy winked broadly. 'He'll not think I'm a thief.' He looked up into her face, a shadow of doubt on his.

'Of course not, Jimmy. The fish offered themselves up, and you just knew where to find them. So we will all have a lucky feast. Now you'd best get home and hand out your day's work. Remember the smallest one for me, there's only one in my cottage. Mind you give your mother the biggest.'

Jimmy smiled, already anticipating his mother's pleasure. As he stooped to pick up the haul, Cecilia looked over his head and saw approaching horsemen bearing down on them. The boy heard the sound of the hooves and stopped in his tracks, alarm now written all over his face.

Caleb Hunter and his companion of the previous day reined in their horses. Cecilia knew, instantly, that they'd been drinking cronies in the village during the storm filled-hours. Caleb, a large framed man, could hold his liquor it was his breath that contaminated the air as pungently as the pile of fish. The fair-haired man could hardly keep his saddle but his words were clear as he pointed to the tell-tale sack.

'What have you there, lad?'

The boy blanched 'I...I was given them, sir.' Cecilia moved to his side and they watched as Byres dismounted. He stood unsteadily leaning against his mount and then gingerly he bent to the sack. He recoiled in disgust as he opened up the neck.

'So, boy, you've been busy I see.'

Cecilia frowned at the man. 'That's too many fish for the boy to have caught. Like he said he found them.'

'Oh, yes, were you there, Miss? It looks like poaching to me. Boys have been sent to the hulks for just one illegal trout.' He glowered at the lad. 'I'm telling you, even a poacher blacking his face is punishable by the gallows.' Cecilia gasped in spite of herself and the man and Caleb laughed at the impact of his words. Cecilia put out her hand and took the arm of the terrified Jimmy, placing herself between him and the excise man.

'The Reverend Felton found them and gave them to Jimmy for distribution around the village. Modern day miracles happen, you know.' She forced a smile. Jimmy's accuser did not look like a man who believed in fairy tales. She could feel the sweat of the boy on his back and she could feel her own heart racing.

Byres stopped in his tracks, his eyes narrowed. 'Felton? So, again you speak of Gregory Felton' A frown crossed the excise man's face. 'Ah, the stranger at Slymefoot I have struggled to remember where I'd seen him before. What did he there?' He looked puzzled. 'No matter, it's you, boy, who interests me now.'

'Like I told you, the Reverend Felton is rector of these parts.' Cecilia sought to keep the man's attention from Jimmy cowering in front of them.

Byres looked irritated. He snapped. 'So, a Reverend gentleman is breaking the law. That sounds serious.' As he spoke he took a step towards the boy. 'And this must surely be his accomplice.'

'Of course he is not.' Cecilia strove to keep her temper with the man bent on making trouble. She thought of Maria Dodds and her dependence on her eldest child. The family needed no further tragedy.

'Surely you should be dealing with things that matter. Fish are below the notice of such an important officer of the law. Is it not whisky that is of interest to you?'

Byres furrowed his brows and winked at the silent Caleb. 'Aye, that is my concern, though only the illegal running of the stuff, I'll have you know.' He peered down at Jimmy. 'And they're a bad lot in these parts, be it whisky or fish. They don't learn the difference between right and wrong at their mothers' breasts. It's time this lad learnt a lesson from me if a Reverend gentleman doesn't set a good example. Come lad.' Jimmy squealed as he placed his hand on the boy.

Cecilia tightened her grip on his other arm. She said tersely, 'The child is small fry but, he can lead you to Kitty Macnab the whisky runner.'

37

Cecilia stared after the retreating figures, the enormity of her Judas words echoing in her ears. What had made her inform on Kitty and therefore Gregory, the man whose return she'd prayed for every single day of his absence in what had seemed an eternity? She stood transfixed, her feet unable to move, even if she'd known which direction to take. The horses and figures, one burdened now by the weight of the boy, disappeared over the horizon before she could blink. The pathetic sack of trout lay abandoned at her feet, left to become a rotting waste.

She turned away from the village and took the track back to her old home. At that moment its isolation beckoned; she wanted no part in her new involved life. She had lived too long with the unworldly man who had been her father.

And how naïve had she been, thinking that she and Gregory were kindred spirits, intelligent and enquiring, and made for a wider world than here in Tynedale? With the chance to leave, that was the very last thing she wanted. She'd reasoned the two of them could find a life together right here in this unlikely spot. And now the dream had come crashing down about her feet. Her jealous reaction to the news of Kitty Linn…the foolish man even had a nick-name for her, Kitty Macnab- would be seen for what it was,woman's jealousy.

She faced the frothing waters of the burn, angry from the ravages of the flood. Likewise the storm had churned her world into a seething lather. The water bubbled white then yellow then brown, a broth mix of disparate ingredients. She looked down into the angry waters and her red hair looked back at her accusingly. Her hasty temper would bring about not only her downfall but that of others. What had she done?

A sensible, uncomplicated face stared back at her, distorted by the fast flowing stream, but there were kaleidoscope shapes for her to see the truth. She'd long since known what the makeshift mirror showed; she was a plain woman, not blessed with the attributes of Kitty Macnab. Her high forehead had no curls to soften, her figure was too angular, her temper too waspish. The moving reflection stared back in its stark reality and her fury with Gregory and the girl subsided with the viewing. A moment's madness had caused her to abandon her innate sense. Gregory Felton had never led her to believe he could be anything but a friend and she, like any foolish chattering girl, had clutched at straws. He had come to her kitchen for companionship and home cooking. For a man's other comfort he had gone to seek Kitty Linn.

She imagined Gregory's incomprehension when he learned of her part in the capture of the girl. Then he would not even want to be her friend.

How she wished that she could turn back the clock, not just a few hours but a few months. Then she would be returning to the goodness of Thomas Howick willing to listen to his daughter and her mundane day. He'd the ability to focus on some trivial point and turn it into something worth debating well after the dinner plates should have been cleared away. The figure standing at the front porch made her stop in her tracks. Even in her state she knew she could not conjure up her beloved father.

The man was tall, a sturdy, dark-skinned presence that spoke of long days out in the open, not cooped up in a study. His fair hair bushed unruly about his uncovered head and his clothes were travel-stained. A stranger, she thought with a feeling of sadness, perhaps the new incumbent. Cecilia felt an unusual reticence. She no longer belonged in this place; her feet trespassed where once she had called home. She drew herself to her full height and said somewhat stiffly,

'Can I be of help, sir?'

Gregory turned to face her and their gasps of recognition echoed about the quiet house. At sight of her, a huge smile of relief illumined his face. She ran to him and they hugged each other. It was Cecilia who withdrew with a strained, embarrassed laugh.

'Anyone would think you had been gone a lifetime, storm-tossed on foreign seas, not just trekking a few miles off into the Cheviot Hills.'

'It feels like it, Cecilia. It's good to be back.' He looked at her, his smile fixed into a broad expanse of white teeth. He is handsome she thought and struggled to hide her chagrin; it had been another woman who had turned him into the tall, upright man that his self-doubt had kept so long bowed.

'So, Gregory, you've come back to your deserted flock. The sheep kept to their hillside, it was the shepherd who got lost.' Her cutting words wiped the smile from his face.

'Oh, Cecilia, I've stayed away too long. I'm sorry.' He took hold of her hand and stood looking down at her as though he were seeing her for the first time.

'You look bonny.'

She laughed and it was the dismissive sound he had heard many times, but he clung to her hand and she made no effort to withdraw it. He would not to rise to Cecilia's reprimand,

'Are you saying that my flock missed me? And therefore, hopefully that would include you, Cecilia? You're a true friend.' At last he let go of her hand. 'I knew you would be the person to come to.'

'What do you want?'

He noted her tone, as he said hesitatingly, 'Cecilia, I've been the shepherd in my journeying. Ninety and nine were safe on their side of the hill, as you say, but I have brought home the lost sheep back into the fold.'

She looked at him. 'Who might that be? Is her name Kitty by any chance?'

Surprise, then alarm showed on his face. 'What do you know of her?' He stared at the angry woman in front of him. 'She is not all bad. And now she is in trouble.'

'Trouble?' Cecilia sounded wary.

'Yes. She is with child and needs a home.'

His words were met with silence and he added, 'She is near six months gone.'

'Oh.' Cecilia's voice was a mixture of emotions as she took in the implication of the time. She strove to sound her old accepting self. 'The girl must be weary. Have you travelled far? Where is she? Is she safe?' She voiced her hope.

Joy, relief, fury, anger, jealousy, all had covered their reunion and now there was fear. Her hasty actions just half an hour ago had opened up what could be a hornets' nest. Her voice was unsure as she said,

'Where have you left the girl? Why is she not with you?'

'I could not take her to Thorneyburn, I knew to turn to you. Meantime she is in a safe place.'

'Good! I will help you.' Cecilia took hold of his hand again and her face showed her concern. 'There is a cottage in the village where she can hide. It's the one next door to the Dodds family.'

'Oh, Cecilia, I knew I could trust you to come up with an answer.' Gratitude flooded his face. 'I will go fetch her. She is in need of a roof over her head and a good night's rest.' He stopped, 'did you say h…hide?'

She interrupted, 'You should delay your return until it is dark.'

He raised his eyebrows then smiled. 'Doubtless you are right; there are many eyes in a village street.' He accepted her suggestion without question and she sighed her relief. She had no wish to spread alarm, better he thought it was just the danger of wagging tongues that threatened the girl.

'For the moment she is comfortable enough. At the meeting of the Tarset and Tarret streams there is a hidden place; I have sought it many times in the past. She can rest there without fear of interruption.'

'A good spot, I know it. Come to the cottage now and I will give you refreshment for her.'

'If it's your cheese scones then I am to be counted too.' He smiled then licked his lips. She returned his smile. He'd not bitten his lip once. It was her turn now to emulate the action. Surely excise man, Byres could know nothing of the secret place and Kitty would be safe as soon as he had retreated back to the border.

38

There was enough water to float a man-of-war. The storm had filled both streams with a white agitation that struggled for supremacy; the usually dominant Tarset rivalled now by the steeper Tarret. Gregory approached from over the encircling high ground, unsure of the depth of the resulting mixture. He remembered the turmoil of his thoughts the last time he'd been there; then the storm had raged in his mind.

He dropped down to the thin shelf of flat land that would have taken but one of Wholehope's buildings, not all four of them. He thought of that place now with almost disbelief. How good it was to be home: what a relief to see Cecilia after the weeks away. Still the same no-nonsense and he had sensed her reciprocal pleasure. Together they would help Kitty in her hour of need.

The girl lay asleep, her head resting on a rock, her legs dangling over the bank just inches from the water. An uncomfortable bed, but she had never sought a soft one. On the opposite bank the ground fanned out in a flat parcel of land at the base of a steep hill. Gregory sat down beside the girl and felt its protection. In the past troubles it had been a hiding place for cattle and men alike, secure from the border raiders. Instinctively he'd brought Kitty here. Why? Was it because in this place she would still feel at home? She would find the village street a hard path.

What of the days to come when the girl was living under the gaze of the villagers, in a cottage with neighbours both curious and hostile? Could he visit her and withstand the gossip? Instinctively he'd wanted to hide her away, for her sake or for his? And what of Cecilia? He minded what her reaction would be. He sighed. The future pointed away from Thorneyburn. And he felt his reluctance.

He saw the boy at the moment his head appeared above the hill on the other side of the stream and felt a surge of anxiety. But all the Dodds children frequented the place whether for sport or fishing or trapping. Gregory frowned, a mixture of annoyance and concern, Jimmy's tracking of them was becoming a habit. And it would ever be. No, Thorneyburn was no place for him and Kitty and the child; there were too many prying eyes. Gently he placed his hand on the girl's arm and shook it.

'Kitty, here is food for you. Cecelia will help us. You may stay with her until we can make other plans.'

Her eyes looked uncomprehending and he whispered his words again. She made no reply, exhausted after their long trek. He stared up at where the boy had been but now there was nothing but a bare hillside. For the time being they were safe in their hiding place. And he knew he was unwilling to leave.

Rocks piled above their heads and alders, wizened and spectral, hung like green witches, their lichen-covered branches caressing the girl's head; at a sudden intrusion of the wind, they shivered. Gregory sat mesmerised by their life-like movement and half expected to hear a cackle of laughter. But instead there was a different noise. It seemed to come from nowhere. A deafening roar of thunder from the hillside as it began to move. Rocks and dust and branches fell about them and the suddenly awakened girl clung to him, fear written all over her face. Gregory shielded her with his body, he could feel her agitation. He shouted above the confusion.

'The wind must have dislodged a tree root and brought down part of the hillside. It's but a small disturbance. This is not a Wholehope event.'

But Kitty, now bolt upright, seized one of the rocks that had narrowly missed her head and clasped it between her fingers. She said, 'It will make a good weapon if we are attacked.'

'But Kitty, there's no fear of that.'

She shivered. 'We are caught in a natural trap. Do you not feel the menace snared in this place?' She looked up at the towering crag on which they rested their heads. 'It wraps itself around you, the rocks are moving.'

'It is your hunger that talks.' Gregory gripped her fingers. Her flesh felt cold and thin.

'Aye.' She half rose to her feet. He thought she has become the stagnant pool, no longer the bubbling linn. He jumped up and lifted her with him. They teetered at the edge of the bank and Gregory pulled her close. He bent and kissed her. She clung to him and he thought she needs me, that is enough. I shall go with her wherever her feet lead.'

They came from the water, the frothing, angry spate that had looked unpassable, the horses, driven by men with intent so that the animals had no time to refuse, their nostrils foaming with the lather of fear. The surprise, the noise, the confusion filled the trap so that Gregory and the girl could only cower together like cornered animals. The terrified horses struggled on to the bank, their floundering feet sounding like frenzied blacksmiths. Caleb Hunter and Vincent Byres kept their seats, towering above them in impressive superiority.

Gregory screamed, 'What the hell are you doing?' He pressed himself against the unyielding rock and felt the vulnerable girl caught between him and the ravine side, her belly hard and ungiving. He shouted. 'Get back you idiots. What are you up to?'

'Looking for you, Gregory Felton.' The man sounded his satisfaction. 'If it isn't my old shipmate, after all this time.'

'We were never mates.' Gregory shouted his defiance.

'No, you speak the truth. You're of no concern to me, be it then or now. We are come to take the whisky runner, Kitty Macnab.' Byres' voice was a pathetic whine, a weak man hiding behind his standing in the law as once he had hidden behind his naval uniform.

'Whisky runner?' Gregory laughed and peered at the silent figure of Caleb Hunter. Surely, the eager consumer of morning dew had not betrayed the girl? 'Caleb, tell Byres he is mistaken.'

Hunter shifted in his saddle. 'I do not know. I'm only here to assist the law.'

Gregory sounded his disgust, 'So then you'll be the first to confirm there is no evidence to justify the accusation.' He edged away from the silent girl and pointed to her. She stood her hands on her belly as though they had become fixed to her body.

Byres dismounted, thrusting his reins into Hunter's unready hands. They slipped and with a whinny of fear his horse shied. Its escape blocked by the steep cliff it turned and headed out the only way it could, back into the swollen meeting of the waters. Hunter tightened his grasp on his own animal.

The excise man swore loudly. 'Take care, Felton. There is such a thing as accessory to the crime.'

Gregory laughed in his face. 'Indeed, I've seen you drink

contraband whisky and I'd say that in a court of law.' Byres' eyes flickered.

'And what tangible proof would you have?' The excise man sought to regain his authority, his voice the sneer that Gregory remembered whenever he addressed anyone below his rank.

'And your proof, sir concerning this lady, is it whisky running that Kitty Macnab is supposed to be engaged in?' Gregory's voice rang with amusement.

In reply Byres snarled, 'illicit whisky trading is a felony with the direst consequences.'

'Look at her. Where is the whisky?'

Hunter laughed. 'True, I see no barrel concealed about her person. Though her belly fits the shape. It will be easy to find out. I'm not squeamish.' His hands shaped an imaginary groping and Gregory felt the girl beside him shudder.

'So then, girl, what does your body hide?' Byres' voice rose a pitch as he moved towards Kitty. Gregory cried out in protest, but Caleb Hunter seated on the horse above him, lunged forward and seized him about the throat. He gasped for air as the farmer's grasp tightened. Byres' hands were on the cowering girl. She screamed and began to struggle, but there was an almost immediate gasp of satisfaction from the excise man.

'So then, Reverend too-good-to-be-bloody-true Gregory, what say you to these?' He held aloft his trophies.

Kitty's skirt lay about her feet, her swollen body straining her chemise. Byre had satisfaction in his voice as he dangled a leather flask in either hand. He brushed one against Gregory's pinioned cheek.

'Here is the evidence, hot from the source. Feel the heat from between her legs, as no doubt we have all done' His voice was choked with excitement, 'She will be cold long before she comes to court, but you are witness, Reverend, of the warmth of her body on the prize evidence for the Crown.'

As he spoke he loosed the stopper from the cask neck and slowly and deliberately poured the whisky over the cringing girl. 'An early baptism for your bastard, Kitty. What could be more fitting?'

Gregory screamed his abuse as the familiar smell invaded his nostrils. Frantically he wrestled with his captor Caleb Hunter but the man had strength. Gregory bit his hand, long and hard; with an expletive Hunter let him go. Gregory threw himself at Byres, his arms flailing in blow after blow. Hunter's horse reared as the farmer attempted to come to his companion's assistance and with a terrified whinny it plunged back into the water. Gregory felt himself falling.

He struggled to keep his footing. Slipping, stumbling he scratched at the bank, his fingers caught at a branch and with super-human effort he pulled himself back on to the land. Kitty lay on the ground, Byres poised above her writhing legs. In slow motion he saw the girl's hand pick up the fallen rock and bring it crashing down on to her tormentor's skull.

39

All eyes were on the girl as she entered the Magistrate's court. She was pale, diminished even in the short time that she had been held in confinement. Clothed in her simple, ill-fitting dress she looked a shadow that if touched could disappear like chaff in the wind. Only the fact that she was large with child made her a figure of substance. Her swollen belly, together with her walker's gait, contradicted her look of innocence and there was a mixed reaction as she made her way to the stand. Market day held no greater spectacle.

The spectators, crowded into the upper room of the local public house, rose to their feet as the Magistrate entered. The show had begun. The noise of scraping wood on wood and the excited babble of voices threatened to flood the low-ceilinged room. Kitty, her head high, gazed back defiantly.

Gregory looked away; he could not bear to see the caged bird that she had so quickly become. He shuddered and stared ahead at a small prism of light trapped and agitated on the bare plaster wall. Her face danced before him as it had done since her arrest. The thought of the imprisoned girl and her loss of freedom weighed heavy. And the fault lay equally with him and Cecilia Howick.

He would do anything to save her. He uttered a prayer as he turned and looked at the girl standing just feet away and the sight of her straight back lifted his resolve. She was not yet the condemned animal.

Gregory looked beyond her to the Magistrate. His eyes had been only for Kitty. Now he stared at the man who held the girl's fate in his hands and his heart beat faster. Fate was as unpredictable as life and God had surely interceded.

The Magistrate took his seat and the others, shepherds, farmers, townsfolk and their wives, obedient as sheep, followed his lead. Gregory could not take his eyes off the girl, centre stage, focus of attention.

She looked more beautiful than he had ever seen her, though her luxuriant hair was shorn like a summer sheep. The revealed fine-boned features looked as fragile as her grandmother's china. He thought of those few precious belongings lost in the flood. Now in this room had started the struggle to save the last, most precious fragment; he remembered the fine cup so out of place in the crude Wholehope shack just as the girl stood misfit here. Was it possible the Magistrate was a man who knew the worth of delicate porcelain?

Byres, her apprehender, stood within feet of the prisoner. In contrast to the accused girl, her accuser was almost hidden by great swathes of bandages. Wrapped round and round, they looked as though they were keeping head attached to body. The pallor of the skin that could be seen matched the bands of white cloth encasing his head, an ugly red gash across his uncovered nose, the only colour to the mummy-like figure. Through it all Byres had not lost his swagger. Along with the girl he was the centre of attention and like her he had every intention of making the most of it. He looked about the room with enough of his mouth on view to show the contempt with which he held those present. Disdainfully, he turned his back on them and fixed his eyes on the Magistrate, a servile look of such cunning that Gregory had to look away. There was more than enough of the man on view to rekindle his loathing.

The Magistrate's voice was clear. 'Kitty Macnab is hereby accused of the crime of illicit whisky running and evading apprehension by the hurting of His Majesty's representative.'

His words were met with a murmur that could only be read as one of approval for the girl and Gregory bit his lip as the Magistrate frowned. The man drew himself up to his full height. He was the man of substance in the room and would brook no dissent.

'Silence! The matter is serious. Mr Byres, you are a well known gauger or as we call them in these parts a Preventive Man. Inform us of your side of the story.'

'Sir, it is my aim to prevent the trade of illicit whisky, as you say. I have had considerable success in my endeavour.' His words were received by a shuffling of feet and Byres raised his voice, a touch of anger that he made no attempt to conceal. 'It's common, reprehensible knowledge that the majority of folk in these parts are for the smuggler. Fortunately, there are worthy figures of society who are willing to support the side of the law.'

Gregory felt his companion stiffen. Cecilia sat beside him, her lips drawn in a tight line, as they had been ever since they'd set out for the court hearing that morning. He'd sat opposite her in the carriage loaned by a local landowner for their journey to the town and the usual open woman had been guilt-ridden quiet. He had maintained the silence; Gregory felt no urge to allay her remorse. Her confession to him had been painful. He could not believe it. What could have been her motive? He had waited for her stuttered explanation to come to an end and had said with no lessening of his stony expression.

'There is good and evil in us all.' He'd never imagined he would ever use the latter in the same context as that of Cecilia.

'It was the village schoolmistress who told me of the girl's presence in these parts. And I am grateful to her.' Byres looked toward Cecilia and a faint pink tinge to her cheeks signaled that the Preventive Man's words had been digested.

'The court will hear her evidence shortly Mr Byres. Pray continue with your testimony.'

'This is a lawless area, and we excise men usually travel in pairs. On this occasion, I was paying a visit to my friend Farmer Hunter, and therefore it is he who is able to verify my story.'

'Was it a social visit? I hear Mister Hunter can offer a good dram.' The magistrate's voice was even. But his words brought laughter to the court, quickly stifled as he raised his hand. Byres waited for the silence.

'We rode out together and found the girl in a known hiding place for ruffians and breakers of the law; enclosed as it is by high cliffs between Tarset and Tarret. She thought herself safe there.' Byres looked smug. 'We'd almost given up the search when the boy, Jimmy, doubled back to tell us he'd spotted the fugitive.'

There was an audible sigh from the gathered company and Cecilia shuffled her feet.

'I searched her and found the whisky hidden about her person; concealed in animal bladders. I received this wound when I sought to relieve her of them.'

'It is a mighty wound, and it must have been delivered with some force. The doctor has already testified to me the severity of the strike.' The Magistrate peered at Kitty and raised his eyebrows. Gregory closed his eyes. 'The girl is slight, can Mister Hunter verify the blow was administered by the accused?'

'Yes...no, Hunter's horse had taken fright and bolted. But...but...' Byres was interrupted by the Magistrate.

'So then what does the girl have to say for herself? Why did you have the whisky about your person?'

'It was for my use and no others.'

'For medicinal purpose, perhaps?' The Magistrate's voice held a note of sarcasm.

'Aye, aye it's so.' The listeners on the benches nodded their heads in agreement and Kitty smirked.

'We know whisky's worth in these parts. Two skins I had, hardly enough for a Happening.' Kitty patted her belly. 'It was intended for a very different event, to aid me at the birth of my child when my time comes.'

'Aye, aye, it's the mothers' medicine.' The women present chorused their support.

The Magistrate banged on the table and again there was instant silence. All present had respect for the law as long as it did not affect them.

'So why did you resist the excise man doing his duty?'

'Because, sir, it is well known that gauger Byres has a taste for whisky, especially when it has the flavour of peat.' The Magistrate raised his eyebrows.

This time the girl's spirited words were greeted with a roar of laughter and Gregory hardly dare look at the Magistrate for his reaction, a man puffed up by his standing in the community. Kitty was enjoying her audience the atmosphere had lightened with her account of events. Gregory bit his lip the girl should take care not to diminish the most important figure in the room. As Magistrate he was all-powerful.

'Order, this is a serious matter. We are here to see if this case should go before the Assize Court.'

There was his fear put into words and Gregory heard a gasp of dismay from Cecilia. Now there was alarm on her face and she clenched her white knuckled hands. Kitty had the sense to look chastened. Silence greeted the words of warning; all knew the Assize was another matter. Guilty verdict there could mean prison or even transportation. Kitty placed her hands on her front and Gregory saw her fear.

The Magistrate looked satisfied at the newly subdued atmosphere. Kitty visibly swayed on her feet and he gesticulated for a stool to be brought for the accused. When the girl was seated he continued.

'You attacked this man who was trying to uphold the law? That is serious.' He frowned, and looked toward the bandaged Byres. 'You could have killed him. Then this would have been the crime of murder.' The words echoed through the packed room. The smell of hot bodies was almost suffocating. There was a collective gasp of horror. Gregory felt panic. It could not be.

'Sir!' Gregory leapt to his feet. 'I have important evidence appertaining to the case.'

The court official turned to him and his eyes narrowed. 'You are, sir?'

'The Reverend Gregory Felton and I was there at the accident.'

'Accident..?' The Magistrate could hardly be heard above the loud excited chatter that erupted at his words.

'A Reverend gentleman you say, so you hardly need to swear on the Bible to speak the truth.' The man smiled at his truism but he frowned as he stared at Gregory just feet from him. 'You say you are a man of the cloth?' He sounded his surprise and doubt.

'I am Rector of Thorneyburn, the place in which the woman was apprehended. I had offered my services to this lady to bring her to the home of Miss Howick, the village schoolmistress, who had kindly agreed to take her in for her confinement.'

'Yes, indeed.' Cecilia's confident voice rang out across the room.

Gregory nodded. 'It's the best possible place for her in her condition. And might I add I understand her need for the whisky palliative when her time comes. I take it for toothache.'

There was a murmur of laughter. 'Aye, for all manner of ills.' A woman on the front row called her support.

'Silence!' The Magistrate eyed Gregory. 'Sir, tell us of this accident as you choose to describe it.'

Gregory looked up at the ceiling. Beyond this confined, claustrophobic room was the sky, vast and unfettered, sometimes blue sometimes storm black that smudged and shifted into grey with the changing wind. Kitty needed her freedom like he needed a stable craft under his feet. He knew that now. There was the difference in them. He remembered their journey on the drove road, his eyes resolutely pointing ahead, the girl turning to look back. He knew her need. He had to save her.

He looked at Byres as he said. 'I regret the state of Excise Man Byres, but it was an unfortunate accident.'

'An act of God, you might say?' The magistrate screwed up his eyes as a shaft of sunshine penetrated the one small window in the room.

Gregory stared at the light. It played cruelly on the girl just inches from him. Sunlight, storm rain, they were as necessary to Kitty as life itself. Was it a sign? He did not know. What he did know was that the words he uttered now mattered above all others. He'd always had a way with words.

'The place of the incident has already been described admirably by the excise man. I could not have done better myself.' Byres stared straight ahead. 'The haugh, wide on one side of the stream, is narrowly confined on the other. In that sheltered place we'd taken time to rest before the final mile or so to the home of Miss Howick.' The Magistrate looked at Cecilia but made no comment.

'The sudden appearance of the horsemen was terrifying. The girl, startled by the aggressive manner of the intruders, huddled against the rock face, and sought to protect herself.'

'Protect herself? What, with a rock for missile?'

'Oh no! She raised her hands to shield her face and then that was when it happened.'

All eyes and ears were on him. Gregory raised his eyes to the ceiling, drew a deep breath and said, 'The hillside began to move.' Gasps of surprise, townsfolk gawped at shepherds, farmers at their wives. An Old Testament happening. Here where they lived their daily uneventful lives in what many thought was a God-forsaken place.

Gregory raised his voice, in for a sheep in for a lamb. 'Saturated by the recent heavy storm, rocks and earth and bushes crashed down the rock face. Excise Man Byres, standing gloating over the small prize of whisky that he had torn from the girl, was in direct line of the falling rocks.' Gregory paused for effect. He said quietly so that the ones at the back had to strain to hear.

'One unfortunately hit him on the head.'

The Magistrate appeared struck by a similar missile. Gregory looked at the man there to uphold the law. He had taken care with his appearance, his clothes pressed, his hair trimmed and his face had an added air of authority from a pair of spectacles. But there was a hardly restrained impatience at his confinement in the court.

'An act of God, to be sure, Reverend, sir,' the man rose to his feet. 'This is no case for the Assize, I dismiss it.' He gathered up his papers. Gregory stood stunned, incapable of movement. The deck of his ship had tilted as he'd begun to speak now he could feel the solid timbers under his feet. He had steered them to a safe harbour.

His God was a good God. He had known it for a fact from the moment the Magistrate had taken his place in the court room. Gregory had exclaimed in surprise as the familiar figure took his seat. Now, the representative of the law bore down on him and local strong man, John Armstrong, held out his hand. His handshake reflected his standing. His influence reached beyond the hills. At Slymefoot Gregory had sensed Armstrong's hardly contained suspicion; in the court he had questioned the man's allegiance.

The powerful farmer raised his eyebrows at Gregory as he grinned knowingly at him. 'So, the man they call Black Rory is not the only one in these parts who can see in the dark. You, Reverend

Felton see beyond the dark uncertainties of life to the truth that matters.' He slapped Gregory on the back.

Gregory smiled. 'We all know life is neither a whore nor an unblemished woman.'

John Armstrong threw back his head and laughed his approval. He was a man who knew such a truth, all hill folk lived where nothing was black or white. Necessity was an equal measure of principle and expediency.

40

Gregory Felton stood at the door of the church, the congregation snaking back up the aisle waiting patiently to shake his hand. Mrs Dodds, as ever was first, fast on the heels of her offspring, impatient to be out in the fresh air.

'Thank you, Jimmy, for the fish you caught and then was turned into delicious potted trout by your mother. I count myself lucky indeed.'

Maria Dodds smiled her gratitude. 'Jimmy is off for a rabbit now. It will be pie for supper. Do you dine alone, sir, or do the ladies join you?'

'Let us ask them.' Gregory looked over the heads of her fidgeting brood and caught the eye of Cecilia. 'Ladies, do I have company tonight?' Already he knew the answer. It was a well-worn track between rectory and village school house, the tiny baby at Kitty's hip or cradled in the arms of her friend. Mrs Dodds smiled her connivance; the child slept equally content in her cottage next door. Cecilia did not bother to consult her companion, but nodded her head.

'You provide a good table, Gregory, but most of all we come for the company, don't we, Kitty?'

'Aye,' her friend grinned, 'sea adventures but we never get seasick. It's good for our diet that you mix salt with our clean air. My baby is healthy.' She patted her sleeping offspring. 'Besides, we shall be more than welcome, I think. John Armstrong travelled through the village yesterday and brought us a skin. You could smell the peat even before we untied the knot.'

'How does friend Armstrong?' Gregory frowned as Caleb Hunter and his mother reached his outstretched hand. Mention of Armstrong unsettled all their lives. It brought the hill country down to Thorneyburn. He could only imagine Kitty's homesickness at the man's appearance. 'Jimmy,' he shouted over his shoulder, 'Make it two rabbits. I want no empty places at my table tonight.'

Hepzibah Hunter looked at her son and spoke for the pair of them.

'Youse spoil us rotten to be sure. 'Tis not just flowery words you dish up, Reverend, but food beyond the taste-blooms of folk like Caleb and me.'

'Taste buds, ma.' Caleb Hunter nodded over Gregory's hand, his eyes averted.

Though his mother had come to every service since the drama with Byres, the two men had met briefly. Gregory took the man's hand, glad to see he'd chosen to be part of the congregation again. He was not all bad; for one reason or another the local man had chosen to stay away from the Magistrates' Court and with his absence, Byres had had no ally. Unsurprisingly, Magistrate Armstrong had chosen to believe one of his own against the strutting outsider. And he, Gregory, the ultimate outsider, had swung the balance so there had been only one possible outcome, the release of Kitty Macnab into the hands of village school mistress and priest of the parish.

Their hands restrained, held her back. But the girl was compliant. Her eyes no longer lifted to the hills but looked down to the daughter in her lap. The baby rested content, but what of her mother?

There were a few hours to go before the arrival of his guests and time enough to work on his labour of love. It was almost complete. He took the steps down to his crypt workshop. The Royal Sovereign lay beached and waiting for launch. His skilled fingers had lovingly replicated every deck, every cabin and mast. He could almost smell the sea and his shipmate, Jock, as they pulled on the ropes together. A toy for Kitty's child, he smiled, what matter little Katherine was not a boy?

'She will love it. There has never been a more beautiful present.' Kitty came down the final two steps to stand beside him.

'Kitty!' He flushed taken by surprise he'd been so engrossed in the model ship though his thoughts had been with her. 'What ails you?'

'Nothing, why should it?' The girl laughed, tossing her head; the lustrous black curls grown back tighter than ever were crumbled peat.

He smiled at her and said, 'I did not sense your presence. You have lost the smell of heather.'

'Aye, it has bloomed purple, and is ready to do so again.'

Gregory did not reply. What could he say? Magistrate Armstrong had placed the girl in no-man's-land. He glanced at her not wanting to see her look of longing. He knew too well that limbo was not a place to be.

'Kitty, you have grown pale in the harbour that is Thorneyburn, you f..find it restricting.' Even now her presence excited, made him the stuttering boy.

She took his hand, 'Sailor Gregory, forgive me, I do not mean to show ingratitude.'

'Ingratitude? That you do not.' Her skin was soft in his hand. She stood too close and he moved from her to the tools on his table. She still could disturb him. It would be ever thus. Kitty Macnab was a beautiful woman.

'Tomorrow John Armstrong returns on his way north.' Kitty hesitated, her large brown eyes sought his, 'Gregory, he has asked me and the child to go h-home with him.' She stuttered her need.

He stared at her, surprise, jealousy, disappointment crowding his vision. His heart beat fast. He'd sat in the courtroom hearing the girl's wings fluttering against the cage. He'd opened the door with his false evidence, and now she was asking him permission to fly. He'd known it would happen.

'So, then, Kitty,' Gregory picked up the toy ship and put it into her hands. 'Take it. There is water aplenty where you go. The streams run wild, but the vessel is strong and sturdy and a survivor as are you.'

She stood on tip-toe and kissed him on his cheek. 'You are a good man, Gregory Felton.'

Gregory stood at the window of his study and looked out over the moors. What he saw could be only in the mind's eye for the rain slanted diagonally across the sky in thick obscuring bands. He sighed. At his own volition he could draw his shutters and shut it out and his study would become the confined comfortable room where he was at peace. Out there in the hills and cleughs of the border land was another world, home only for those animals born and bred to its ways.

The mind is its own place that would be his Sunday text from poet Milton. It created its own heaven or hell. His journey had been tortuous and difficult. Had it been Devil sent or God led? He knew it to be both. A path led in two directions. His drove road had taken him into the dark core of the hills, to a place too far. But he had taken the way back to Thorneyburn and he knew now it to be the safe craft under his feet. He bent his head and began to write. He had much to say.

Bands of white light reflected across the page. He had not entirely closed the shutters. He got up and opened them again. The rain had cleared, the moon had risen high into a cloudless sky. The outline of the church stood out solid and belonging in the landscape. The path, edged by the fledgling oaks that led to its door, was already well marked. In a hundred years time the steps would be grooved. They would be no cleugh, but it was a beginning.

His eyes lingered on the churchyard. There would be his resting place. The first family vault? He knew Cecilia looked no further. He looked up to the hills. The oak trees, however tall they grew, would never obscure his view. Somewhere out there was the free spirit that was Kitty. There, in time, would rest her bones, like the dried bent grass and the roots of heather that gave back their own to the land from which they came.

Historical Note

At the end of the Napoleonic Wars much of the English fleet was mothballed and there were many out of work sailors.

In 1818, the Greenwich Naval Hospital, owners of the Earl of Derwentwater's sequestered land in Northumberland, commissioned Newcastle Architect, H H Seward to design four replica churches and rectories for their Simonburn Parish, to provide new livings for naval padres without a ship.

Little account was given to the fact that in this remote region, close to the Scottish border, there was a strong Presbyterian following and the Church of England was neither needed nor welcomed.

While the places mapped in the story are real, the plot and characters (with the exception of Admiral Collingwood) are fiction woven round the name of Black Rory who lives on still in Cheviot Hill folklore.

The late Joan Eddershaw fired my interest in the 'SOLUS' carvings on her husband Francis' rectory shutters in Falstone. Then when I trekked the Cheviots and heard the smuggler tales, *Devil's Drove* was born. Painting the landscape in gouache and pastel was no longer enough.

Exploring the background of this story through *Whisky Smuggling on the Border* by John Philipson, 1991 and *Upper Coquetdale* 1903, by David Dippie Dixon provided endless days of pleasure. Any mistakes are entirely of my doing.